"Hepworth dazzles [...] three generations of midwives in Providence, Rhode Island. This intelligent, well-plotted debut will draw readers in from the very first word and keep them engaged until the end." —*Publishers Weekly* (starred review)

"Hepworth's debut is deftly told. . . . This thoughtful intergenerational story will delight readers." —*Library Journal*

"Hepworth's promising debut is a chorus in three voices not so much about the consequences of keeping secrets as it is about the cathartic effect of finally airing them. . . . Ah, families, their conflicts made all the more poignant here by the shared profession of the three women." —*Booklist*

"Strong, compelling female characters drive an intriguing narrative." —*RT Book Reviews*

"Sally Hepworth's novel enchants." —*Us Weekly*

"A heartwarming story . . . In addition to the interesting characters, the book contains fascinating medical information about childbirth and the evolution of the role of midwives in recent decades." —*Manhattan Mercury*

"The midwifery information is fascinating. . . . The author has clearly done a lot of homework, and my respect for the profession of midwife has grown tremendously." —*The Providence Journal*

"For some mothers, this book will trigger almost fond memories of labor pains, which in itself speaks to the depth of Hepworth's research into midwifery." —*Star Tribune* (Minneapolis)

"A good story of the lives of three generations of relatable women, this story speaks to family and strength."

—*The Parkersburg News and Sentinel*

"*The Secrets of Midwives* is women's fiction at its finest. Sally Hepworth has written a wonderfully satisfying story about three generations of midwives. It's touching, tender, and obviously meticulously researched, giving the reader a fascinating window into the amazing world of midwifery. A delightful read." —Liane Moriarty,

author of *The Husband's Secret*

"From the first page, I could not put *The Secrets of Midwives* down. Sally Hepworth delves into family secrets and family love in two different eras, adding mystery and plot twists at a breathless, exhilarating pace. I simply love this book!" —Ann Hood,

author of *The Knitting Circle*

"*The Secrets of Midwives* is a compelling exploration of life, loss, and love. Family secrets test the bonds between three women—Neva; her mother, Grace; and her grandmother, Floss—as they bring babies into the world and navigate their own complex paths. The story deepens and enlarges as it moves through their varied perspectives to its powerful conclusion." —Christina Baker Kline, author of

Orphan Train

"With empathy and keen insight, Sally Hepworth delivers a page-turning novel about the complex, lovely, and even heartbreaking relationships between mothers and daughters. *The Secrets of Midwives* is that rare tale that weaves together the past and the present in a totally absorbing narrative. Sally Hepworth illuminates one of the most important moments in a woman's life—when she becomes a mother—and spins a story that will hold you captivated till the very end."

—Emily Giffin, author of *The One & Only*

"Hepworth's debut enchants . . . as three midwives unravel their secrets in the path of a classic New England storm . . . combines vibrant and nuanced characters with a breathtaking plot."

—Beatriz Williams, author of *A Hundred Summers*

Also by Sally Hepworth

The Things We Keep

The Secrets of Midwives

SALLY HEPWORTH

St. Martin's Griffin ⚹ New York

THE SECRETS OF MIDWIVES. Copyright © 2015 by Sally Hepworth. All rights reserved. Printed in the United States of America. For information, address St. Martin's Press, 175 Fifth Avenue, New York, N.Y. 10010.

www.stmartins.com

Designed by Molly Rose Murphy

The Library of Congress has cataloged the hardcover edition as follows:

Hepworth, Sally.
   The secrets of midwives / Sally Hepworth. — 1st. ed.
      p. cm.
   ISBN 978-1-250-05189-9 (hardcover)
   ISBN 978-1-4668-5263-1 (e-book)
   1. Midwives—Fiction.   2. Family secrets—Fiction.   I. Title.
   PR9619.4.H48S48 2015
   823'.92—dc23

                                              2014033628

ISBN 978-1-250-05191-2 (trade paperback)

Our books may be purchased in bulk for promotional, educational, or business use. Please contact your local bookseller or the Macmillan Corporate and Premium Sales Department at (800) 221-7945, extension 5442, or by e-mail at MacmillanSpecial Markets@macmillan.com.

First St. Martin's Griffin Edition: December 2015

10 9 8 7 6 5 4 3 2

For mothers and babies everywhere, especially my own

Acknowledgments

Thank you to my editor, Jen Enderlin, for your insight and wisdom. Working with you is a joy and a privilege. Thank you also to the team at St. Martin's, particularly Katie Bassel, Caitlin Dareff, Angie Giammarino, Elsie Lyons, Lisa Senz, Eliani Torres, and Dori Weintraub, for making me look better than I am.

To my agent, Rob Weisbach: Thank you for always making me dig deeper. Heartfelt thanks also to May Wuthrich, for giving me my start.

To Joan Keaney, for reading this manuscript and providing midwifery expertise, and to Grace Owen and Clare Ross, who fielded my questions about high-risk deliveries: Thank you. Any errors are mine, not theirs.

To my critique partners, Anna George and Meredith Jaeger: Thank you for reading and for always asking the tough questions. Also to my first readers, Kena Roach, Angela Langford, Inna Spitzkaia, and Dagmar Logan—for your kind eyes and generous words.

To my girlfriends—the inspiration for the incredible women I create: Thanks for always sharing your flaws, or, as I like to call them, your best features.

To the Carrodus family: Thank you for your quirks and dysfunctionalities. You have given me enough material to fill a lifetime of books.

To Oscar and Eloise—you gave me the words to describe the boundlessness of a mother's love. Without the two of you, this book would be unwritten.

To Christian, thank you for being my person.

Finally, to those special men and women who dedicate their lives to the safe birth of our babies: We might forget to say it at the time . . . but thank you.

1

Neva

I suppose you could say I was born to be a midwife. Three generations of women in my family had devoted their lives to bringing babies into the world; the work was in my blood. But my path wasn't as obvious as that. I wasn't my mother—a basket-weaving hippie who rejoiced in the magic of new, precious life. I wasn't my grandmother—wise, no-nonsense, with a strong belief in the power of natural birth. I didn't even particularly like babies. No, for me, the decision to become a midwife had nothing to do with babies. And everything to do with mothers.

On the queen-sized bed, Eleanor's body curved itself into a perfect C. I crept up farther between her legs and pressed my palm against her baby's head. Labor had been fast and furious and I wasn't taking any chances. Eleanor's babies liked to catch us off guard. I'd almost dropped her first son, Arthur, when he decided to make a sudden entrance as Eleanor rocked over a birthing ball. She barely had time to gasp before he began to crown and we all had to rush into position. Her second son, Felix, was born in the birthing pool, five minutes after I'd sent Susan, my birth assistant, on break. This time, I was going to be ready.

"You're nearly there." I pushed a sweaty strand of hair off Eleanor's temple. "Your baby will be born with the next contraction."

Eleanor squeezed her husband's hand. As usual, Frank had been silent, reverent even. Dads varied enormously on their level of involvement. Some adopted the poses of their wives and girlfriends, panting and pushing along with them; others became so fixated on whatever small task they had been assigned—be it working the iPod or keeping the cup of ice chips full—they nearly missed the birth entirely. I had a soft spot for the reverent ones. They knew they were in the presence of something special.

The baby's head turned to the right and Eleanor began to moan. The room fired with energy. "Okay," I said. "You ready?"

Eleanor dropped her chin to her chest. Susan stood at my side as I eased the shoulders out—first one, then the other—until only the baby's legs remained inside. "Would you like to reach down and pull your baby out, Eleanor?"

Eleanor's sons had come too quickly to do this, but I was glad she'd get the chance now. Of all the ways a baby could be delivered, this was my favorite. It seemed only right that after all the work a mother did during labor, her hands should bring her baby into the world.

A ghost of a smile appeared on Eleanor's face. "Really?"

"Really," I said. "We're ready when you are."

I nodded at Susan, who stood ready to catch the baby if it fell. But it wouldn't. In the ten years I'd been delivering babies, I'd never seen a child slip from its mother's grip. I watched as Eleanor pulled the black-haired baby from her body and lay it against her heart—pink, slippery, and perfect. The cry was good and strong. Music to a midwife's ears.

"Ah, how about that?" I said. "It's a girl."

Eleanor cried and laughed at once. "A girl. It's a *girl*, Frank."

She was a good size. Ten fingers. Ten toes. Eleanor cradled her baby, still attached via cord, with the perfect balance of tenderness and protection. Frank stood beside them, awe lining his features. I'd seen that look before, but it never got old. His wife had just become more amazing. More miraculous.

Susan beckoned Frank for cord cutting and began giving instructions. Seeing Frank's expression, I couldn't help but laugh. Susan had lived in Rhode Island since her nineteenth birthday, but forty years later, her thick Scottish accent meant she was largely incomprehensible to the American ear. On the upside, this made her the ideal person to share confidences with; even if she did disclose your secret, no one would understand. On the downside, I spent a lot of time translating.

"Just cut between the clamps," I theater-whispered. Susan turned away, but her gray, tight-bound curls bounced on her head, so I was fairly sure she was chuckling.

Once the placenta had been delivered and the baby had breast-fed, I tended to Eleanor, settled the baby, and debriefed with the night nurse. When everything was done, I stood at the door. The room was calm and peaceful. The baby was on Eleanor's bare chest getting some skin-on-skin time. Frank was beside them, already asleep. I smiled. The scene before me was the reason I'd become a midwife and, in my opinion, the real magic of childbirth. No matter how arduous the labor, no matter how complete the mother's exhaustion, the men always fell asleep first.

"I'll see you all tomorrow," I said, even though I wanted to stay.

Eleanor waved at me, and Frank continued to snore. I peeled off my gloves and was barely into the corridor when fingers clamped around my elbow and I started to fall. I thrust out a hand to catch myself, but instead of hitting the ground, I remained suspended in midair.

"Hello, gorgeous."

Across the hall two young midwives giggled. I blinked up at Patrick, who held me in a theatrical dip. "Very cute. Let me up."

Patrick, our consulting pediatrician from St. Mary's Hospital upstairs, was forever coming down to our birthing center, getting the nurses all excited with his ridiculous gestures. But I didn't bother being flattered. Yes, he was young and charming—and good-looking in a disheveled, just-rolled-out-of-bed kind of way—but I knew for a fact that he dropped the word "gorgeous" with more regularity than I used the word "contraction."

"Your wish, my command." In a heartbeat I was back on two feet. "I'm glad I ran into you, actually," he said. "I have a joke."

"Go on."

"How many midwives does it take to screw in a lightbulb?" Patrick didn't wait for an answer. "Six. One to screw in the lightbulb and five to stop the ob-gyn from interfering." He grinned. "Good one, right?"

I couldn't help a smile. "Not bad."

I started walking and he fell into step beside me. "Oh . . . Sean and I are heading to The Hip for a drink tonight," he said. "You in?"

"Sorry," I said. "Hot date."

Patrick stopped walking and stared at me. That's how unlikely it was that I would have a date.

"I'm kidding, obviously. I'm going to Conanicut Island to have dinner with Gran and Grace."

"Oh." His face returned to normal. "I take it you're not getting along any better with your mom, then?"

"Why do you 'take' that?"

"You still call her Grace."

"It *is* her name," I said.

I'd started calling her Grace when I was fourteen—the day I delivered my first baby. It had seemed strange, unprofessional, to call her Mom. Saying Grace felt so natural, I'd stuck with it.

"You sure you can't come for one drink? You haven't come for a drink for months." He adopted a pouty expression. "We're too boring for you, aren't we?"

I pushed through the door to the break room. "Something like that."

"Next time, then?" he called after me. "Promise?"

"Promise," I called back. "As long as you promise to learn some better jokes."

I was confident it was a promise he wouldn't be able to keep.

I arrived in Conanicut Island at ten to eight. Gran's house, a shingle-style beach cottage, was perched on a grassy hill that rolled down to a rocky beach. She lived on the southern tip of the island, accessible only by one road across a thin strip of land from Jamestown. When I was little, my parents and I used to rent a shack like Gran's every summer, and spend a few weeks in bare feet—swimming at Mackerel Cove, flying kites, hiking in Beavertail State Park. Gran was the first to go on "permanent vacation" there. Grace and Dad followed a few years ago and now lived within walking distance. Grace had made a big deal about "leaving me" in Providence, but I was fine with it. Apart from the obvious fact that it meant Grace would be a little farther away from me and my business, I also quite liked the idea of having an excuse to visit Conanicut Island. Something happened to me when I drove over the Jamestown Verrazzano Bridge. I became a little floppier. A little more relaxed.

I stepped out of the car and scurried up the grassy path. I let myself in through the back door and was immediately hit by the scent of lemon and garlic.

Grace and Gran sat at the table in the wood-paneled dining room, heads bobbing with polite conversation. They didn't even look up when I entered, which showed how deaf they were both getting. I wasn't exactly light on my feet lately.

"I made it."

They swiveled, then beamed in unison. Grace, in particular, lit up. Or maybe it was her orange lipstick and psychedelic dress that gave the effect. Something green—a bean, maybe?—was lodged between her front teeth, and the wind had done a number on her hair. Her bangs hung low over her eyes, reminding me of a fluffy red sheepdog.

"Sorry I'm late," I said.

"Babies don't care if you have dinner plans, Neva," Gran said. A smile still pressed into her unvarnished face. "No one knows that better than us."

I kissed them both, then dropped into the end chair. Half a chicken remained, as well as a few potatoes and carrots and a dish of green beans. A pitcher of ice water sat in the center with a little mint floating in it, probably from Gran's garden. Gran reached for the serving spoons and began loading up my plate. "Lil hiding?"

Lil, Gran's painfully shy partner of nearly eight years, was always curiously absent for our monthly dinners. When Gran had announced their relationship and, as such, her orientation, Grace was thrilled. She'd yearned her whole life for a family scandal to prove how perfectly tolerant she was. Still, I had a bad feeling her avid displays of broad-mindedness (one time she referred to Gran and Lil as her "two mommies") were the reason Lil made herself scarce when we were around.

Gran sighed. "You know Lil."

"Mom's not the only one who can bring a partner along, Neva," Grace said. "If you'd like to bring a guy alo—"

"Good idea." I stabbed some chicken with my fork. "I'll bring Dad next time."

Grace scowled, but one of my favorite things about her was that her attention span was short. "Anyway, birthday girl. How does it feel? The last year of your twenties?"

I speared a potato. "I don't know." How *did* I feel? "I guess I'm—"

"I'll tell you how *I* feel," Grace said. "Old. Feels like yesterday I was in labor with you." Grace's voice was soft, wistful. "Remember looking down at her for the first time, Mom? All that red hair and porcelain skin. We thought you'd be an actress or a model for sure."

I swallowed my mouthful with a little difficulty. "You're not happy I followed you into midwifery, Grace?"

"Happy? Why, I'm only the proudest mom in world! Of course, I still wish you'd come and work with me, doing home births. No doctors hovering about with their forceps, no sick people ready to cough all over the precious new babies—"

"There are no doctors or sick people at the birthing center, Grace."

"Delivering in the comfort of one's own home, it's just . . ."

Magical.

"Magical," she said, with a smile. "Oh! I nearly forgot." She reached for her purse and plucked out a flat, hand-wrapped gift. "This is from your father and me."

"Wow . . . You shouldn't have."

"Nonsense. It's your birthday."

Gran and I exchanged a look. Of course Grace had ignored the no-gifts directive—the one thing I'd wanted for my birthday. I hated gifts: the embarrassment of receiving them, the awkwardness of opening them in public, and, if it was from Grace, the pressure of ensuring my face was adequately arranged to demonstrate sheer delight, a wonder that I'd ever been able to get through life before this particular ornament or treasure.

"Go on." She pressed her hands together and wriggled her fingers. "Open it."

An image of my thirteenth birthday flashed into my mind—the first time since elementary school that I had agreed to a party. Maybe the fact that I was in the middle of my second-ever period and was cramping, bleeding, and wearing a surfboard-sized maxi pad in my underwear skewed my judgment. Grace wasn't happy when I insisted we keep it small (just four girls from school) and she was positively broken-hearted when I refused party games of any sort, but she didn't push her luck. With hindsight, that should have been my first clue. My friends and I had just gotten settled in the front room when Grace burst in.

"Can I have your attention, please?" she said. "As you know, today is Neva's thirteenth birthday. We are celebrating her becoming a teenager."

She looked like a children's stage performer, smiling so brightly that I thought her face might crack into three clean pieces. I willed her to vanish in a cloud of smoke, taking with her the previous thirty seconds and the crimson crushed-velvet dress she had changed into. But any notion that this might happen faded along with my friends' smiles.

"My baby is no longer a baby. Her body is changing and growing. She's experiencing the awakening of a vital force that brings woman the ability to create life. You may not know this, but the traditional name for first menstruation is 'menarche.'"

Panic broke out; a swarm of moths over my heart. I no longer wanted Grace to disappear and take the last thirty seconds—I wanted her to take my future. To take Monday, when I would have to go to school and face the fact that I was a social outcast, now and forever. To take the coming few weeks, when I would have to go about my life, pretending I didn't hear the whispers and snickers.

"In some cultures," she continued, oblivious, "menarche inspires song, dance, and celebration. In Morocco, girls receive clothes, money, and gifts. Japanese families celebrate a daughter's menarche by eating red rice and beans. In some parts of India, girls are given a ceremony and are dressed in the finest clothes and jewelry the family can buy. I know for you young ones it can seem embarrassing or, heaven forbid, dirty. But it's not. It is one of the most sacred things in the world, and not to be hidden away, but celebrated. So, in honor of Neva's menarche, and probably some of yours too—" She smiled encouragingly at my friends. "—I thought it might be fun to do like the Apache Indians here in North America, and—" She paused for effect. "—dance. I've learned a chant and we can—"

I can't believe I let it go on for as long as I did. "Mom."

Grace's smile remained in place as she met my eye. "What is it, darling?"

"Just . . . stop."

I barely breathed the words, but I know she heard them, because her smile fell like a kite from the sky on a windless day. A steely barrier formed around my heart. Yes, she'd gone to a lot of trouble, but she'd also left me no choice. "Dad!"

Our house was small; I knew he would hear me. And when he appeared, his frantic expression confirmed he'd heard the urgency in my voice. He surveyed the room. The horrified faces of my friends. The abundance of red everywhere—Grace's dress, the balloons, the new cushions, which amazingly, I had only just noticed. He clasped Grace's shoulders and guided her out, despite her determined protest and genuine puzzlement.

But now, as Grace hovered over me, I didn't have Dad to help me. I turned the gift over and began to open it tentatively, starting with the tape at one end.

"It's not a puzzle, darling. You're not meant to unpeel every little bit of tape, you're meant to do *this*!"

Grace lunged at the gift with such vigor, she rammed the table with her hip. Ice cubes tinkled. The water pitcher did a precarious dance, teetering back and forth before deciding to go down. Glass cracked; water gushed. A burst of mint filled the air. I shot to my feet as the water drenched me from the chest down.

Usually after a commotion such as this, it is loud. People assigned blame, gave instructions, located brooms and towels. This time it was eerily quiet. Gran and Grace stared at the mound that was impossible to hide under my now-clinging shirt. And for maybe the first time in her life, my mother couldn't seem to find any words.

"Yes," I said. I cupped my belly, protecting it from what I knew was about to be let loose. "I'm pregnant."

2

Grace

"You can't be pregnant," I said. But as I reached out to touch Neva's round wet belly, I could see that she was. And reasonably far along. Her navel was flush with the rest of her stomach. Her breasts were full, and I was certain if I looked under her hospital top, I'd find them covered in bluish purple veins. "How . . . far along?

A touch of pink appeared in Neva's cheeks. "Thirty weeks."

"Thirty—" I pressed my eyelids together, then opened them again, as if doing so would render the news less shocking. "*Thirty* weeks?"

It wasn't possible. Her face was fresh and clear of spots and she didn't appear to be retaining water. Her wrists were tiny. She didn't have any additional chins. In fact, apart from the now-obvious bump, I couldn't see a single sign of pregnancy, let alone a third-trimester pregnancy. The whole thing was very hard to believe. "But . . . your polycystic ovaries!"

"Doesn't mean I can't get pregnant," Neva said. "Just that it's a little less likely."

I knew that, of course, but it was too much to comprehend. My daughter was pregnant. I was a midwife. How was it possible that I hadn't known?

A steady stream of ice water dripped off the table's edge, landing at Neva's feet. The way she stared at it, you'd think she'd never seen water before. "Your table's going to stain, Gran," she said slowly. "Have you got any paper towels?"

I stared at Neva. "Paper *towels*?"

"I'll get the paper towels," Mom said. "Grace, take Neva into the front room. I'll make tea."

I followed Neva to the front room, observing her closely. Her waddle now was so apparent, I couldn't believe I'd missed it. As she lowered herself onto the sofa I noticed she looked pale. Her skin was translucent—so fair. I could practically see the blood moving about underneath. When she was little, that skin had been a liability. In the summers, I'd had to keep every inch of her covered up, which was against my instincts to let her run naked and free. But to see her now, so perfectly alabaster, without so much as a freckle—it was worth it. She ran a hand through her auburn ponytail, which was thick and glossy and another pointer to her pregnancy I hadn't noticed.

"I'm sorry," she said. "I wanted to tell you earlier, it's just taken me some time to get used to the idea. I haven't told anyone apart from Susan, and that's only because she's doing my prenatal care."

I nodded as though it were perfectly reasonable to hide a pregnancy for thirty weeks. Though, in some ways, it *was* classic Neva. Once, when she was in elementary school, I was greeted at the school gates by her teacher, asking why we hadn't attended the school's performance of *Goldilocks*. It turned out Neva had been cast as one of the three bears. When I asked her why she didn't say anything, Neva had simply said, "I was going to."

"So . . . I'm sure you have questions," Neva said. "Fire away."

My mind began spewing out possibilities. Why hadn't she told us earlier? Had she had proper prenatal care? Would she consider a home birth? Was I the last to know? But one question was more pressing than the rest, and I had to ask it first.

"Who's the father?"

Something in Neva's face captured my attention. It was as though she had closed up. It was strange. It wasn't a difficult question. And she *had* asked what I wanted to know. She hesitated, then looked at her lap. "There is no father."

I blinked. "You mean . . . you don't know who the father is?"

"No," Neva said carefully. "I mean . . . I'll be raising this baby alone. For all intents and purposes, there's no father. Just me."

A tray clattered against the coffee table and I glanced at Mom. If she'd heard, she wasn't giving it away.

"I know this is a shock," Neva said. "It was a shock to me too. Especially given that—"

"—the baby has no father?" I didn't mean to sound judgmental, but I think I did. I couldn't help it. It was an even more unsatisfactory answer than her not knowing who the father was. How could the baby not have a father? Unless . . . "You mean a sperm donor?"

"No," she said. "Not a sperm donor. Though you can think of him that way if you like. Because he's not going to be involved."

"But—"

"Well, this *is* big news," Mom said, pouring the tea. "How do you feel about it, dear?"

A touch of color returned to Neva's face. "I guess . . . excited. A little sad I'll be doing it on my own."

"But you won't be on your own, dear," Mom said. She handed me a cup of tea.

"Of course you won't," I echoed. "The father might want to be involved, once you tell him. Stranger things have happened. And if he doesn't, good riddance! Your father and I will do anything we can to support you."

"Thanks, Grace. But like I said—"

I banged my cup onto the table, spilling a little into the saucer. "Neva. You don't have to be cryptic, darling. Honestly, I don't care who the father is. This is my grandchild. This baby will know nothing but love, even if its father isn't part of its life. But at least tell us who he is."

Neva's jaw clamped shut. She met my eye, almost defiantly. And I knew the subject had been closed. Despite my shock and frustration, a pleasant surge of adrenaline rushed through me. It started in the sternum, then spread pleasantly through my center, like ice cream into hot pudding. Neva didn't do things like this. She never got into any trouble, not interesting trouble. She'd always been so bookish that I'd actually looked forward to her teenage years, when I was sure she'd come into her own and make her mark on the world. But her teenage years had come and gone and her twenties were worse. She'd studied hard, then loyally followed Mom and me into our profession, where she'd quickly eclipsed us both in skill and success. Now, at twenty-nine, Neva was rebelling. And despite my desperation to know the parentage of my grandchild-to-be, I was excited.

"I'm tired," she said. "Can we talk more tomorrow?" Neva stood with some difficulty and peeled the damp shirt away from her skin. Immediately, it stuck again. "Dinner was great. I'll call you both tomorrow."

"Wait!" I sprang to my feet. I didn't know what I'd say, but I knew I couldn't let her leave. "Aren't you . . . going to open your present?"

She paused in the archway leading to the hall. "Oh. Uh . . . yes. Sorry."

I darted past her into the dining room and returned with the box, which I thrust at Neva. "You open it this time." I held my hands up and away from the gift. "No interference from me. Promise."

Cautiously she opened the box and tipped it up. The silver frame slid into her waiting hand.

The photo was an old one, taken when pictures were smaller and browner and rounder at the edges. Mom sat in her wicker garden chair on the piazza, her salt-and-pepper hair collected in a coil at her nape. In the foreground, I knelt with a four- or five-year old Neva in front of me. The hem of my skirt was pulled up and I was hiding behind it, while Neva—serious even as a child—gave her Gran an exasperated look. I'd stumbled over the picture in an album, and even though Neva said no presents, I thought she might make an exception.

A smile inched its way onto Neva's face. "Who took this?" she asked, staring at the picture.

"Probably your father. Do you like it?"

I watched her closely. Her eyes, I noticed, were dry but filled with emotion. Perhaps for once I'd gotten it right with my daughter?

"I love it, Grace," she said, looking up. "And I'm sorry. I know this is a shock. I just need some time. Is that okay?"

What could I say? If she meant accepting that her baby didn't have a father, then, no, it wasn't okay. I'd never heard anything less okay in my whole life.

"Of course, darling," I heard myself saying. "Whatever you need."

I was pleased to see the bedroom light on when I turned into the driveway. I knew I'd never sleep if I couldn't debrief the night's events. I locked the front door behind me, slipped out of my shoes, and hurried to the bedroom. Just as I turned the door knob, the night-light went out.

"Honey?" I scurried into the dark room and turned on the lamp. "Wake up. You won't believe what has happened."

Robert made a noise that sounded like "hmmm" but his eyes remained closed.

I jostled him. "Rob. I need to talk to you."

He muttered something, which sounded like "talk in the morning," and rolled over.

"Neva's pregnant," I said finally.

There was a pause, then he rolled back, opened his eyes.

"Six months along," I continued. "Mom and I only found out because she spilled water down the front of her blouse and there was no hiding it."

I waited for Robert to snap to attention and beg for more information. Or at least display some overt signs of surprise. But in true Robert style, his movements were slow. Measured. Once, I had loved this about him. Now it made me want to punch him in the face.

"Who's the father?" he asked.

"There isn't one, she says."

Despite my frustration, it gave me a certain satisfaction saying that. And even more when Robert sat up and reached for his glasses from the side table. Now I had his attention.

"What on earth do you mean?" he asked.

"I don't know what it means. But that's what Neva says. That there's no father."

"As in, the virgin birth?"

"Who knows? Whatever it is, she's not talking. And the more I pressed her—"

"The more she clammed up, yes." He sighed and thought. "Well, there's no point in speculating. I'll call her in the morning to get to the bottom of it." He took off his glasses and returned them to the table. "Why don't you go to sleep, love?"

He shut off the light, leaving me in darkness. I resented his insinuation that one phone call from him would get all the answers we needed, even though a small part of me believed it was true. Neva often confided in her father, possibly just to irritate me. But whatever the reason, I hoped she did tell Robert. I needed to know who the father of that baby was. And the sooner, the better.

With nothing left to do, I stood, slipping out of my clothes and underwear. I was too pumped up to sleep. And experience told me that only one thing helped with pent-up energy at this time of night. I peeled back the covers and slipped into my husband's side of the bed. His skin was rough and warm and I shimmied against it.

"Grace," he protested, but I silenced him with a kiss and rolled him onto his back.

"Just lie back."

I followed the trail of salt-and-pepper hair south. He'd had a shower before bed, I could smell—and taste—the soap on his skin. It made me want him more. I needed intimacy. Needed someone to want me. It would be a tall order from my sleepy husband, but I had my ways of convincing him. I'd gotten as far as his navel when his hands curled over my shoulders.

"I have to work in the morning, Grace. And honestly, after the news you've given me, I'm a little distracted." He tugged me upward and pressed my cheek to his chest. "Why don't you try to get some sleep? It's a full moon tonight—someone is bound to go into labor. You'll want to have had some rest before you get the call."

His voice was controlled, completely uninfluenced by desire. The tone of a master to its dog. *No more catch tonight, Fido.* These dismissals had been happening more often lately. A sudden headache, an immediate steadying of his breathing when I came to bed. But this rejection was the most overt. How many times had I sat around at book club, listening to my friends complain that all their husbands thought about was sex, sex, sex? And, if they did submit, it was for three minutes of missionary, no foreplay, no fellatio. I was ready to give my husband the whole shebang and . . . was I that repulsive? Once, Robert had found me irresistible. We'd prided ourselves on being part of a couple who maintained their "spark." What had happened to us?

I lay in his arms for as long as I could, probably no more than a minute, and then whispered, "I think I'll get some water."

Robert didn't protest, nor did I expect him to. By the time I had slipped into my dressing gown he was snoring. In the kitchen, the reeds lashed against the house so loudly it sounded like the wind might lift our cottage right off the ground and toss it into Mackerel Cove. I sat in the blue chair with my sketchbook on my lap and face-planted into it.

What was going on with Neva? When it was all boiled down, there were only two possibilities: Neva didn't know who the father was, or she didn't want me to know. Whichever it was, there wasn't going to be a father in the picture for this baby. It was something my grandchild and I would have in common.

A tractor rolled onto my father while my mother was pregnant. I'd always thought that was a tragic, freak thing to happen, but Mom was pretty matter-of-fact about it. "It was the country," she'd say. "Stuff like that happened." Mom had done a good job of picking up the slack my father left behind—an exemplary job—but I always knew something was missing. I saw other children being carried by their fathers long after their mothers had lost the strength. Girls giving perfunctory, embarrassed pecks to their fathers' cheeks at the school gates. Kids asking for—and receiving—wads of notes from their father's wallets, together with a promise *not to tell your mother*. Endearments like "princess" and "honey." Gestures and generosities somehow more special from a father than from a mother.

When I was eight I spent a week with my friend Phyllis at her grandmother's summer home. On the Saturday night, Phyllis's dad was instructed by her mother to "wear us out." He bustled us onto the huge green lawn and asked us to line up. From the way Phyllis's sister and brother started to giggle, they'd clearly played this game before. I couldn't see a ball or a Frisbee, so when he said "Go!" I remained where I was, even after the others scampered off in different directions. A split second later, I was flying.

"Gotcha!" Phyllis's dad said, tossing me high into the air. His voice was animated. "That was too easy. What am I going to do with her, kids?"

Phyllis shouted out from the tree branch on which she sat with her sister. "Tickle her, Dad." She laughed hysterically. "You have to tickle her."

"Death by tickling, eh?" He pinned me to the grass and observed me with mock seriousness. "I'm not sure Grace is ticklish. Are you, Grace?"

"Yes," I said, already feeling giddy. "I am."

He waggled his fingers in the air, then brought them down on my stomach, my sides, my neck. Giggles rippled through me until my stomach ached and I thought I'd explode. I rolled around until my pajamas were covered in grass stains. I'd never experienced a greater feeling of content, not before or after.

Eventually he let me go and went after the others. They sprinted away squealing, climbing trees and tucking themselves into small cavities under the house. I didn't understand. Were they trying to avoid the tickling and the throwing? If it were my Dad, I would have just lain there, a sitting duck to his tickling hands.

No, Neva didn't realize what she was doing by keeping her baby's father a secret. She had a doting father. She'd had shoulder rides and tickling and nicknames. She would have a Papa for her children one day and, if she chose it, she would be walked down the aisle.

I knew what her baby would be missing out on. And I wasn't going to let it happen.

3

Floss

It was the same nightmare I'd had for sixty years. There were different versions, but they were fundamentally the same: I go into my baby's room or pick up my little girl from school and she's not there. Initially I stay calm; there must be some kind of explanation. She's rolled under the bed. She's hiding. It's someone else's turn to pick her up. But my neck already feels sweaty and I can't hear my thoughts too well past the sound of my thundering heart. It's not long before the hysteria starts. I start thrashing around the nursery or school parking lot, searching for a glimpse of that soft red hair or freckles. Instead I see another face. The face that is synonymous with the end of life as I know it. The end of life with my daughter.

I jerked upward into darkness, my fingers twisted in the bedcovers. Lil was by my side, her warm body a stark contrast to my chilling dream.

I lay down again, mimicking her slow breaths—in out, in out—until my heart began to slow. It felt like déjà vu. The situations weren't exactly the same, but the similarities were striking. Neva was going to be a single mother. The father of her child remained under a shroud of secrecy. And if her reasons for this were anything like my own, well . . . that was what terrified me.

I needed to go to sleep. But when I closed my eyes, all I could see were gray clouds and seagulls. Wind tangling my hair and briny sea air in my lungs. It was 1954 and I was on my way to America. As I strolled the windblown deck, newborn Grace peeked out of my wool coat, perhaps wanting a glimpse of the new life we were about to start. I continued to stroll until, on the third trip around, she drifted off. I waited until I was sure she was completely out, then gingerly lowered myself onto a plastic seat.

"Do you mind if I have a look?"

A woman about my age hovered over me, tugging the hand of the young man beside her. She strained to see inside my coat. Grace's eyes flickered under her lids with new sleep, but seeing the woman's enthusiasm, my motherly pride rose up. I opened my coat an inch.

"Oh, Danny, look—it's so tiny! A boy or a girl?"

"A girl. Grace."

"You lucky thing. We're desperate for a baby, aren't we, Danny? She's beautiful. How old?"

"Two weeks."

"Two weeks? But . . . shouldn't you still be in hospital?"

I opened my mouth, releasing a cloud of smoggy air but no words.

"Well," the woman said, "your husband must be taking very good care of you."

Ah, my husband. There wasn't one of those, of course. But my mother, unable to completely turn her back on me, had prepared me with an answer to *that* question.

"Actually, my husband . . . passed away. He was a farmer. There was an accident."

"Oh no." The woman looked at her husband and then back at me. "You're raising the baby alone?"

"A lot of people have worse luck."

Again, the woman turned to her husband. She just couldn't seem to get her head around it. Life—and love—had obviously been kind to her. "That's so sad. You're going to America alone?"

"No." I smiled at the ginger-haired bundle in my arms. "I'm going with my daughter."

At some point I must have drifted off. When I woke, it was with a flying start. It was going to be one of those nights. Jolting in and out of consciousness. Skating along that foggy line between reality and dream. Usually, when this happened, I'd take a book into the study—just because I was restless, didn't mean I had to disturb Lil. But tonight, I didn't get the choice. Because the phone was ringing.

I sat up and dropped my legs off the side of the bed. In the dark, I located the red numbers of the clock—1:03 A.M. Grace.

Lil, ten years my junior and perpetually nervous of bad news coming at night, was already on her feet.

"I'll get it, Lil," I said. "It'll be Grace." I reached for my dressing gown on the bedpost, and by the time I'd reached the hall, Lil held the receiver to her ear.

"Hello?" she said. She nodded, then held the phone out to me. "Grace."

"Thank you, dear. You go back to bed."

I rubbed her arm as she horseshoed around me. Poor Lil. First she spent the evening huddled in our room reading a book—her choice, of course. But now her sleep was being interrupted. She was as sweet and tolerant as they came, but sometimes I wondered if Grace was wearing her thin.

By the time I lifted the phone to my ear, Grace was already talking.

"I know, I'm sorry. It's late. It's just . . . I'm stunned, flabbergasted, horrified—"

I lowered myself into the seat by the hall table. My old body felt like a sack of rocks. "Yes. It was a big shock."

"You didn't know, did you?"

"No. I didn't."

"How could I not have known?" Grace whined. "I'm her mother. I'm a *midwife*. Can she really be thirty weeks? She doesn't look thirty weeks."

"You were the same when you were pregnant," I said. "Nothing more than a thickened waist until the eighth month."

"And why won't she tell us who the father is? She didn't tell you, did she?"

"No. She didn't."

"It makes no sense. I'm not judgmental, am I? I might have been a little shocked at first, but I'd have gotten over it. Why didn't she come to me . . . or you, for that matter? You of all people would know how she feels."

"You know Neva," I said. "It just takes her a little while. She'll come around."

"Maybe. Maybe not." Grace groaned. "It's just so frustrating. Why doesn't she come to me? Maybe if I was more like you—"

"She didn't come to me either, remember?"

"No. I suppose not." This sated her a little.

"Besides," I said, "Neva wouldn't want you to change. She loves you."

"Maybe, but she doesn't like me very much. My husband doesn't either. You are my mother, so you have to love me—biology forces it." A short pause followed. "Would my father have liked me, do you think?"

I hesitated. Stupidly, I hadn't expected that Grace would draw a parallel between her grandchild's absent father and her own. Stupid, because I'd already made the connection myself. "I . . . yes. Of course he would."

Another silence ensued, this one long enough to unsettle me.

"Did you ever love him, Mom?"

Grace had asked a million questions about her father over the years. The color of his hair when the sun hit it. The lilt of his accent. Whether he was so tall he would've hit his head on the top of the doorway if he wore a top hat. She liked details. The one, single photograph I had of Bill, a wedding photo, was tattered and bent from spending so much time in Grace's pocket or under her pillow. But this question, she'd never asked before.

"Yes, I did. Once."

She sighed and I wasn't so deaf I didn't hear her relief. I hoped we could leave it at that. Because when Grace needed answers, she didn't leave a door unopened. And this particular door was one best left shut.

"So what should I do, then? About Neva, I mean."

"It's not for me to say."

"But if you were me?"

"I'm not you. But if you're asking what I'm planning to do . . . I'm going to accept her at her word—that her baby has no father—and ask her how I can best support her."

I wondered if any of this was getting through. Hard to tell with Grace. One minute she could be all emotion, and the next—who knew? Robert had once described a date with her as an emotional bungee jump. Grace had thought it was hysterically funny at first, but once she thought more about it, had become cross with him. Case in point, I suppose.

"You're right. As always. But . . ." Grace sounded unsatisfied. I could picture her by the phone, jiggling back and forth as she used to as a child when she couldn't make sense of something.

"But *what?*"

"How can you stand it? A secret like this? Isn't it eating you alive?"

I almost laughed. If only she knew.

"Secrets are hard," I said. "But if keeping the secret allows you to have a relationship with your daughter? I, for one, think it's worth it."

4

Neva

When my mother doesn't know what to do about something, she talks about it. *I've got this problem,* she'll start, and then vault into whatever's on her mind. It doesn't matter if it's a stranger, a client, my father, or my grandmother, she's happy to air her linen, dirty or otherwise. Generally speaking, she already knows what she wants to do. I get the feeling she just likes the sound of her own voice.

When I was twelve, Dad got a bonus. He'd promised me for years that if he got a bonus, we could go on vacation—anywhere I wanted to go.

"So where's it going to be, Nev?" he had asked. "Disneyland? Hawaii?"

"I don't know. How about . . . Seattle?"

It was the first place that sprang to mind. But once I'd said it, I was pleased with my answer. I could picture the three of us moseying around the Pike Place Market in our rain jackets, ducking into a café for clam chowder when the heavens decided to open. "I liked the movie, *Sleepless in—*"

"Seattle!" Grace said. "Of course, I loved that movie. That scene where they meet on the top of the Empire State Building and . . . hang on—" Grace clapped a palm to her cheek. "New York! *That's* where we should go. That'd be cool, right?"

"Grace," my father warned. "It's Neva's choice."

"Uh . . ." I was caught off guard. My thoughts scrambled to catch up. "New York would be kind of cool . . . I guess."

"Just think about it," Grace said. "We can go to the top of the Empire State Building just like Meg Ryan and Tom Cruise—"

"Hanks," I corrected.

"—and we can go ice skating at Rockefeller Center!"

Dad frowned. "It's August, Grace."

"—and we can picnic in Central Park!" Grace was beaming from ear to ear. It was hard not to get caught up by her enthusiasm.

"Now, wait just a minute," Dad said. "The destination is Neva's choice. Not yours."

Grace pouted. "She said it sounded cool—"

"Maybe it does. But if she wants New York, I'm going to have to hear it from her lips, understand? Her lips?"

Two heads swung to me. And because they were staring at me, and because I did think New York would be kind of cool, I nodded. But a few days later—once Grace had booked the tickets—I realized I didn't really want to go to New York. I wanted to go to Seattle.

* * *

I rolled over in bed, trying to get comfy. It was no good. My belly felt heavy and it wasn't just my belly. This wasn't how I'd wanted things to go. I knew, with the rational side of my brain, that people would find out I was pregnant sometime. But another part of me believed that as long as I could keep it to myself, I'd be in control.

Giving up on sleep, I headed for the kitchen. I had visions of warm milk with cinnamon and honey, but as I had neither cinnamon nor honey, it would have to be plain milk. As I stood waiting for my mug of milk to heat in the microwave, a shadow appeared on the floor beside me.

"Geez, how's a man supposed to get any sleep?"

I smiled. "Don't you have your own place, Patrick?"

"You gave me a key!"

"For emergencies. Three years ago."

I removed my milk and turned around. Three years ago, Patrick had been a new divorcé, drowning his sorrows in the bars that were a lot closer to my College Hill apartment than to the East Greenwich home he'd shared with his wife. He never told me the details of the split and I didn't ask. I didn't need to. Patrick was a good guy, and a wonderful doctor, but when it came to women, he was like a fat man at a buffet: he couldn't help himself. After several weeks of him ringing the buzzer—or climbing up the fire escape—to my apartment in the small hours of the morning when he'd had too much to drink, I relented and gave him a key. I expected that once Karolina moved back to Germany he'd start spending more time at his own home, or maybe buy himself an apartment in town. But three years on, I still regularly found him on my couch, snoring after a big night out or catching some z's before an early shift at the hospital. The strangest part about it was . . . it wasn't strange.

"I'd have thought that as a well-respected, well-paid doctor, you could afford a hotel, or at least have a girlfriend in the area. I mean . . . what?"

Patrick's face was pale. He stared at my stomach, and after a silent curse, I followed his stare. My hospital shirt was dry now, but it had become stiff, making my belly look, if anything, larger than it actually was. I assessed my options and found only one. I had to tell him. I was going to tell him sometime and there was no hiding it now. I may as well have screamed, *Hello! There's a life growing inside me! Come and take a look!*

"You're pregnant."

"Yes."

For once, smooth-talking Patrick couldn't seem to find any words. "Who's . . . who's the father?"

I sighed. "This is awkward. I don't know how to say this, but . . . it's yours."

Apart from his lips, Patrick's face didn't move an inch. "It's mine?"

"Yes."

"You're sure?"

"One hundred percent."

He wandered over to the chair in the corner and sank into it. I watched, unspeaking, as he picked up a matchbook from the table and turned it over between two fingers. "That's weird. Since we've never had sex."

"Oh, right!" I forced a laugh. "So it's not yours. Whew! That must be a relief."

Patrick didn't laugh. "I can't believe you're joking about this. Whose is it, Nev?"

I couldn't believe I was joking either. What was wrong with me? I should just tell him the truth. He wasn't Grace. He wouldn't fire questions at me or demand answers. And the idea of sharing the burden—well, it was like a hot shower after a brisk swim at the beach. But something held me back. "It's . . . mine."

"And who else's?"

"Just mine." I downed my milk and turned to wash out my mug.

"Have you told your mom?" he asked.

With my back to him, I nodded. Patrick hadn't met my mother, but he knew enough to know the minefield I'd be facing when I told her. My hand cupped my belly. *It won't be that way for us, little one. Not a chance.*

"Does anyone else know?" he asked.

"Gran. You. Susan. That's it. Although there's no hiding it now, is there?"

"Not Eloise?"

"No."

Eloise, my roommate, was perhaps the obvious person to tell. She was sweet, considerate, reliable. But she'd met Ted, her very nice, very time-consuming, boyfriend shortly after moving in and we'd never quite made the journey from roommate to friends. It was fine by me. I'd more or less given up on female friends in the seventh grade when I realized that female friendship was practically a religion. Thou shalt not sit next to another friend at lunchtime. Thou shalt insist you wear my favorite jacket and then get mad when you spill soda on it. Thou shalt not talk to anyone currently being shunned by the group. In contrast, hanging out with male friends felt like sliding into a pair of old jeans: comfy, predictable, unpretentious. I especially felt this way with Patrick.

I upended my mug on the draining rack and with nothing else to do, spun around. Patrick was right in front of me—so close, my belly skimmed his. "You mean you've gone through this alone?"

I tilted my head up, but for some reason, couldn't look at him. He pulled me against his warm chest. "Oh, Nev."

I didn't bother protesting. Patrick was too strong to push away and besides, I didn't want him to see the rogue tear that streaked down my face. Our friendship had always been more about laughter than tears. Laughter was what had brought us together, five years ago, at The Hip. It was quiz night. Susan and I had just completed a successful vaginal twin-delivery at the birthing center and it seemed like a good excuse for a drink and some mindless trivia. We had just ordered a jug of beer when Patrick and Sean, an ob-gyn whom I'd met in surgery, sidled up to our table.

"So?" Sean pulled out a free chair and sat down. "Team of four?"

Sean was so assuming, so confident. I had an overwhelming urge to tell him *Sorry, our table is full.* But my eye had already slid over to Patrick. I knew him—I knew them both from the hospital—but Patrick, I liked. He was a good guy. The kind of doctor who stayed late to help his patients and never hurried them even if his shift had long finished.

"Sure," I said after Susan nodded. "Why not?"

"Nether, isn't it?" Sean asked.

Patrick elbowed him. "It's Neva, you goose."

"Nev-a?" He helped himself to a glass of our beer. "Unusual name."

"More unusual than Nether?" I asked.

"I don't know," Sean continued, unperturbed. "You could have been conceived in the Netherlands. . . . Hey, I work in obstetrics, I've heard it all."

I started to laugh, but stopped when I noticed something playful in Patrick's expression. "Not a fan of unusual names, Sean? Weird, given your middle name."

Susan and I swiveled to Sean. He paled. "Now just a sec—"

"Tiffany," Patrick announced proudly.

Susan's hand shot to her mouth. A snort bubbled from me.

"It was my mother's maiden name," Sean muttered.

We couldn't hold it in any longer. At least I couldn't. It tore from the depths of my stomach. Beside me, Patrick was doubled over and tears streamed from Susan's face. Everything Sean said only made it worse.

I can't remember the last time I'd laughed so much. Patrick admitted his middle name was Basil, like the herb. Susan told us she had an uncle named Esther. But nothing beat Tiffany. As obnoxious as Sean was, there was something so . . . likable about him. Particularly after he told us about Laura, the Texan cashier at his neighborhood grocery store. He told us he always gave her large notes because he loved hearing her count back the change in her smooth American-pie drawl. *Fave, Tayn, Twenny dahllars. Thare you gow, kand sir. You have yerself a good day, now.* He planned to wear her down until she finally agreed to become his wife. Patrick said he didn't have a hope. At least, not after she found out his middle name.

We made a pretty good team, the four of us. There was the odd debate over the right answer, a given with Sean on our team. But Patrick, I noticed, always sided with me. Even the time I was wrong. He pulled my ponytail playfully throughout the evening, and though I always shook him off, I found myself hoping he'd do it again.

When the MC announced that we had won, Patrick lifted me off the ground and spun me in a circle. My legs bumped the table, knocked over a chair. A glass smashed. Patrick either didn't notice or didn't care. Then, abruptly, the spinning stopped.

"*There* you are, Patrick!"

Patrick's arms loosened around my waist, and my feet found the ground. His body, so fluid just a moment earlier, became stiff. "Karolina."

The pretty blonde crept to Patrick's side and he took a small but distinct step back from me. "Karolina, this is Neva," he said. He laughed, though not the same guffaw that I'd heard all evening. It was more stilted. Nervous. "Neva's a midwife at the birthing center."

"It's nice to meet you," I said.

A hand clasped my upper arm. It was Sean. "Want to come accept our prize?"

I nodded woodenly. As I followed Sean to the stage, he ducked his head casually to my ear. "Don't waste your pretty pink cheeks on Patrick," he said. To his credit, he spoke softly. Kindly. "He flirts in his sleep. He can't help himself."

"Who was that girl?" I heard myself ask.

I recognized the expression on Sean's face immediately: pity.

"His fiancée."

It wasn't as bad as it could have been. As my memories of the night faded, I was able to be in the same room with Patrick without having to feign an excuse and leave. And after a while, I realized it was for the best. Patrick would be a terrible boyfriend. By the sound of it, he was a worse husband. But as a friend, well, he wasn't bad. Not bad at all. Now, I relaxed into his arms.

"Oh. Sorry."

Patrick and I sprang apart. Eloise stood sleepily in the doorway in her nightie. "Sorry," she said again, "I was just getting some wat—Oh my God!"

She stared at my stomach.

"Yeah," I said. "I'm pregnant."

Her eyes rushed up to mine, then dropped again to my belly. "But . . . you're *really* pregnant."

I nodded. Under her gaze—and Patrick's—my stomach felt twice as large, my secret twice as ridiculous.

"Do you want to talk?" she asked, flicking a glance at Patrick. "I can make coffee."

I shook my head. I knew this was the time to explain but I didn't trust myself. "Actually, I'm really tired. Do you mind if we talk tomorrow?"

Without waiting for a response, I squeezed past them both into the hallway and then into the bathroom. It was steamy and it smelled of Eloise's strawberry bubble bath. I sank onto the tiles. Deep vibrations rumbled through the wall—Patrick talking to Eloise about my revelation. I cocooned my belly with my arms. There'd be a lot more people discussing it soon.

But I'd survived this far. Every time I had to steal a new, larger shirt from the birthing center. All the times I'd made up obvious lies to get out of after-work drinks. Even the time I told Anne at reception I had a urinary tract infection to explain my frequent trips to the bathroom. I'd survive this too. And it would be worth it.

I hugged myself a little tighter, and a fist or foot jabbed against my ribs. I think it was my baby, trying to hug me back.

5

Grace

I dragged a stool up to the bed. "I'm going to take your blood pressure, Gillian. Can you roll up your sleeve for me?"

It was the day after Neva's announcement and I still felt faint. Neva was pregnant. Thirty weeks in. No father had been named. Thankfully I'd had back-to-back prenatal appointments to take my mind off things. Gillian was my last for the day. And as soon as we finished I would get to the bottom of this nonsense.

Gillian pushed up the sleeve of her shirt so it bunched under her shoulder. I slid the cuff to the fleshy part of her arm and felt down the cord for the hand pump. "So how have you been feeling?"

"Fine. Excited."

"You should be," I said. "This experience is going to be life-changing for you."

Gillian beamed and I wondered if she was the same woman who'd crept into my office seven months ago, newly pregnant and trembling at the very mention of the word "birth." During that consultation, she told me that the first time around she'd hoped to have an active, drug-free hospital birth. She wanted to breast-feed as soon as possible after birth and have the baby sleep in her room. But Gillian's labor was long and arduous. She didn't dilate as fast as the doctors would have liked. After twelve hours, the doctor artificially ruptured her membranes and, after seventeen hours, they gave her drugs to speed things along. The drugs brought on such strong, painful contractions, Gillian agreed to an epidural. She wound up flat on her back, surrounded by cords and intravenous drips. Though the baby was never in distress, the doctor performed a "routine" episiotomy before dragging the baby out with forceps and placing her into the hands of a waiting nurse. Gillian's daughter spent the first night in the hospital nursery because after the epidural, the nurses didn't think Gillian could care for her on her own.

I cringed as she recounted her experience, but it wasn't the first time I'd heard a story like that. Instead of providing support, the hospital system provided pain medication. Instead of patience, they provided drugs to speed along labor. Instead of empowering women, they undermined their ability to give birth naturally. *Well, get ready*, I told Gillian at that first appointment, *because we're taking your power back.*

"I just wish I'd known about you earlier," Gillian said. "I knew about home birthing but I was worried it wasn't safe."

"So no concerns now?"

"None. In fact, I have more confidence in your ability to handle this birth than I did in those doctors that delivered my daughter. And

I know that if anything goes wrong, we're an eleven-minute ride away from Newport Hospital."

"That's right," I said. It was funny . . . when I heard clients talk like this, I felt validated. Not just that home birthing was okay, but that I was okay too.

"And now that I've seen your birthing suite, I'm ready," she continued. "The bedspread, the pillows, the birthing pool, the oil burners . . . it's exactly what I was hoping for. And I love your sculpture."

Gillian was looking at my new creation, a three-headed clay sculpture with a swollen belly. It was supposed to represent the coming together of mother and child, but as so often happened with my artwork, my sculpture had other ideas. A third head had presented itself—covered in stubble and with a large knobbly nose. The father. I was pleased with how it turned out. "I'm glad you like it."

"Do many people use your room?"

"Some. Most clients like to give birth in their own home, but many folks don't have the space. And I have a few out-of-towners that live too far away for me to travel to them."

I scribbled down Gillian's blood pressure, then released the cuff. The air hissed out of it. "Your blood pressure's fine. Now if you'll just lie down, I'll measure your belly. See how this baby is growing."

I held Gillian's arm, taking some of her weight as she lifted her legs and lowered her torso down. Beside the bed, on a small table, was a picture of Neva in her graduation cap and gown. "That *has* to be your daughter," Gillian said.

"It is." I smiled at the picture. In it, Neva looked happy, if a little uncomfortable to be having her photo taken. "The day she graduated."

"She's a midwife too, isn't she?"

"Not just *a* midwife. One of the best midwives around." I located the baby's head—low down in the pelvis, engaged—and placed the tip of my measuring tape there. "And she's pregnant herself. Her first."

"Congratulations," Gillian said. "Are you going to deliver the baby?"

My smile waned. I stretched the tape up the middle of Gillian's stomach to the baby's buttocks, right under her ribs. "Actually, Neva works at a birthing center in Providence, so she'll probably deliver there."

"Oh." Gillian studied my face. "Well, I've heard good things about birthing centers."

I sighed. "They're not the worst option in the world, I suppose. Their rates of intervention are lower than the hospital's, at least. But the one that Neva works at is attached to a hospital! It's nowhere near as intimate as the home. Ob-gyns and pediatricians roam the halls, desperate to jump in and take over."

"I suppose I hadn't thought of that," Gillian said. "Well, hopefully your daughter won't run into any complications and she can have a natural, intervention-free birth at the birthing center. With any luck, she won't even have to see a doctor."

"Yes. Or his forceps . . . Anyway, we shouldn't be talking about my daughter. This is about you. I'm looking forward to meeting your sister. Is she still planning on assisting me with delivery?"

"Yes, if you don't mind. She's almost finished her midwifery studies and I'd love to have her there."

"Mind? You're saving me the trouble of getting a birth assistant. And I also happen to think it's wonderful having female family members in the room when you give birth." I thought of Neva again and my heart broke a little. "It's how births used to be. The women of the community—mothers, grandmothers, sisters, aunts—all came together to support the mother in labor. Secret women's business, they called it. I'd like to see more of that. Now that dads are present in the delivery room—which is a great thing, don't get me wrong—we've lost a bit of that camaraderie." I checked the measurement against last week's. Good growth. "When does your sister arrive?"

"A week before I'm due." Gillian rubbed her belly. "Let's hope this little one can wait until then."

I hauled her into a sitting position. "Don't worry. Only about five percent of mothers deliver on their due date and most mothers deliver late. Don't look so worried. Worst-case scenario, we find another birth assistant. You'll be fine."

I finished up Gillian's appointment and saw her out. Immediately my thoughts turned to Neva. Why was she doing this? Why wouldn't she let me in? Even as a brand-new baby, Neva had done things her own way. I'd intended to co-sleep and breast-feed and baby-wear into toddlerhood. Neva had other plans. After three weeks of strapping her to my chest while she screamed, Robert settled her in two minutes by wrapping her up and settling her in her crib. When she was six months old, she decided she'd rather drink from a bottle than from me, so after a couple of weeks of pumping to give her breast milk, I switched to formula and she was much happier. Mom assured me that with time, we'd become close, and I clung to that hope with all my might. But now she was twenty-nine. Pregnant. If we weren't close now, what hope did we have?

Something was going on with her. Hiding her pregnancy until the seventh month. Keeping the father a secret from everyone. It made no sense. On some level, I could understand why Neva would keep the secret from me—perhaps she was afraid I'd demand she have a home birth or do something to embarrass her—but why would she keep it a secret from the father?

An idea came at me before I could stop it. And no matter how hard I tried, I couldn't shake it off. There was nothing else for it. I had to see my daughter.

The traffic wasn't bad and I got to Providence in forty minutes. Anne was behind the reception desk at the birthing center. Her gray hair was streaked with purple and her skin was tanned. She'd been on vacation somewhere glamorous like the Swiss Alps, as I recalled. Or was it the Greek Islands? Either way, together with her burgundy cardigan she resembled something of a red wine grape.

"Hello, Anne. How are you, darling?"

Anne beamed, her white teeth creating a line in the sea of purple. "Grace. Decided to come and help us again? We could use an extra pair of hands around here."

"I'll think about it," I said, although it was a lie. I'd assisted them a couple of times when they were short staffed, but only because I foolishly assumed that I'd get to do a delivery with Neva. Both times I'd been assigned to another midwife. Probably at Neva's request. "Neva about?"

"She arrived an hour ago, but her client has been transferred for a C-section. She's probably gowning up now, but you might just catch her."

I was already turning toward the door when I had an idea.

"Oh, Anne? Would you mind if I took a copy of the birth notes from one of my deliveries here? I've got a new apprentice and I wanted to tell her about the shoulder dystocia delivery I did when I was here. Kena Roach was the mother's name."

The phone rang, and Anne waved me behind the desk. "Go ahead, just leave the originals." She reached for the phone with one hand, and with the other opened her top drawer and fished out a tiny cabinet key. "Here you go. St. Mary's Birthing Center, this is Anne speaking."

With a fluttering heart I scooted behind the desk into the file room. I approached the archive file cabinet where Kena's file would have been and, after a quick glance over my shoulder, proceeded to the next filing cabinet, marked CURRENT CLIENTS. The lock was stiff and I had to jiggle it about to get it to turn. Then, with a slight tug, the top drawer slid open. My heart did a little leap. Before I could lose my nerve, I scanned the *B* names;

Ball, Emily
Barry, Lisa
Beaumont, Isabelle
Bradley, Neva

I gave myself a congratulatory hug. Exactly what I needed. I slid the file out and opened it. The first page was the document I was look-ing for.

Client: Bradley, Neva
Date of LMP: Uncertain (PCOS)
Due Date: December 31, 2014

Medical History: Polycystic Ovary Syndrome. Irregular bleeding for 3+ years. LMP not known.

I scanned over the address and medical history until I got to the field I was looking for.

Father's Name:

The adrenaline left my body like the wind from a sail. I don't know what I expected. That the name of the man would be written there plain as day? Maybe. Or perhaps that something else telling would be there. Like "Father Unknown" or something. But blank? It gave me nothing. Less than nothing. It actually supported Neva's ridiculous theory that her baby had no father. Something I refused to accept.

Anne was still on the phone and I dropped the key on her desk on my way out. With new determination I marched toward the hospital. If I couldn't get the information I needed from her file, I'd get it from Neva.

I found her in Labor and Delivery, looking at some charts. Beside her was the ob-gyn. The white coat gave it away, but even without it, I would have known. Something about the look of importance he wore like a badge. Neva was leaning toward him, listening so intently that she jumped when I spoke.

"Grace, hi," she said. From the way she looked at me, you'd have thought a Martian had just entered Labor and Delivery. "What . . . what are you doing here?"

The doctor, I noticed, was watching us keenly. He was close to good-looking—tanned, with radiant white teeth—but his nose was slightly too big and his eyes slightly too small. He did, however, have height on his side. It made me think of the old expression: Tall cures all. "Neva, I'll leave you to it," he said.

She nodded. "Be right there, Doctor."

I seethed at the inequity. He, the high-and-mighty ob-gyn, was "Doctor," while my daughter—just a midwife—was "Neva."

When he was gone, she looked at me. "Grace, I'm sorry but I can't chat. A client is about to go in for a C-section."

"Does she need a C-section, or did that doctor bully her into it?" I knew it was a risky comment, but I couldn't help myself. "Anyway," I said, "can we talk while you robe up?"

"Gown up?"

I rolled my eyes. "Potato, potahto."

Her lips twitched; a good sign. "Fine," she said. "But I've only got a minute."

I followed her into a room filled with lockers and sat down on the central bench. She stripped down to her underwear and then flipped through a pile of scrubs in plastic packets, looking for her size. As I stared at the mound on her belly, I wondered once again how I could have missed that she was pregnant.

"So? What can I do for you?" She stepped into a pair of wide-legged hospital pants and knotted the waist string.

"It's about the father of your baby," I said. No point in beating around the bush. "I want you to know that none of this is your fault. Or the baby's. We will love that baby unconditionally and so will you. And I don't think you need to use the pregnancy as a reason not to press charges either. In fact, the baby's DNA could prove—"

Neva held a palm toward me. "What are you talking about?"

"You were raped." I scanned Neva's face for any sign of affirmation. "Weren't you?"

Neva closed her eyes. It frightened me. Either I was right, or she was trying very hard to stay calm.

"Honey? Am I right?"

"No, Grace." Neva spoke slowly. "I wasn't raped."

I continued to watch her face. "Are you sure?"

"One hundred percent sure. Look, I really have to scrub up for surgery."

"Okay, it's just . . . if you weren't raped, then . . ." I didn't get it. If she wasn't raped, then why wouldn't she want anyone to know who the father was? Unless . . . I gasped as it dawned on me. "He's married!"

"Oh my God," Neva said.

I stayed on Neva's tail as she exited the locker room. "That's it, isn't it? He's married. You're protecting him. His family?"

When Neva turned, her face was taut. I was on her last nerve. "No. That's not it."

"Then *what*?"

I must have yelled because several people stopped in their tracks and stared. Neva took my arm and led me toward the elevator. Her nails pinched my skin. "Just go home. I'll call you later. I promise."

"But—"

Neva peered over her shoulder and I followed her gaze. The ob-gyn—Dr. Cleary, according to his badge—stood in her eye line. "Everything okay here?"

"Yes," Neva said. "Fine."

I froze. My daughter might not be forthcoming with personal information, but some things a mother could tell on sight. Chemistry—it was palpable. I could feel it now. Neva was involved with this doctor.

I tried to catch a glimpse of his left hand but before I could see anything, Neva had shoved me into the elevator. When the steely doors clamped shut, I slumped against the wall. Suddenly I understood why Neva didn't want to tell me who the father of her baby was. Whom did I hate more than anyone in the world, including parking inspectors and tax collectors?

Ob-gyns.

6

Floss

The day after receiving Neva's news, I was anxious. I hadn't slept much. And during the brief minutes of sleep I did snatch, I'd dreamed of Grace's father. Now I made myself my fourth coffee for the day and carried it into the sitting room. It was a warm, clear day, and through the window I could see a pair of young tourists carrying a kayak down the sand-edge road toward Hull Cove. Usually just a glimpse of this was enough to relax me—to remind me how fortunate I was in life. Not today.

Lil was on the couch, reading a book. When I sat beside her, the cushions bounced. "Let me guess," she said. "Grace?"

Lil didn't usually weigh in on my relationship with my daughter, but I knew she found it curious. She wasn't familiar with the relentless worry that went along with having a daughter. I got the sense she found

Grace a little codependent and over the top. Perhaps she was. But Lil didn't understand Grace the way I did. More important, she didn't understand the circumstances that had made her that way.

"No." I lifted my legs onto the ottoman and sank into the cushions. "Well, not directly."

Lil set down her book: an invitation to talk. But I was hesitant. I'd told her Neva was pregnant, of course, and that her baby didn't appear to have a father. But I hadn't told her of the wound it had reopened for me. I'd never told Lil anything about Grace's father—she'd caught on to the fact that he was dead and left it at that. Now, part of me wanted to talk, but after all my years alone, I found the concept of talking through my troubles foreign at best, and at worst, frightening.

"I'm not saying I can do anything," she said, reading my mind. "But I can listen."

"You're a love," I said. "But it's nothing I haven't been dealing with all my life. Daughters, granddaughters—"

Lil reopened her book. "Yes. So you say."

I hesitated. "You all right, dear?"

"Fine. Just fine."

Lil's downturned face appeared calm, unflustered. Mine, I was certain, was not. Though she never said so, I knew Lil thought I needed to take a step back from my family. Under normal circumstances, she may have been right. But this particular drama wasn't over the PTA or the Board of Nursing or a fight with Robert. This was something I'd set in motion, all those years ago, when Bill McGrady strolled into my life, and changed it forever.

Watford, England, 1953

In the smoke-filled front room of the Heathcote Arms, I tried not to let my boredom show. There'd been a wedding in town, which to all the single women in Watford meant one thing: eligible men. I was with Elizabeth and Evie, two fellow midwives who, like me, had moved from London for their midwifery training in Watford. We all lived at the nurses' home (or virgins' retreat, as it was nicknamed) in town. Sister Eileen had told us to be home by ten thirty sharp, but as we knew she was always in bed by nine thirty, we didn't worry.

Evie and Elizabeth were dressed to the nines, but while they'd turned several heads, no one had bought us a drink so far. It must have been my fault. Elizabeth and Evie were both widely accepted as magnificent, but with enough imperfections to make young lads think they were in with a chance. I, on the other hand, had a face my mother had once described as "handsome." My bottom was wide rather than curvy and my hair was so determinedly straight that any attempt to curl it always ended in hot, frustrated tears. As such, I was forced to accept that our lack of success in the drinks department was something to do with me.

The room continued to fill and I was beginning to feel a little light-headed when the door opened and a gush of fresh air poured in, along with a pair of young men. All heads in the room turned to look. Through the smoke I could see that one of the men was tall and lean, with a large forehead and dark brown hair teased into a peak. Together with his mate, he did a rotation of the room then rambled over to our table.

"Can we buy you ladies a drink?"

The tall, handsome one was looking directly at me.

"Forgive me," he said, "I'm being rude. This is my mate, Robbie. And I'm Bill McGrady."

Evie and Elizabeth stared up at him from our bench seat, marveling as if Jesus Christ himself were standing before us. And, indeed, Bill McGrady was something rather special.

"I'm Floss," I said, clearing my throat. "This is Evie and this is Elizabeth."

Bill tipped his nonexistent hat. "Pleasure to meet you ladies."

His gaze remained fixed on me. I knew I should look away, but somehow, I couldn't. I cursed the gods. In the past few months, I'd virtually accepted that men, on the whole, didn't interest me. I had a niggling feeling that perhaps women did. As if I wasn't confused enough—now *this*.

"I'd like a drink," Elizabeth said. "A shandy, please. Same for you, Evie?"

Evie nodded.

"And for you, Floss?" Elizabeth asked. Sometimes, when she leaned in close like she was doing, I had the urge to scoot forward and kiss her perfect, pink mouth. But today, I was thinking about another set of lips. "Nothing for me. I'm fine."

"Go on, Floss," Bill said. I didn't want to be flattered or swept up, but looking at his cheeky, half-cocked grin it was difficult.

"Fine," I said. I felt the blush, so I could only imagine how it looked. I'd probably broken out in a heat rash. "A sweet sherry would be lovely."

When Bill turned to talk to Robbie, Elizabeth leaned closer to me and lowered her voice. "Go on, love," she said. "He's a doll. Go for it."

"No, no," I said. "You go for it."

"He was staring at *you*, Floss."

"He wasn't. Anyway, he's not my cup of tea."

"*He's* not your cup of tea? Mr. Marlon Brando?"

I insisted that no, he wasn't. And after a few seconds of assurance, Elizabeth sighed. "Well, if you're sure." She waited until I confirmed yet again, and then leapt to Bill's side. "How 'bout I give you a hand with those drinks?" she asked him.

I watched as Bill guided Elizabeth to the bar, his hand near, but not touching, the small of her back. Most men I knew would use a crowded bar to their advantage, but Bill appeared to be the perfect gentleman.

When they arrived at the bar, Bill cast a glance over his shoulder and I quickly joined a stilted conversation between Evie and Robbie. By the time I looked back, Bill was looking at Elizabeth. In an emerald green belted dress, she was looking particularly pretty, and from the look on Bill's face, he'd noticed. Her long auburn hair was out and curled, and she somehow looked demure but risqué at the same time. She was beaming and making theatrical hand gestures, perhaps telling the story about the young virgin who'd turned up at their prenatal clinic, convinced she was carrying the Lord's next child. Whatever she was saying, Bill was clearly enamored. And the brief moment we'd shared was clearly forgotten.

Bill and Elizabeth were married six months later.

It was a small wedding. Money was hard to come by then—the war had taken it from those who had it, and taken the lives of those who didn't. Bill's family never had money to begin with and Elizabeth's parents, who fancied themselves as society people, had married four daughters before her and now had little left other than their good name. As maid of honor, I'd been the first one to walk down the aisle. I'd smiled at the guests, the floor, the flowers—everywhere but at Bill. But when I reached the altar, I had to steal a look. His stance was relaxed, his smile traveled all the way to his eyes, and there wasn't a trace of nerves. This wasn't a man having second thoughts.

It was Elizabeth who'd spent the morning in a state of pre-wedding jitters: tense, teary, quiet. But when she appeared in the church's double doorway, her nerves were nowhere to be seen. Everything sparkled—her eyes, her smile, the antique jeweled comb in her hair. She'd decided to wear her hair out, a last-minute decision that her mother had fought, calling it "common," but Elizabeth had stuck to her guns, and no one could argue with her now. With it flowing over the capped sleeves of her A-line gown, she was as whimsical and delicate as the peonies she carried.

Elizabeth and Bill were to spend the wedding night in the town's hotel, before moving to Bill's house in Kings Langley. According to Elizabeth, it was nothing but a humble cottage, but she didn't mind. What Bill lacked in money, he made up for in charm. And charm, we all agreed, was something he had in spades.

"I want to thank you all for coming tonight," he'd said when he opened his speech. "It's humbling for a man such as myself to be in the presence of you fine folk, and even more so to have married into a family such as the O'Hallorans. Most humbling of all"—he smiled at Elizabeth—"is to be standing here as the husband of this beautiful creature. I won't pretend to be anything more than I am—the son of a farmer who spent a few years in the service. A lot less than Elizabeth deserves. But I promise that I will work hard every day of the rest of my life to make myself worthy."

The room came apart at the seams. What a delightful young man! Isn't Elizabeth lucky? Many of the guests were in tears. I also shed a tear, though perhaps for different reasons.

The bridal waltz followed, then all the dances after that. Father–daughter, mother–son, in-laws, bridesmaids. Bill and Elizabeth swept around the floor, gazing at each other, as indeed they should have been. Evie and her new beau, Jack, pressed up against each other like a pair of magnets. Meanwhile, I took my maid of honor duties seriously, powdering Elizabeth's nose, keeping her quarrelling aunts apart, dancing with the best man. As the event drew to a close, I helped Elizabeth's parents pack up the hall. As I bundled the last of the gifts into Elizabeth's father's car, two fingers tapped impatiently against my shoulder.

"Does the groom get a dance with the maid of honor?"

I slammed the trunk and turned around. Bill was glassy eyed, his top three buttons undone and his bow tie hanging open. He gave me a cheeky grin.

I consulted an imaginary piece of paper that I pulled from an imaginary pocket. "I don't see it on the run sheet, I'm afraid."

He moved in closer beside me and I caught a whiff of the carnation in his pocket. He looked at my pretend run sheet. "Are you sure? I think I see it—" He pointed a finger in the air. "—right here."

"I think you're seeing things. Elizabeth is about to throw the bouquet. We'd best get inside."

"Are you hoping to catch it?" he asked.

"No. Evie should be the one tonight."

"And why, may I ask, not you?"

I looked at my feet. I worried that if I looked directly at Bill, I might not be able to look away. Ever. "Well . . . she and Jack have been dating for months, and I—I don't have a lad."

"Well, then . . . ," Bill said, "how about that dance?"

I scanned the space around us. A few guests hovered by their cars, saying good-byes. "I really don't think that's a good idea."

Bill opened his arms in a waltz stance. He grasped my right hand in his left and pointed them at the sky. "Bill," I said. "We really should get back to Elizabeth."

I heard a car engine, then watched as the small group who'd been hovering outside drove away. Bill looked from the car to me and waggled his eyebrows. "All alone."

He pulled me a little closer. Our bellies pressed together. My heart started to race, and I had no idea if that was good, or bad.

"Elizabeth has had my attention all day," he said into my ear. At the same time, he moved his right hand a fraction lower. "And you, not having a lad and all, are in need of a bit of attention, I'd say."

7

Neva

I decided to become a midwife on a Wednesday. I was fourteen. After school, my teacher had passed me a note with the address where Grace was delivering. This happened from time to time, when the client's house was within walking distance from school. This day it took me about twenty minutes to get there and when I did, a piece of lined paper was wedged between the wrought iron and the mesh of the screen door. The handwriting was Grace's.

Door is open. We're in the back.

"I'm here," I called as I let myself in. I stood in the hallway, waiting for Grace to shout out a greeting. After a few minutes, she'd come and update me on how it was going, and either give me cab money or tell me Dad would pick me up on the way home. Not this day. Instead, the bedroom door peeled open. Her face was pale.

"Neva—thank God. Quick. Come in."

I froze; a deer in the headlights. "What?"

"My birth assistant is sick, she's had to go home. Agnes is nine centimeters dilated—I need someone now."

When I was younger I was often in the room while Grace's clients delivered. On those days, she jokingly called me her assistant. I may have passed her a towel or held a client's hand for a while. I may even have whispered a few motivating words. But she'd also had an actual assistant. Someone experienced with childbirth. "I can't."

"Course you can."

She ducked back into the room. Despite my reservations, I dropped my bag onto the floor and slowly followed her.

The woman—Agnes—sat on the edge of the bed, wrapped in a cream waffle-cotton robe. Her elbows were pressed against her knees and she rocked back and forth, moaning softly. Her husband sat beside her, rubbing her back.

"This is my daughter," Grace said. "She's attended more births than you've had hot dinners."

I wasn't so sure. The man was at least thirty. I'd attended about twenty births—fifty, if you included those I'd heard from my bedroom but didn't see. Unless he'd eaten a lot of cold dinners, Grace's stats were off.

"How old is she?" he asked.

I opened my mouth.

"Sixteen," Grace cut in. "And we don't have a lot of choice, Jeremy. My birth assistant had to leave. We're just lucky we have an experienced person here to help us. Unless you'd like to transfer Agnes to a hospital?"

"No," Agnes said.

Her husband, Jeremy, turned to her. "Honey—"

"No hospital! I'm not sick and neither is my baby. Why should we go to the hospital? I want my baby to be born right here in its home, not in some stark, sterile hospital room surrounded by strangers in surgical masks."

Agnes's tone left no room for doubt. I could tell Grace was trying not to look smug. She failed. "Right, then," she said. "It's decided. Neva, I have to prepare. Can you stay here with Agnes?"

She was gone before I could respond.

Another contraction was upon Agnes, and she curved in on herself again. She was in the advanced stages of labor, clearly, but I'd heard worse. I let her finish the contraction, then spoke.

"I'm Neva," I started, feeling self-conscious. I squatted down, bending to see her face. It struck me that she might not be in the best position for this stage of labor. "Are you feeling comfortable there?"

She sat upright. I didn't expect, after the strength of her no-hospital declaration, to see anguish on her face. "I'm just . . . exhausted."

"I know," I said, though I didn't. I was a fourteen-year-old girl— what did I know about labor? I tried to think of what Grace would say to this woman, but all the options were too airy-fairy for my liking. *You are a warrior* was one of her catchphrases. *Think of your precious little angel, ready to grow its wings.* Neither of those things felt like me.

"Would you like to try standing?" I said. That was one thing my mother had taught me that was based on science, rather than fairy dust and sunshine. Good old gravity. "Your husband and I can take your weight, and you can hug one of us through contractions."

I must have got her at the right time, because she seemed happy to get up, and reported that it helped a lot. Strangely, Agnes chose to hug me during contractions, rather than her husband, but I attributed it to height. Her head rested on my shoulder and we got into a good rhythm, pacing and adopting the slow-dance position when the pains came on. With each contraction, her face locked up—but she remained purposeful. She listened to all my suggestions and followed them.

"Shhh, you're okay," I told her, rocking back and forth, working through a contraction with her. "You're okay."

In fact, she was better than okay. I was impressed. Though I didn't share my mother's disdain of doctors and hospitals, there was something to admire about a woman's determination to stick to her guns to have a natural home birth. She was certainly being tested. As I rocked back and forth with her, an unexpected feeling came over me. A feeling that I was an integral part of something. Something greater than myself.

"You're amazing, Agnes." Even as I spoke, the words sounded like they had come from someone else. "You're doing it. Soon, the pain will be over, but you'll have done something extraordinary. I'm very proud of you."

It was an odd thing for a teenager to say to a woman in her twenties or thirties. But it just came out. Odder was the fact that she responded to it. She nodded. She *believed* me.

By the time Grace returned to the room, Agnes was feeling pressure in her pelvis.

"Looks like you're ready to push your baby out, Agnes," Grace said. "Let's get you into position."

To my surprise, Agnes looked at me. "Is it best to stand while I deliver too?"

"It's best to be in whatever position feels right to you," I said, not missing a beat. I felt Grace staring, but I didn't break Agnes's gaze. "So you tell us."

She frowned as she thought. "I'd like to squat."

When Agnes was in position, squatting over the end of the bed with her husband and me at each side, Grace raised her eyebrows at me. "Go ahead."

"Really?" I mouthed.

Grace nodded. If she had any concerns, she kept them well hidden. It bolstered my confidence. Maybe, just maybe, I could do this. I paused, trying to think what to say. But when Agnes whimpered, the words just came.

"Try to blow while you push," I said, kneeling by Grace's side at Agnes's feet. "We don't want the baby to come too fast or it can cause a tear."

Agnes did as I said. Grace moved to the side as the baby emerged, and I continued to guide Agnes, drawing on words of support that had obviously been buried deep in my subconscious. By the time the baby boy spilled into my arms, I knew. Women *were* warriors. And I wanted to be part of it.

Erin lay on the operating table, gripping her husband's hand. She blinked up at me tearily. "What's happening?"

I peeked over the curtain. Sean's forehead was gently pinched in concentration. Beside him, Marion, a gossipy middle-aged nurse who for some reason I'd taken an instant disliking to upon meeting, stood, suction at the ready. Patrick was in the corner, whispering to Leila, a pediatric nurse, who was chuckling. Everyone was going about their business, and the atmosphere told me everything was well. Still, I knew the patients liked to hear it from the doctor's mouth.

"How's it going, Dr. Cleary?" I asked Sean.

"We'll have this little one out in a minute," he said. "The heart rate has stabilized."

I squeezed Erin's hand and smiled at her husband, Angus. "Did you hear that? You're in good hands."

"Very good hands," Marion echoed. "Dr. Cleary is one of the best doctors in the country."

Marion smiled preemptively at Sean. But when he kept his head down, her smile thinned. Marion made it her business to stay on the right side of doctors, if only to give the impression that she had more clout around the hospital than she actually did. It drove her crazy that Sean didn't buy into it, particularly as he wasn't opposed to a bit of hero worship. What she didn't know was that he was a private person and his disdain for gossip took priority over his need to have his ego stroked. It was one of many things I liked about him.

On the operating table, Erin started to well up. "I just wanted so much to do this myself."

I squatted down beside her. Erin's two older sisters had delivered their children at the birthing center. Of all my clients, this family had perhaps been the most moved by the experience. Both sisters had raved about the transformative quality of natural birth, and about how afterwards, they'd felt superhuman. I knew Erin had hoped that she would experience this superhuman feeling today. And I was going to make sure that she did.

"I know. But Dr. Cleary said everything looks good. We're lucky that we have access to expert medical attention when complications arise. The most important thing is that your baby is safe."

A tear dripped onto the table. "But why did complications arise? What did I do?"

I felt a stab of resentment toward my mother and her bitter diatribe about doctors and hospitals. While I was a huge fan of a natural birth where it was possible, I was a huger fan of doing what was safest for mothers and babies. Some women chose to have a C-section, some needed one for their own, or their baby's, health. Scaremongering and quoting intervention statistics did a lot more harm than good, in my opinion.

"I'll let you in on a little secret, okay?" I lowered my voice. "That superhuman feeling people describe? It has nothing to do with the way the baby comes out. It's about what happens to the mother. *You* become superhuman. You'll grow extra hands and legs to look after your baby. You'll definitely grow an extra heart for all the love you'll feel." Erin was watching me intently. "The second you see this baby, you won't care if it came out your stomach or your nose." About this, I was certain. "You'll feel it, I promise you. Just wait and see."

"A nasal delivery?" Sean's voice was loud and contemplative through the screen. "Is that what you midwives get up to in your birthing center? I always thought you lot were a little unorthodox."

Erin's lips curved up slightly. That was another thing I liked about Sean. He knew when and how to lighten a mood.

"Here we go," he said, and a tiny cry came through the thin sheet. Erin sucked in a breath as a little face appeared over the top of the curtain. "No! Already?"

"It's a boy!" Sean said with delight that was hard to feign. "Just a bit of cord around his middle. He's fine."

"A boy!" Erin cried. "Did you hear that, Angus? It's a boy."

I stood and peeked over the screen. Sean handed Patrick the baby and he carried him over to the baby warmer. "He's a good size," I said. "Looks perfectly healthy. The pediatrician and nurses are checking him out, but I'll go hurry them along. We want him in your arms as soon as possible."

"Oliver," Erin said. "His name is Oliver."

I nodded. "I'll bring Oliver back as soon as I can."

Leila, the pediatric nurse, was rubbing Oliver with a warm towel while Patrick did the suction. He was pinking up beautifully. "Looks good," I said.

"Yes," Patrick said. "Very good."

"Making you broody, Dr. Johnson?" Marion said. "My daughter Josie is about your age, you know."

My gaze bounced to Patrick's, but I quickly looked away. What was I doing, getting territorial over Patrick? Just because he slept on my couch occasionally didn't mean he was in my jurisdiction.

"If she's a daughter of yours, Maz," Patrick said, "she's too good for a scoundrel like me."

"Far too good," Sean echoed.

"She could do worse, of course," Patrick said. "Then again, Sean isn't single."

Both men had smiles in their voices, but there was truth in their words. How two people could be such good friends but be so competitive at the same time was beyond me.

"Now," Patrick said to the baby, "let's see how you are doing, little fella."

As with Sean, Patrick's delight in his job was obvious. As he checked Oliver over—testing reflexes, rotating his hips—he chatted continuously, telling the baby what he was going to do before he did it. He spoke in a natural voice, the kind he would use over a beer with an old friend. Leila stared unashamedly. Even I could admit, there was something sexy about a man who was comfortable with a baby.

"So, I hear congratulations are in order, Neva?" I lifted my head before I realized what Marion was saying, giving her a ringside seat to my horrified expression. "About the pregnancy, I mean."

I busied myself checking the baby's fontanels. "Oh. Thank you."

"And due quite soon, I hear," she continued. "You must be excited."

Casually, I scanned the room, assessing the fallout. Patrick winced. Leila's mouth hung open. Sean had frozen, his hands still half-buried in Erin's abdomen. He scanned what he could see of my stomach. "Neva, you're expecting?"

"Yes." I didn't look at him. I held my hands out to Patrick. "Baby, please."

I must have sounded authoritative because, rather than joke with me over one last check as he usually did, Patrick wrapped the baby and handed him over. I crossed the room, back to Erin.

"I hope I haven't put my foot in my mouth," Marion said. Her tone made it clear that she hoped she'd done exactly that. "Eloise mentioned it this morning. It wasn't meant to be a secret, was it? Because I'd hate to think—"

"*I'd* hate to think you weren't paying attention, Marion." Sean's voice was quiet but sharp, and it silenced the room. Marion's cheeks colored. "Because as you can see, I'm still stitching the patient. And I need a lap sponge."

"Yes, Doctor." Marion fumbled for the sponge, and I could tell she was not happy. I almost felt sorry for Sean. Ignoring her attempts to ingratiate herself was one thing, but a public reprimand was quite another. She'd make him pay for that.

I tried my best to focus on the task at hand, pressing the baby's face against his mother's cheek, letting him see her, smell her breath, feel her touch. With any luck, we could start him breast-feeding as soon as we made it into recovery. I needed to concentrate on that.

"When are you due, Neva?" Sean asked me after a minute or two of silence. His voice had lost its sharp edge; in fact, it was a little quieter than normal.

I met his eye over the curtain. "December thirty-first."

"A New Year baby," he said. He frowned, then his gaze returned to Erin's stomach. "What a miracle."

"Yes," I agreed. "It really is."

I pushed my scrubs into the overfull laundry basket and dragged myself toward the elevator. Now that my urgent tasks were done, the familiar weight of tiredness anchored me to the ground like cement boots. I still had to check in at the birthing center on my way out, to make sure none of my clients had gone into labor. If not, perhaps I'd have a lie down in one of the suites. It took less than ten minutes to walk to my apartment, but somehow that was too far.

As I waited for the elevator, I leaned against the wall. At the far end of the corridor, Patrick held court with three student nurses, who were taking notes and giggling at intervals. Although Patrick was professional enough never to cross the line with a student, it was easy to see he loved the attention. Marion stood at the nurses' desk, whispering furiously and stealing glances over her shoulder. I'd have assumed she was gossiping about my pregnancy, but thanks to Sean's reprimand in theater, there was an equal chance she was slandering him. I couldn't help but be grateful.

I sighed and allowed my eyes what I called an extra-long blink.

"Should I be hurt?"

When I opened my eyes, Sean stood before me in blue scrubs, blue cap, and puffy blue shoe covers. My first instinct was to run. To locate the nearest exit and hurtle toward it as fast as my legs would carry me. But even if I had the energy to do that, it wouldn't help me for long. "No. You should be relieved."

"Were you planning to tell me?"

"Actually, I was waiting for you to guess. For someone who is usually quite perceptive, and an ob-gyn, I'd have thought—"

"Neva."

His tone made me pause. "Yes?"

"Are you sure you have your dates right?"

"Yes."

"Is that all you're going to say? Yes?"

I was about to say that if the answer to his questions continued to be yes, then yes, that's all I was going to say, but before I could respond, he towed me into a corner. "Are you *sure*? Because if you're just a few weeks out—"

I stopped him before he could say the words. "It's okay. I'm sure."

I rested a hand on his chest, partly to calm him, partly to regain some personal space. Finally he sagged like a day-old balloon. "God, Neva. I don't know what I'd do if . . . well, I'm just glad it's not."

I let Sean bask in the relief. I only wished I could have shared his joy. "Me, too."

"So?" he said. "Whose is it?"

"It's mine."

"I realize that." A look of bafflement appeared on his face, followed by a short laugh. "And who else's?"

I was already so sick of saying it, and it hadn't even been twenty-four hours since I'd made the announcement. I longed for a stack of flyers of FAQs that I could hand out. *This should answer most of your questions*, I'd tell people as I pressed a flyer into their hand. *And there is an e-mail address at the bottom if any of your questions remain unanswered. It is questions@nevaspregnancy.com.* Alas, I had no printed flyers.

"No one's. Just mine."

He cocked an eyebrow. I sighed.

"The father's not going to be involved, okay?"

Sean took a minute to digest that. "I see. Well, I'm sorry to hear that."

He did look sorry. He started that awkward, mumbly thing guys did when they were uncomfortable. Which, of course, made me more uncomfortable.

"If there's anything I can do—"

I pointed to the wedding ring, which he wore on a band around his neck during surgery. "I don't think that's a good idea, do you?"

One of us had to bring Laura up. True to his word, Sean had wound up marrying that Texan cashier from his grocery store. With frizzy, peroxide-blond hair and hips to match her enormous breasts, she was far from classically beautiful, but she had a pretty, friendly face and a sweet disposition. The kind of woman who, after three years of being married to an ob-gyn, still got choked up when he told her about delivering a baby. Not the kind of woman you felt good about betraying.

"Probably not."

"How *is* Laura?"

"Fine," he said. "Thanks for asking."

"Tumor's still shrinking?"

He nodded. "Now they're saying it's the size of a pea."

Nine months ago, the tumor had been the size of a baseball. Her illness started with a headache. Sean had popped Laura a couple of Tylenol before work one morning, and by the time he got home, it was a migraine. Three days later, she was blind in one eye. Thanks to Sean's connections at St. Mary's, Laura was able to get in for a CT scan straightaway. The prognosis hadn't been good. But according to Sean, Laura liked nothing more than proving people wrong.

"She thinks it's this green tea diet she's been on. Loves telling me that doctors know less than nothing when it comes to people's health." Sean laughed, shaking his head. "It's more likely to be the surgery, chemo, and radiation therapy. But I'll credit the tea, if that makes her happy."

"Whatever it is, I'm glad it's working," I said.

"Yes," Sean said. "Yes, me too."

"Anyway," I started; then my mouth stuck on what I was supposed to say next.

Anyway . . . give Laura my regards?

Anyway . . . glad to have brought you the good tidings?

Anyway . . . you're off the hook?

No appropriate sign-off existed for this particular conversation. Best that I just end it as soon as possible.

"Anyway . . . ," I tried again. "I guess I'll see you later."

As I waited for the elevator doors to close, I saw Patrick at the end of the corridor. The nurses still stood in front of him, pretty and eager as ever. But his gaze was focused over their heads and down the corridor. Directly at me.

8

Grace

Usually as I drove across the thin strip of Beavertail Road that links the south part of Conanicut Island with the north, I was at peace. With Mackerel Beach on my left and Sheffield Cove on my right, it was hard not to be. Right now the beaches were stuffed with swimmers and skin divers. Windsurfers tore across the sparkling green water at the mouth of the cove, and boats nodded good evening to one another. Still, as I drove the short distance home from a delivery, I wasn't at peace. My mind was too full even to spare a thought for the healthy baby girl I'd delivered three hours before.

The mystery of Neva's baby was driving me crazy. I hated secrets at the best of times, but this one would do me in. I was going over it all in my head yet again as I pulled onto the grass in front of our stone-and-shingle beachfront home, next to Robert's car. Odd. It wasn't even five thirty; Robert was never home at this hour.

My phone vibrated on the way to the door. I located it in my bag and shouldered it to my ear. "Hello?"

"Oh, um . . . hi, Grace, it's Molly. Is this a bad time?"

Molly. I did a quick calculation in my head. She wasn't due for another month. Not a labor call. "Not at all, Molly. You okay, darling?"

"Yes, I think so, but . . . I just wanted to check . . . I've been getting really thirsty lately. Like, almost a gallon and a half of water today thirsty. I know I'm probably being paranoid, but I thought I'd check if this was normal. I mean . . . my baby's not dehydrated or anything, is it?"

Molly Harris was twenty-two, and it was her first pregnancy. She was a natural neurotic, and I received a call most days about something. Once, she'd accidentally eaten some unpasteurized cheese. Another day, she'd thought her bladder leakage was her water breaking. But I was happy to take her calls. Molly had lost her mother to cancer shortly before she became pregnant, and I liked to think I'd become something of a mother figure to her.

I fished for my keys in my bag. "Absolutely not. It's completely normal for thirst to skyrocket during your third trimester. Your body has created about forty percent more blood to provide nutrition and oxygen to your baby, and all that extra blood uses up a lot of water." I found my keys and inserted them into the lock, but when I turned, found it already unlocked.

"Oh, okay. Jimmy told me I was being silly. I'm so sorry to bother you, Grace."

"Do I sound bothered? Call anytime. That's what I'm here for."

I hung up and pushed open the door. The scent of something hearty hit me. It smelled like food, but it couldn't be. Robert hadn't cooked a proper meal in thirty years, save for some grilled cheese sand-wiches and instant noodles when I was called out on a delivery. I took a step toward the kitchen, stopping short as Robert appeared in the doorway.

"Hi," he said. He grinned like there was nothing strange about him being home at this hour. "How was your day?"

I stared at him. He had a glass of red wine in his hand. My floral apron was knotted around his waist, and behind him, steam fogged up the stainless steel backsplash. "Is everything okay, Rob?"

He laughed. "Yes."

"Then . . . what are you doing here?"

"A man can't surprise his wife with dinner anymore?"

"A man can," I said, "but he rarely does."

He handed me a glass of wine and kissed my cheek. But I still didn't get it. "Seriously? You cooked?"

"Reheated," he admitted. "Meatballs from Isabella's. Consider it an apology. For these last few weeks. I've been a beast."

"Weeks?"

Robert winced. "Months?"

"More like yea—"

He cut me off with a poke in the ribs. I laughed. "What's brought this on?"

"More layoffs. Today I lost half my team."

"Oh, no."

"There'll be more too. Projects are on hold. We're having to cut our margins to win new work. We're going to offshore a bunch of jobs."

We strolled side by side to the kitchen, where a pot of pasta was boiling over. I turned it off and looked at him. Behind the wrinkles and the salt-and-pepper hair, I could still see that handsome boy I'd married. I could also see Neva in him. The high, angular cheekbones, the flying saucer eyes and straight nose.

"Is your job safe?"

Robert tried determinedly to separate a clump of overcooked spaghetti. "Finance is a cost center, so no. But since I'm doing the calculations for severance pay, I'm probably okay this month."

"Well, we'll be all right, whatever happens," I said. "We have each other, we have our health."

He cracked a weary smile. "Yeah. The important stuff."

"At least I've got a recession-proof job," I said. "People will continue to have babies. If it paid better, I'd tell you to shove the job and take up golf."

"Don't worry about golf. Just keep doing what you're doing. We can't afford to have both of our jobs in jeopardy."

Robert continued to stir the pasta as if it would magically separate. I had my doubts. "How about we throw this out and start over?"

Robert smiled. "What would I do without you?"

We started again with some fusilli, and soon the house smelled like a starchy, herby Italian kitchen. As I cooked, Robert got under my feet, full of offers to stir this or salt that. I frowned and shooed him away, smacking his hand as he tried to taste. But I loved every second of it.

"I spoke to Neva today," Robert said after a few minutes. His tone indicated he'd thought carefully about how and when to bring it up.

"Oh?" I continued stirring the pasta but my senses went on high alert. "What did she say?"

"She wanted to apologize to you for running off at the hospital."

I tapped the spoon on the side of the saucepan and turned around. "Did she say anything else?"

"Not about the father of her baby, no."

I deflated.

"But she is coming to dinner," he said.

A squeal tore from me before I could stop it. "Tonight? Really?"

"Yes. But I want us to have a pleasant dinner together. I don't want you interrogating her about the baby's father."

"But it would be such a good opportunity to—" I stopped when I saw Robert's face. "Fine. Anyway, I know who the father is."

"She told you?"

"No. I figured it out."

Robert frowned. "I see."

"Don't you want to know who it is?" I didn't give him the chance to answer. "It's an ob-gyn that she works with—Dr. Cleary. He's tall, handsome-ish, and as arrogant as a room of doctors. Rob? Did you hear me?"

"Mmm-hmm."

"As soon as I saw them together, I knew. Che-*mist*-try. And it makes sense. Neva wouldn't want to tell me she was having an ob-gyn's baby, would she?"

"I'm not sure."

I waited for Robert to say more, but he didn't.

"You think I'm wrong, don't you?"

"Not necessarily. I just wonder if your dislike of medical intervention would be enough to evoke such a strong stance from Neva."

I thought about that. "You're right," I admitted. "Neva wouldn't bother creating such a lie for my benefit."

"I didn't say that. I just think there might be a bit more to it. Neva wouldn't create a drama unless she had no choice."

I frowned. "You don't think—?"

"What?"

"I don't know . . . that there really *isn't* a father?"

Robert coughed, then swiftly covered his mouth with his hand. "No. I don't think that," she said. "Even if it were medically possible to become pregnant without a father, do you think Neva would be the first one to get her hands on the technology?"

"I have to consider all possibilities. She's a midwife. What if she was part of an early trial?"

"You're not serious, Grace."

I allowed a smile. "I was. But you're right. It's silly."

Robert came to my side. "You make me laugh, you know that?" He reached over and turned off the heat on the pasta and sauce. "Why don't we eat this . . . later?"

There was a distinct glint in Robert's eye. I hadn't seen it for a while. "But Neva—"

"—won't be here for forty-five minutes."

I hesitated, but only for a millisecond.

We could always make more pasta.

Fifteen minutes later, I lay partially naked in my husband's arms. The sex had been perfunctory and unimaginative, but I fought my inclination to be disappointed. Robert was making an effort. He'd made dinner. He'd invited Neva over. He'd initiated sex for the first time in God knows how long. And given the horrible time he was having at work, the least I could do was pretend to have enjoyed it.

In the corner of the room, a large canvas leaned against the wall, drying. A blend of reds, blues, and purples—an abstract piece, in theory. But who was I kidding? It was so obviously a vagina that as I looked at it, I actually blushed. Had I left it there as a message to Robert? *Here I am, a woman with needs. Make love to me before I explode?* Was that how things were now?

Before we got married, sex had been our strong suit. Not that I blamed marriage. Marriage changed things, but not in the way I'd expected. I hadn't considered myself the marrying type, thinking it was a foolish ritual for people who required material security. I thought it would make me feel trapped. But it didn't. In fact, with Robert's surname where mine used to be, I felt invincible. Where I once had weaknesses, I now had Robert, the perfect yin to my yang. I'd always been excellent at anecdotes, but until Robert came along, they often fell flat when people wanted supporting "evidence" or worse, "studies." With Robert by my side, he'd unobtrusively fill in the gaps in my arguments with "evidence," shutting up all the naysayers with his gentle, authoritative tone. And afterwards, as we lay in each other's arms on the sofa or the kitchen floor or wherever it was that had taken our fancy that night, we'd drink wine and marvel at what a perfect pair we made.

When I became pregnant with Neva, it was the beginning of a funny patch of our sexual relationship. I initiated a sex-free first trimester for fear of miscarriage, and though I didn't encounter any resistance from Robert, things began to change. Without that intimacy, I noticed Robert was less affectionate with me, less likely to tell me his innermost thoughts. Once we were out of the "danger zone," we did resume inter-course, but it was different somehow—more of a necessary release than a way of connecting. And the more my belly grew, the less effort Robert made. I'd thought after Neva was born things would go back to normal, but they didn't.

What Robert lacked in the bedroom, he made up for in attentive-ness to his daughter. He adored her. I'd expected that he'd love her, of course, but having no father of my own in the picture, I'd never had a point of reference. Neva returned his feelings. The way she settled in his arms, the way she lit up when he entered the room—it was some-thing I hadn't foreseen. Something wonderful. It was a shame, though, that during this period, sex slipped down a couple of rungs on our ladder of importance. It simply wasn't a priority.

By the time Neva left home we'd fallen into what I believed was a typical pattern of noticing that it had been a while between drinks and deciding we may as well get on with it. The frequency wasn't des-perate, and I still had the odd orgasm, so when I complained to my friends, they simply rolled their eyes and said they wished they had my problems. And outside the bedroom, Robert and I still had our laughs. We cuddled at night and, occasionally, held hands in the street. We celebrated birthdays and anniversaries, and Robert always put thought into the messages he wrote on the card. I'd asked myself more times than I could count if this was enough, and I'd come to the conclusion that it was. But now that Neva was gone and my mother was happily involved with Lil, lovemaking was creeping back up my list of priorities. So, I should have been pleased that Robert was initiating sex, even average sex. Why instead did I feel like I'd been kicked in the guts?

"Shall we finish getting dinner ready?" he asked after a minute or so of obligatory cuddling.

I rolled into a sitting position, invigorated as I remembered Neva was on her way. "Yes. Neva will be here soon."

I stood, letting my dress fall over my hips to the floor. The doorbell rang.

"Oh. Here she is!"

Robert stomped toward the door and I hurried into the kitchen. The pasta was ruined yet again, so I tossed it out and flicked on the burner again. Our third attempt. While I waited for it to boil, I checked my reflection in the microwave. A little disheveled perhaps, but no more than normal.

As I stirred the meatballs, Neva and Robert rounded the corner. She delighted me by planting a kiss on my cheek. "Hi, Grace."

"I'm glad you could fit us into your busy schedule."

"Sure. Can I help?"

"Just sit down and relax," I told her, pointing at a bar stool. "I'll take care of everything." But Neva and Robert were already halfway to the dining room, lost in their own world of conversation. I watched them through the pass-through—Neva smiling, Robert's arm casually strewn across her shoulders. It irritated me no end.

"Red, Robert?" I called out.

He paused, mid-conversation. "Please."

"And you, Neva?"

She half turned, but her eyes remained locked on her father. "Juice, please. Thanks, Grace."

As I poured their drinks, I continued to watch them. They were so relaxed, so at ease. Robert showed no signs of worry over his job and

Neva, no concern for her baby's apparent lack of a father. As they talked, they mirrored each other—scratching the same ear, crossing the same leg. It was a habit I'd always found endearing. I should have been pleased that Neva had such a kindred spirit in her father. But today, for some reason, it hurt.

When dinner was ready, I set their plates down and took a seat at the head of the table. They were talking about politics or the economy or something. But I would put a stop to that.

"Okay, okay," I said. "Enough about politics. Why don't you tell us about work, Neva? Any interesting births today?"

Neva and Robert exchanged a look. I frowned. "What?"

"You're not interested in hearing about the new state senator, Grace?" Robert asked. "Mr. Hang Seng?"

"Puh-lease," I said. "No."

"What do you think about the new minority leader, Grace?" Neva asked. "Ms. Dow Jones?"

"Dow? Frightful name." I forked some pasta. I hoped I could turn the conversation onto baby names, and then, with any luck, the baby's father. But when I looked up, Neva and Robert were snickering. "What? What?"

All at once, the penny dropped: They were mocking me. "You weren't talking about politics," I said slowly. "Were you?"

Neva and Robert were now full-on laughing. I glared at Robert and he registered it. "Sorry, Grace. I'm sorry."

Neva's face straightened. "Yes, sorry, Grace."

"Yes, well," I said. "I should think so."

Neva and Robert bowed their heads. And the mood, which had

been happy and playful was soured. I shouldn't have been surprised. I had a talent for killing Neva's joy, it seemed.

"I must admit I'm relieved," I said, wanting to fill the silence and pep up the mood. "Dow Bradley is terrible name."

I hadn't intended to be funny, but I noticed the corner of Robert's lip starting to twitch. Then, so did Neva's. Before long they were chuckling, and even though I knew it was at my expense, I did too. I was powerless against laughter. Even the smallest little snicker, particularly in the most inappropriate of situations, was all it took to set me off. Now my mouth curved upward and giggles forced their way out from between my clenched lips.

I pasted on a silly grin. The night was young, and with all the laughter and good feeling, perhaps we'd find out the father of the baby yet.

"So," I said, reaching for the serving spoon. "Who's for more meatballs?"

9

Floss

I looked into the sea of expectant faces. It was the busiest session yet. For most instructors this was unusual in week three of a six-week course, but for me, it often happened this way. People enjoyed the course and then brought a friend, a parent, a grandparent. Not bad for the oldest instructor at the Jamestown community center. The oldest by twenty-five years.

"Welcome back, everyone. We are already in week three of Birthing Naturally. We have talked about proper prenatal care, the cycle of intervention, and techniques for managing your pain without drugs. Tonight you're going to hear from my granddaughter, Neva Bradley, about delivering in a birthing center."

I located Neva in the second row of the auditorium. It had been two weeks since she announced her pregnancy, and we still hadn't had the chance to talk properly. I hoped we would tonight. Neva sat next to a wicker basket full of materials. On top I could see her plastic pelvis and baby dolls. Neva had delivered her presentation to my class several times now, and it always featured in the highlights in the course evaluation.

"But first," I said. "I see we have some new faces in the room tonight, so let me start by introducing myself. My name is Florence Higgins, Floss for short. I am retired now, but I was a practicing midwife for over forty years, first in my native England and then right here in Rhode Island. I've delivered babies at home, in birthing centers, in hospitals—you name it, I've done it. Now, at eighty-three, I'm happy to be part of the cliché: 'Those who are too old—teach.'"

That got a few laughs, as it always did.

"Neva is a Certified Nurse-Midwife. She currently works at St. Mary's Birthing Center in Providence. She has delivered babies in hospitals as well as in birthing centers, so she will be well equipped to answer any questions you might have. So without further ado, I'll hand you over to Neva."

I took a seat at the side of the room. It was always a treat watching Neva's class. Like her mother, when she talked about midwifery, she came to life. Today was no different. Within minutes, Neva had the class engaged, laughing, excited. People were passing the plastic doll through the pelvis. Men were wearing the baby suit, a fabric device, heavy in front, designed to allow the father of the baby to feel pregnant. By the time Neva was finished, I couldn't help but feel enthused. And judging from the faces in the room, everyone else felt the same.

After the class, a few people remained and Neva waited around to answer questions. People seemed genuinely interested in the idea of birthing centers and had a lot of questions. While Neva answered them, I packed up the room. I was almost finished when a father-to-be, whose wife was speaking to Neva, came over to give me a hand.

"My wife and I have been debating the origin of your accent," he said with a grin. "My money is on Surrey."

His own accent, I noticed, was English. I smiled. "London. But I practiced as a midwife in Watford and Watford Rural."

Neva and the man's wife finished speaking and joined our circle.

"London!" the man said to his wife, who clicked her fingers as though she should have picked it. He grinned at me. "But you practiced in Watford Rural, you say? My grandfather lived in Abbots Langley. He was a farmer."

"So was Gran's husband," Neva said. "Small world."

"Oh, yes?" The man lit up as though he'd discovered we were long-lost relatives. "Abbots Langley?"

"Uh, no. Kings Langley."

"Kings Langley?" He slapped his thigh. "That's a stone's throw from where Pa lived. I practically grew up there. He was a dairy farmer."

"Is that right?" I yawned, hoping it would politely conclude the conversation. No such luck.

"What kind of farm was yours?" he asked.

"Oh, just . . . a normal farm, you know. A few cows, a few horses."

"Not a working farm, then?"

"No."

Neva gave me an odd look. "I thought it was a cattle farm? That's what Mom said."

"Ah—so it was. My mind's going. It's the old age." I smiled, playing the doddering old lady. The couple accepted it, though I wasn't sure about Neva.

We waved off the couple and sat down on two of the folding chairs. Neva stared at the basket in front of her. The animation she'd shown during the class was gone and she seemed flat. Tired.

I reached out and touched her belly. "How are you doing, dear?"

"Not bad." Neva continued staring at the basket. "Better than Mom, probably."

I smiled. "That's probably true."

"She doesn't want my baby to grow up like she did. Without a father."

"Is that what she said?" I asked.

"That's what she's thinking," Neva said. "That scar runs pretty deep with her, doesn't it?"

"It does appear that way."

"Makes me wonder what my baby will be in for. . . . I've been thinking about you a lot, actually, Gran. You went through everything I'm going through, but worse. You started single motherhood in a new country."

"It was tough, initially," I said. "But I wanted us to have a fresh start."

"Weren't your parents upset that you left?"

I looked at my hands, crossed in my lap. "They understood my reasons."

"And my grandfather's family? Didn't they want to see their granddaughter?"

"Perhaps they did," I said after a time. "But I had to make a choice. I chose the path that I thought was best for my daughter."

"You didn't ever think the best path would be to stay on the farm in Kings Langley?

I looked up sharply. "No. No I didn't."

It wasn't like Neva, firing questions at me like this. It was more her mother's style. I could see she was concentrating on keeping a neutral face, but the blood rose to the surface of her pale skin. She was trying to make sense of her own situation.

"I guess I just feel so alone. I can't imagine putting myself in a situation where I'd feel more alone."

"You'll understand when you become a mother, dear. Once you see your baby, you'll forget about your own needs and you'll do what's best for them."

"But that's what I don't understand," she said. "Why was it best for you and Mom to travel to the other side of the world, where you didn't know a soul?"

It was the obvious question. I actually couldn't believe that no one had asked it before. What *would* make a young lady leave her friends and family for a faraway place with a newborn baby in tow? Or rather, who *would*.

Bill's face sprang to my mind. His eyes. His cocky half smile. That air of likability that penetrated a room like killer gas. The same man who held me close outside the church hall on his wedding day. I still remember blinking at him, waiting for him to release me with a laugh and a joke. Because it had to be a joke. Bill McGrady wouldn't proposition *me*.

Eventually I managed a dry laugh. "We'd best get inside, Bill. I've maid of honor duties to attend to, and you need to cut the cake."

Bill didn't let go. His gaze was eerily piercing, like he was looking through my skin, to the bones and muscles underneath. I opened my mouth, suddenly on full alert.

"Bill!"

It wasn't my voice that rang through the silence. It was Elizabeth's.

"*Bill?* Are you out here?"

She stood at the door to the hall, cupping one hand around her mouth. Her singsong voice transformed Bill's face, smoothing his lines and lifting his features.

"Over here, my darling." I wriggled out of his grip and he stepped around me, into the light. "Floss and I were just packing the last of the gifts into the car."

"Well, good," she said. "It's time to cut the cake."

Bill jogged up to meet her on the stairs. At the top, he turned around. "Coming, Floss?"

The Bill standing before me looked like a normal, carefree young groom. Happy, friendly, and yes, a little drunk. I tried to conjure up his expression just a second ago—the piercing gaze, the pinch of his fingers on my waist—but it was already fading like a dream. As if it had never happened.

"Yes. Yes, of course."

I didn't see Elizabeth for months after that. I thought she'd visit Evie and me regularly, particularly given her love for midwifery and her (rash, I think) decision to leave it when she got married. But apart from one letter, which did little more than detail the strangeness of living on a rural property, I didn't hear from her. Not a dicky bird. Evie thought she'd be busy getting settled into married life. I expected she was right.

The world kept ticking along. Babies were born. Evie and Jack got engaged. A month passed, then another. When I still didn't hear from Elizabeth, I began to worry. What if Bill had told Elizabeth about what happened the night of the wedding, but twisted things to make it look like I'd been the one to try it on with him? *Had* I been the one to try it on with him? The whole thing had been so strange. Sometimes I wasn't even sure it happened at all.

Finally, I decided to ride out to their property on my bike. Even if the worst turned out to be true and Bill had told untruths to Elizabeth, it couldn't be more terrible than the torture of not knowing. On my next day off, I was wheeling my bike down the front path when I passed Evie. A wad of envelopes was tucked under her arm and she waved a sheet of cream stationery under my nose.

"Elizabeth is coming to my engagement party," she said. "So you needn't worry your dear head about her anymore."

"Oh," I said. "That's . . . wonderful news."

It *was* wonderful news. And I was certainly relieved that she was all right. But I was confused. If Elizabeth had responded to Evie's invitation, why hadn't she got in touch with me? Still holding the bike, I hesitated, then returned it to the shed.

The engagement party came around before I knew it. Evie's family was from East London, so the celebration was a good deal less formal than Elizabeth's pre-wedding functions. Everyone was ready for a good time. The room was decorated with nothing more than balloons and streamers. The food was good and hearty, not an hors d'oeuvre in sight.

"Floss! There you are."

Before I saw her, I was choked by a faceful of auburn hair. "Don't hate me," she said into my ear. "I'm a terrible pen friend. I got your letters. I've just been so busy, you know, getting settled and all. I'm so sorry."

In her arms, I blinked, then softened. "Of course I don't hate you, Elizabeth. I just wanted to make sure you were okay."

"I am," she said. "I'm fine."

When she pulled away, I did a visual assessment. She certainly looked fine. In a pretty white sleeveless dress with a wide, red sash and a full skirt, she looked demure and fashionable. Her lips were fiery red and her hair, which had a tendency to become flyaway, was thick and shiny. She gave me a sheepish smile. With it, I realized how much I'd missed her.

"So tell me," I started. "—Oh, goodness!" A whirl of air went by, and suddenly I was flying. I was in Bill's arms—I recognized his scent: booze and smokes and country air. He spun me in a little circle. "Floss, old girl. Long time no see."

He set me back on my feet and I patted down my blouse, which had become untucked. "Hello, Bill."

"Look at you." He whistled. "A sight for sore eyes. Are you well?"

Bill smiled as he awaited my response. Most of the people I'd spoken to that night had the curse of the wandering eye—continually glancing over my shoulder for someone better to talk to. Not Bill. His gaze didn't waver. I felt a surge of warmth toward him, and in an instant, my worries melted away. "Very well, thank you."

"And there she is . . . the beautiful bride-to-be."

Bill greeted Evie in the same way he'd done me, swinging her about in circles. Elizabeth raised an imaginary glass to her mouth. *He's full,* she mouthed.

I chuckled. "What can you do? He'll be embarrassed tomorrow."

"If he remembers," Elizabeth complained. But her smile was tolerant and she seemed every inch the happy, understanding wife. I suppose anyone would be tolerant, with a husband like Bill.

As the evening progressed, I began to enjoy myself. Everyone was happy and Elizabeth didn't have a bad word to say about Bill or marriage. Not even a regret about leaving midwifery. It was unexpected. I'd thought an adjustment period would be normal for anyone. Not for Elizabeth. Perhaps marriage with Bill was enough to cancel out any feelings like that? I couldn't help feeling a little jealous that I didn't have a relationship that fulfilling.

A spoon chinking against a glass stole our attention. Bill, red cheeked and smiling, was standing on a wooden barstool. "Ladies and gents, if I can have your attention, please. I'm sorry to hijack the celebration. This is Evie and Jack's night, but I've an announcement to make as well."

I looked to Elizabeth. She was watching Bill. Her smile was wide but stiff; it seemed to be fixed in place.

"My bride and I have been blessed," Bill said. "Just when you think life can't get much better . . . we're going to have a baby!"

The room fired with gasps and claps on backs. I drew in a breath. That explained Elizabeth's glowing skin and thick hair. I pasted a smile to my face, but my heart felt heavy. Elizabeth smiled back guiltily. "Sorry. I was about to tell you."

My eyes drifted over her, looking for any other sign of pregnancy that I might have missed. But she was thin as a whippet, even thinner than usual, and as flat-chested as ever.

Bill beckoned her. "Come up here, darling."

The crowd parted and Elizabeth made her way to where Bill stood.

"Here she is," he said. He reached for her, pulling her up onto the stool. I watched uncertainly. The chair, inadequate even for one person, wobbled, but Bill didn't seem to notice. He was grinning like a fool. "Now. I've only been married a few short months, but already I'm

a changed man. And when this one comes along"—he patted Elizabeth's flat stomach—"life will be perfect. And so I'd like to make a
toast to my wife. Now, where has my drink got to?"

Bill reached behind him in search of his beer, and the stool rolled
with him, going up on two legs. Elizabeth started to fall. A gasp rippled
through the room. Men stepped forward, arms extended. I stepped forward too. Somehow, Bill managed to tighten his grasp on Elizabeth's
waist with one hand and, with the other, steady them against the bar.
Collectively, the room exhaled.

"That was close," Bill said with a laugh. "You all right, darling?"

Elizabeth nodded. She started to get down from the chair, but Bill
held her tight. "I've got you," he said. "Don't worry."

Elizabeth looked nervous. "I really think I should—"

Bill shook his head almost imperceptibly. I had no idea what it
meant. I did know, however, that Elizabeth immediately stopped protesting.

"Let. Her. Down."

The room hushed and people looked to where Evie's father, a tall
man with a ruddy face and a no-nonsense attitude, stood. His tone was
affable but firm. Given his height and stature, I wouldn't have wanted
to argue.

"She shouldn't be standing on chairs in her condition, and you're
in no condition to hold her up, young man." He nodded at one of his
sons, a man who shared his father's stature, who lifted Elizabeth to the
ground. "All right," Elizabeth's father said to Bill. "Continue your toast,
if you must."

The room stilled, apart from a few snickers at the back of the room.
Elizabeth also stilled. Bill locked eyes with Evie's father. He looked as

though he were carefully contemplating his next move. I was overcome by an urge to leave, to flee the room, but another part of me couldn't look away. What was going on? What was he thinking?

Finally Bill's lips curved up—the signature half smile. "You're right, we can't be too careful." His face brightened, as if a switch had been flicked. "As I was saying, I'd like to raise a toast to my new bride. I'm going to need at least four boys to help me run the farm, and Elizabeth has done a great job of getting things started. To Elizabeth."

"To Elizabeth," chorused the room.

Everyone was grinning and swilling. Everyone but me. Was I the only one who'd felt that? Evidently, I was. Conversations had resumed and from what I could hear, they weren't talking about Bill. Even Evie's dad was making small talk with Bill, and it appeared to be amicable. And why not? Nothing had happened other than a man being a little careless with his wife after a few too many drinks. Many men were guilty of worse. But the feeling in my stomach said it was something more.

"Gran?"

"Yes?"

Neva was watching me with an expression that made me nervous. "Why would you travel across the other side of the world with a brand-new baby?"

Silence engulfed us. I realized my misstep. Like Grace, Neva saw the parallels between our situations. But Neva's secret gave her insight Grace didn't have. She was right, of course. It didn't make any sense for me to cross the ocean with a new baby in tow.

Unless I had something to hide.

"What aren't you saying, Gran?"

I shrugged a little. "Perhaps it was a strange thing to do, but hindsight has a way of making things clear. In the moment, things are muddier, less obvious."

Neva nodded, but her face was still wary. It worried me. She wasn't like Grace. She wouldn't press me on an issue I didn't want to discuss. But she also wouldn't forget about it the way her mother would. Her unresolved questions would sit, just under the surface, a palpable but invisible wall between us.

This wouldn't be the end of it. My granddaughter was on to me.

10

Neva

It was the first time I'd been home in days. Usually as I dashed from here to there, always late for the next thing, I courted a healthy lust for the idea of free time, the sleep-ins, the lazy breakfasts, the newspaper reading. Not today. The day ticked by in seconds, not minutes, and by late afternoon, I was climbing the walls.

When the buzzer rang at five P.M., I perked up. A visitor. I heaved myself into a standing position, and then I found the button and tapped it down. "Hello?"

"Hi, darling."

I opened my mouth, but I couldn't seem to project any words. Grace hadn't been to my apartment in years, not since she'd moved to Conanicut Island and developed a sudden intolerance for the "big smoke" of Providence. "Grace? Is that you?"

"Yes, it's me."

Suddenly it was crystal clear. Grace was staging a surprise visit to try to catch me off guard. Perhaps she thought she'd find my baby's father crouched behind the sofa or, failing that, his wallet or football jersey in the bedroom. "Okay. Come on up."

"Oh no, I can't stay," she said. "Could you come down?"

My finger froze, poised over the button. *Seriously?* She'd come all the way to Providence and she wasn't even going to come inside? "Er . . . sure. Just a sec."

As I took the stairs, it occurred to me that I liked the fact that my mother could still surprise me. Like the time when I was in the third grade, and as the rite of passage went, asked my parents for a dog. We were all living in Providence back then, and Dad said our yard wasn't big enough. Grace asked if I was upset and I remember saying "I guess not." Being upset, I figured, wouldn't change the size of our yard.

That night, when Dad and I were watching TV, Grace crawled into the room on all fours, dressed in a white, furry bunny costume. Before we could even ask what she was doing, she barked, said they didn't have any dog outfits at the costume store, and that we could call her Rover. I had a strong urge to hug her, but instead I patted her furry back.

The next day she met me at the school gates, still dressed as the bunny. That, in essence, was the problem with Grace. She never knew when to quit.

I peeled open the door, and there she was. In her slightly too-long tie-dyed sundress with her wild strawberry hair, Grace looked small. Innocent. Well meaning.

"Well," I said. "This is unexpected."

Grace reached into a bag and produced a yellow Tupperware container. "Bell pepper and bean sprout soup. Rich in folic acid, vitamin A, vitamin C."

"You made me soup?"

"Got to make sure my grandchild is getting its nutrients."

Her smile was full and wide, exposing two rows of teeth. The steel gate around my heart opened and I stepped back, allowing the door to open further. "Come in, Grace. Have some soup with me."

She pressed the soup into my hands. "I wish I could, but I have to get back. I don't want your father attempting to cook again."

With a hand on each cheek, she kissed me. She smelled like essential oils—lavender and perhaps cedar. Grace loathed perfume, but thanks to the oils that burned constantly at her house, she always smelled lovely. "Let's talk soon okay, darling?"

I nodded dumbly as she turned and hurried away, her tangled hair trailing after her like a leashed puppy. As I watched her, I had an overwhelming urge to scream, *Wait! Stay. Have soup with me.* But it was too late. She was gone.

An hour later, I was still perched on the stoop of my building. Somehow the bustle of the street was preferable to the silence of my apartment. The sky was navy blue and dusted with lavender clouds, and the damp, earthy reek of an impending storm hung in the air. It was funny; Grace's visit, which was meant to be an act of kindness, had managed to make me feel even more alone than I had before.

People mooched along my street, nicely dressed, ready for a night out. There were no strollers about. People with kids were at home, out in the suburbs, cooking dinner and organizing carpools for the morning. Not these people. Some wore wedding bands; others were clearly new to each other—a first or second date. If things worked out for them, they'd probably do things the traditional way—an engagement, a wedding, then a baby. Or maybe they'd mix things up. I had to admit, I'd never minded the idea of doing things out of order, or perhaps never getting married, but I never expected that the baby would come before the man.

"Neva? Is that you?"

I blinked. "Mark?"

"It *is* you," he said. "I thought you'd disappeared off the face of the earth."

I smiled, wishing I'd done exactly that. It was all Eloise's fault. She had joined Sean, Patrick, and me for a drink at The Hip one night last year, and as usual, Patrick and Sean (but mostly Patrick) grilled her about my love life. Usually I found it pretty easy to ignore them, but this day, for some reason, they got under my skin.

"So tell us," Patrick had asked, "does Neva ever bring guys back to the apartment?" Eloise told him the truth—that it was rare. Which was fine until she added that she'd be happy to introduce me to some eligible bachelors. The next thing I knew, her phone was out and she was preparing to text my number to a cute Italian accountant. I started to object, but as Patrick jotted down the number of Eloise's friend Amy, I heard myself say, "Sure thing. Text the accountant."

Mark had done all the right things. Picked me up at the door, kept my glass full, asked me about myself. He even paid the bill while I was in the ladies' room. I laughed more than once and he disagreed with me a couple of times in a way that didn't get my back up. One glass of wine turned into a bottle, then another. As we made the journey back to my apartment, I was feeling pleasantly buzzed.

"So, do you want to um, come up for uh . . . coffee or something?" I asked on my doorstep. A pleasant beat of electricity fizzed between us.

"I don't drink coffee," Mark said, taking a step toward me. "But, yes, I'd like to come up."

As his lips touched mine, something stirred in me. It had been a long time. Somehow we made it up the stairs, across the apartment, and into my room, but we didn't make it as far as the bed. Afterwards, as we lay staring up at the roof, my head spun.

"Hey," he said. "You wanna hear a joke?"

"Sur—" I rolled to face him, then paused and blinked hard.

Mark reached up and touched my cheek. "What is it?"

It was the strangest thing. I'd just been on a date with Mark. I'd *slept* with Mark. It might have been all the wine, but . . . when I looked at him, I expected to see Patrick. No, not expected. I *wanted* to see Patrick.

"Nothing." I threw him a smile. But my buzz was gone. "I'm fine. What was the joke?"

The joke was funny. Not hilarious, but funny. I thought of Patrick again. Usually I had to fight to keep my mouth straight when he told me a joke. He loved it when I laughed. He said I was a tough audience, but it wasn't true. Sometimes his jokes were terrible and I'd still chuckle. Something about the way he looked at me right after he'd delivered the punch line—so cautiously hopeful—would set me off. And later, as I lay in bed or walked home from my shift, I'd think of that look and smile again.

The next time Mark tried to kiss me, I closed my eyes. But it didn't matter. The passion was gone.

I hadn't expected to hear from Mark again. But a few days later, I did: Did I want to catch a movie? Did I want to try that new French restaurant? Part of me did. But every time I tried to respond to his texts, my thumbs froze. Eventually he stopped texting, and I was grateful. Until now.

Mark turned to the woman to his right, as if remembering she was there. "Oh, uh . . . Neva, this is Imogen."

"Hello, Imogen," I said, forcing myself into a standing position. "Nice to meet you."

Her lips pressed together in a tight smile. "Hello."

This, I knew, was the part when we would mutter something about being late, and shuffle off in separate directions. I was about to start the ball rolling when Mark's expression darkened.

"Could you give us a minute, Imo?" His voice was falsely bright, but his gaze, I suddenly noticed, was fixed on my stomach. "I'll meet you at your place."

Imogen's puzzled expression must have matched mine. She looked from me to Mark and back again. Then her eyes found my belly. "Oh-kay," she said, frowning. "See you at home."

Mark smiled at her reassuringly. But when Imogen was gone, his smile fell away. "You're pregnant," he said to me. It sounded like an accusation.

"Yes."

"It's not—" He cleared his throat. "—it's not mine?"

"No. Oh God, no." At least now I understood why he'd asked his girlfriend to leave.

"When are you due?" he asked.

"December thirty-first."

I waited as he did the math. Then, satisfied, he nodded. "Well. Congratulations, I guess. I wish you luck."

We bobbed our heads, the mood once again awkward. Drops started to fall from the sky, all at once heavy and separate, like tiny, teeming water balloons. The timing was good.

"Well, I guess I'd better—" Mark jabbed his thumb in the direction Imogen had headed.

"Yes," I said. "Me too. Nice to see you, Mark."

"You too," he said.

I watched as Mark jogged away. Then, while I fumbled in my pocket for my keys, my phone began to ring.

I pressed the phone to my ear. "Hello."

"Neva, I need your help."

"Grace?" My heart beat a little faster. "What's wrong?"

"I have a client in labor. Her sister was meant to be my birth assistant but she's from out of state and the baby is coming early. I've tried Mary and Rhonda, they can't come. Any chance you could assist?"

I processed the information she'd given me. Grace did home births. The baby was early. The equation didn't add up. "If the baby's premature, Grace, you need to take her to the hospital."

"She's thirty-seven weeks along, so there's no need for a hospital. She's having the baby at my place."

A man leaving the building held the door open for me, and I gave him a wave as I slid inside. "What stage is she at?"

"I haven't examined her yet, but I'd guess she's five to six centimeters dilated, water intact, contractions six minutes apart for the last hour. Second baby."

"When did labor start?" I started up the stairs.

"A couple of hours ago, but it's progressing at a reasonable rate." I could hear the desperation in Grace's voice. "Darling? I really need you."

I heaved the door open and plodded into my apartment. "I'm on my way."

"You are?" Grace's voice broke. "You're really coming?"

"Of course I'm coming," I said. The idea that she thought I wouldn't brought on a wash of shame. Sure, Grace and I had our troubles. But she was my mother. And no matter what problems existed between us, if she needed me, I'd come.

11

Grace

"Okay, Gill, just relax. I'm going to give you an internal exam, see how you're progressing. Lie back for me. Perfect."

I snapped on my gloves and knelt at the end of the bed. Gillian's husband stood to my right. "David, I need you to help me slide her down the bed. You grab her shoulders, and Gill, you lift your bottom and shimmy down. Ready? Go."

When Gillian was in position, I started my examination. "Eight centimeters. My, my. Well done, you."

I smiled, then felt for the head, pausing as my fingers found a hard bone in the center of the skull. I concentrated on keeping my face neutral. What *was* that? I splayed my fingers, feeling the soft surrounding tissue. It felt like a buttock but . . . it couldn't have been. The baby had been head-down last time I examined Gillian. With my right hand I felt the outside of her stomach. Yes, it felt like a head.

Gillian started another contraction, and I removed my gloves and drifted to the sink. I couldn't make sense of it. If the baby was head-down, what was I feeling? Even though it was unlikely, I couldn't rule out a breech. If it was—it was high-risk. Too high-risk for a home birth. She'd have to be transferred to the hospital.

"I'm here."

I turned. Neva stood by my side in sweatpants and a hoodie that strained over her belly. Her hair was wet and windswept. I exhaled, suddenly grateful that none of my other birth assistants were available. "Neva! Thank goodness."

Neva turned to Gillian and David. "My name's Neva," she said. "I'm a Certified Nurse-Midwife, and I'll be assisting with your birth. Looks like you're doing a great job so far. I'll go wash up, and then we should get you up and about. Let gravity do some work for you." She hesitated then, and looked at me. "I mean . . . if that's okay with Grace."

"Uh . . . yes," I said. "It's fine with me."

As Neva chatted to Gillian, an image of my little strawberry-haired baby daughter popped into my mind, so at odds with the woman I saw before me. She touched Gillian's stomach gently but not too familiarly. Her facial expressions were professional but warm. All her best qualities were in play.

When Neva finished her chat with Gillian, she joined me at the sink. "How is it going? Have you done the internal yet?"

"Yes, though . . ." I lowered my voice. "The baby was head-down at thirty-five weeks, but when I examined her just now, it felt a bit like a breech. Hard in the middle, soft at the sides. I'm not sure."

"Thirty-five weeks? That'd be late for it to turn," she said, echoing my thoughts. "Could it have been the nose you were feeling? A face presentation?"

"I suppose." But I doubted it. I'd felt faces before. This was different.

"Would you like me to have a look?"

I sagged. "I'd love it."

Neva smiled and my concerns vanished, just like that. With Neva by my side, we'd work this thing out. The idea brought on a small bubble of joy.

I went to Gillian's side. "Would it be okay if Neva did another examination before we get you up? The baby's not in the position I expected, and I want a second opinion."

Gillian's face clouded.

"This happens sometimes," I continued, trying to be upbeat. "We're monitoring the baby's heart rate, and there is no sign of distress. We just need to know what's going on."

Gillian still looked tense. "But . . . are you worried?"

"Do we look worried?" Neva grinned as she snapped on rubber gloves. "Now, I want you to relax for me. Wonderful. Deep breath. This won't take a minute."

Neva chatted throughout the examination, keeping the couple calm and reassured. But I could tell from the length of time she spent feeling around that she had concerns too. After a minute she withdrew her hand and removed her gloves. "Well, I'm baffled. From the outside, it feels like its head-down but to feel it, I'd swear it was breech." She clicked her tongue as she thought. "My advice is that you go to the hospital. That's what I would recommend for a client of mine."

The atmosphere in the room took a dive. Hail pelted against the window, Mother Nature's way of agreeing.

"But . . . can't you deliver a breech baby here?" Gillian asked.

"It's really not safe," Neva started, then Gillian rose to her feet.

"But I . . . I can't go to the hospital!" she cried. "Not after last time. Please, Grace."

Neva put her hand on Gillian's shoulder. "It will be all right, Gillian, I promise. But a breech birth is high-risk, and—"

Gillian started to flap. I reached for her hand. "Just stay calm, it's not good for the baby if you get upset. Perhaps there is something we can do. Let me speak to Neva, see if we can come up with a plan."

I gestured for Neva to join me outside and she nodded. But as I shut the door behind us, her face became a mask of disbelief. "*Perhaps* there's something we can do? You're not suggesting that we deliver a breech baby at home? Six miles from the hospital accessible by only one road. Tell me you aren't suggesting that."

"You've delivered a breech baby before—" I started.

"—I've *assisted* with a breech delivery during my midwifery training. That was in a hospital with an ob-gyn and a pediatrician, not to mention all the drugs and lifesaving machinery I had by my side! Delivering a breech baby vaginally is majorly high-risk. Doing it in a home setting is unethical. If something went wrong, they could both die."

"Neva"—I fought to keep my voice even—"Gillian had a traumatic first birth and she's terrified of hospitals. That isn't good for the baby. Besides, we don't even know for sure that it is a breech we are feeling. You said yourself it wasn't clear. It could be something else. A face presentation, a nasal bone—"

"—That's the problem, we don't *know* what it is! It didn't even feel exactly like a breech. Below the bone I felt . . . a hole."

"The mouth?" I asked hopefully. If she felt the mouth, that meant it was head-down.

"I don't think so. There was no space between the bone and the hole. If it is face presentation—" She sucked in a breath.

"What?" I asked.

"It could be a cleft palate."

A short silence followed, then Neva slumped against the wall. I thought about it. If the baby was face presentation, it could have been the nose we were feeling. And the cleft could be the hole Neva was describing.

"That's it, isn't it?" she asked. But her tone said she desperately wanted to be wrong.

I felt sick. In my entire career, I'd had to give this kind of news only a couple of times. Once when I'd delivered a child with a hemangioma birthmark covering the entire left side of its face. The other time was when I'd delivered a little girl with only two full fingers on her left hand. "I guess we're going to the hospital, then," I said after more than a minute of silence. "If the baby has a cleft palate, there could be a host of other problems. We'll need a pediatrician present." I braced myself and took a step toward the door.

"Wait," Neva said. She took a deep breath, as if weighing up her thoughts. "I know a pediatrician. I might be able to convince him to come here."

I paused, afraid to hope. "Really?"

"Maybe. At least that way Gillian wouldn't have to have a hospital birth on top of hearing this news."

"But . . . do you think your pediatrician would come to a home birth?" I asked.

"Not sure," Neva said. "Give me two minutes."

She tugged her phone out of her pocket and jogged down the stairs. I waited where I was. I wouldn't go in until I knew for sure; I didn't want to get Gillian's hopes up for a home birth if this pediatrician didn't come through. But I was also delaying the inevitable. Was it the right thing, giving Gillian the option to proceed with a home birth? Even with a pediatrician present, we didn't have the resources of a hospital. If the baby required a blood transfusion or operation, we would lose precious time transferring it to the hospital. On the other hand, keeping Gillian in an environment that she was comfortable with benefited everyone. I was still going back and forth when Neva appeared in front of me.

"The pediatrician is on his way. Let's go chat with Gillian."

Neva pushed past me into the room. If she had any doubts, I couldn't see them. And if Neva, Miss By-the-Book, was comfortable, I didn't have any reason to worry.

Gillian and David sat up straight as we entered, and I took a seat at the end of the bed. I placed a hand on Gill's thigh. "Neva and I have discussed what we felt, and we are not convinced that your baby is breech after all. We need to confirm, but we think what we were feeling is—" I took a breath. "—a cleft palate."

Gillian looked blank, then turned to her husband.

"A cleft palate is when the baby's top lip is missing or deformed," David said, not to Gillian but to himself. His own lip thinned as he spoke, perhaps in solidarity with his child.

"No!" Gillian's face became alarmed. I wanted to assure her that a cleft palate was no big deal. That her baby would still be beautiful, and most likely, the deformity would be minor. But I owed her more than that.

"David's right," I said. "The baby may have a minor or significant deformity to the lip and palate, usually a hole between the top lip and nasal area. Now that we know what we're looking for, we'll check for the rest of the face to confirm, but we both think that is what we are dealing with." I paused as another contraction took hold. Gillian worked through it and her husband helped her. When it was over, I continued. "A pediatrician is on his way. He will examine the baby once it is born. And that might be the end of it—"

"But it might not?"

"There's no evidence of any other problems at this stage," I said. "But we don't know anything for sure until the baby is born. Once we confirm that the baby is not, in fact, breech, we can still try to deliver here, if you'd like."

"Yes," Gillian said. "I want to have the baby here. More than anything."

I smiled at Neva, sending her a silent thank-you.

"Okay," I said to Gillian. "Now, why don't you lie down again?"

An astonishingly good-looking young man arrived an hour later. Even mid-contraction, Gillian was silenced at the sight of him. Thanks to the unforgiving rain outside, his hair was stuck to his head and his clothes were sodden. When he pushed his hair back off his face, I actually gasped. Out loud. With his strong jaw and pronounced forehead, he had a look of Elvis Presley but more chiseled, more defined. I silently cursed my daughter. It would have been nice to have some warning.

"Sorry I took so long," he said, peeling off his soaked jacket and hanging it over the back of the chair. "I could hardly see with all the rain. The thin part of Beavertail Road was terrifying, the waves were actually crashing onto the road—I'm surprised it wasn't closed."

"Thank God it wasn't," Neva said. "That road is the only way in and out of this part of the island. If it closes . . ." Neva trailed away, obviously not wanting to frighten Gillian, but we all heard the subtext. *If it closes, we're stuck here. No one comes in, no one leaves.* "But the rain seems to have eased off now, so we should be fine."

He looked at me. "You must be Grace. It's nice to finally meet you."

He grinned, revealing almost-perfect-but-not-so-perfect-that-they-looked-fake white teeth. I raised my eyebrows at Neva. Finally? How long had he been around?

"I'm Patrick," he said. I waited for the rest. *Patrick Whoseummy-whatsit, doctor of this and that, and God of all things medical.* That was how all doctors introduced themselves in my experience, particularly when they were addressing midwives, who—according to them—were a bunch of uneducated cowboys. But not Patrick. He didn't even give me his last name. And before I could ask him for it, he was already wandering over toward my clients.

"Hi, there, Gillian, David," he said, pulling up a chair and sitting. "I'm Patrick. I'm a pediatrician. Neva's filled me in on what's going on. I'm sure you are worried, but try to leave all the worrying to me and concentrate on delivering this baby. Cleft lips and palates can be corrected with surgery. And you've had proper prenatal care, so I say we remain optimistic. In fact, let's get excited. We're about to meet one of the most important people in your life."

I glanced at Neva and she shrugged. *Yes he's special,* her expression said. Indeed, he was rather special. In a couple of sentences, he had managed to turn the somber mood in the room around. It was very undoctorlike. I liked him immediately.

"Okay, I'm going to sit back now and let the pros do their thing," he said. "Neva is one of the best midwives in town, and if Grace is her mother, then you're in fantastic hands."

Patrick rose even further in my opinion. A doctor who wasn't taking over? Who called us—the midwives—pros? Where did Neva find him? And more important, how could I make sure she kept him?

"Right, let's get you moving," Neva said. "I'd like to see this baby come before sunup!" She brushed past Patrick, giving him a nudge with her elbow. He smiled at her, and I saw something in his eyes. He *liked* her. Hope fizzed inside me, but I tried to push it down. Dared I even *hope* that this gorgeous man was the father of my grandchild?

Neva moved Gillian onto a birthing stool, where she spent the next three hours. Labor progressed steadily, and as the sun peeked through the blinds, she began to bear down.

"Try not to push," I told her as she began to crown. I squatted by her feet. "Just pant. Slowly, slowly. Good girl. I want the head to come out slowly."

"Here it comes," Neva said, moving in close with a towel.

As the baby's face came out, Neva cooed. Patrick had moved in closer and was studying the baby's face. The baby had a cleft lip and palate, no doubt about it. But Patrick smiled encouragingly at the parents. I had an overwhelming urge to hug him. What a wonderful doctor. What a wonderful man.

"The head's out," Neva said.

I hooked my fingers under the baby's shoulder to bring it under and around the pubic bone. Then we waited for the next contraction. The atmosphere was exuberant, exactly as it should be for a first-time home birth.

"Here we go," I said as Gillian began to moan again. Neva moved Gillian's husband down next to me so he could watch his child being born. "I want one more big push."

"Come on, Gill," Neva urged.

With the next push, I caught their baby girl. She was big, maybe nine pounds or more. She cried immediately.

"A girl!" we all cried.

With the baby in my arms, I hesitated. It had been so long since I delivered a child with a doctor present, I'd forgotten the protocol. I always gave the baby straight to its mother, to allow it to be comforted by her smell, her touch, but from memory, doctors liked to examine the baby first.

"Give her to her mother," Patrick said. "She wants to meet her parents before she sees my ugly mug. And there's obviously nothing wrong with her lungs."

I didn't know whether to be glad or disappointed that Patrick was disproving so many of my preconceptions about doctors.

We moved Gillian to the bed, and I placed the baby, still covered in vernix and blood, on her mother's stomach. Neva stood at Gillian's side, rubbing the baby with a warm towel. I watched the scene, holding my breath. Gillian lifted the towel from the baby's face to look at her daughter. I thought about saying something, but decided against it. They needed time.

"Oh!" Gillian said eventually, in a half sob. She tried to swallow, blinked back tears. "Her face."

I nodded to Neva to come and take my place at the end of the bed. The placenta was still to come, but I had to be with Gillian. I joined her at the head of the bed and gazed down at the newborn squirming on her mother's breast.

"Oh, Gillian." My hand flew to my mouth. The baby's top lip rose to meet the base of the left nostril, leaving a gaping black hole in the center of her face. The rest of her face was fine—perfect, in fact. I peeled the towel back farther, revealing ten perfect fingers and toes, and a big round belly. She squinted up at us crossly. My heart exploded. "She's . . . beautiful."

I couldn't keep the beam off my face. Neva was smiling too, but she wasn't looking at the baby. She was looking at me.

"She *is* beautiful," Gillian said, as if seeing her for the first time. "Look, David. Look at her little hands and feet."

I smiled as the new parents marveled at their new daughter. Had it really been twenty-nine years since I'd done this myself? Just like then, these parents had fallen hopelessly in love with their child in an instant. Everything was as it should be.

"Okay if I take a look at her?" I stood back as Patrick approached.

Gillian closed her arms around her daughter. "Do you have to take her?" A look of fierce protectiveness covered her face.

"Maybe just another few minutes, Patrick?" I asked.

Patrick smiled. "I'm not taking her anywhere. I can examine her right where she is, if that's okay. It's the best place for her, right next to Mom."

Gillian loosened her grip slightly. She nodded. "Yes. That's okay."

"Good. Now, let me see." Patrick opened the towel. "Hello, beautiful."

Neva was watching Patrick. Her expression was soft and unguarded.

"Does she have a name?" he asked.

"No. Not yet."

"Okay, well, I'm just going to have to call you 'little one.'"

Without removing the baby from her mother, he did a once-over, listened to her lungs, checked her reflexes. "Good. Very good."

Patrick smiled throughout the examination and when he was finished, he rewrapped her towel. "I'm sure you're anxious about the lip, so let's talk about that first. The good news is that we can do a lot with surgery. The operation is very common, and very successful. The palate is a little more complicated, but the prognosis is good. . . ."

Patrick continued, patiently answering the parents' questions in layman's terms, not a trace of the arrogant brush I liked to paint doctors with. He was so likable. I sidled up to Neva, who was inspecting the placenta in a kidney dish. "So—?"

Neva didn't even look up. "No. He's not the father. And I'm not interested."

"All right. All right." I held up my hands. "Keep your hair on—"

"Anyway, he's not the type to settle down with one woman. Why would you, when you can have them all? For God's sake, *you're* already in love with him! Can you imagine how it is around the hospital?"

I nodded slowly.

"What?" she asked.

"Nothing. It's just . . ."

"Spit it out, Grace."

"Well, he *did* drive an awful long way, in the middle of the night, to help you out, Neva. And you *were* very comfortable asking him to do that. Maybe there's more going on than you—"

"Grace?" Patrick approached from behind, and Neva studiously returned her attention to the placenta. "I'm going to arrange for a transfer to the local hospital," he said. "I want the baby to be looked at sooner rather than later."

"Already?" I said.

"We can't!" Neva said. "Gillian has a tear that needs stitching."

"Well," Patrick said. "I could always take David and the baby—"

"No." Gillian crossed her arms over her baby. "If she's going to the hospital, I'm going too."

I smiled. The mother's instinct was primal, even after just a few minutes. "Okay," I said. "We can tend to the stitch at the hospital. Let me just clean you and get you some fresh pads and we can go. Where's your other daughter? Is there someone you'd like me to call?"

"She's with a neighbor," David said. "I'll go get her once we know everything is okay here."

Neva had already got some pads down from the cupboard and was filling a dish with warm water. "I'll stay, Grace," she said. "I know all the birth details, I can write the notes and clean up here. You go with Gillian. I'll call the hospital and let them know you're coming."

A few minutes later, we loaded Gillian, David, and the baby into my car. Patrick started up his own vehicle, ready to follow us there. Neva held my car door open for me. "Good luck."

I gave her a chaste kiss, and she caught my waist and pulled me into a quick hug. "You did good today, Grace," she said into my ear. "And you were right. It *was* magic."

Before I could gather my thoughts enough to speak, she was striding back toward the house.

12

Floss

The first time I laid eyes on Lil, she was in the third row of my Birthing Naturally class. In a black trouser suit with a mulberry scarf, she was dressed more for a wedding than a birthing class. Clearly she was too old to be pregnant. The empty seats beside her indicated she wasn't accompanying her daughter. She was a fine-boned woman with a pure white bob and a dainty, angled face. The opposite of myself, physically speaking. As I introduced myself to the class and handed out my reading material, I couldn't help stealing glances at her. She appeared a little out of place, but then, so did a lot of people. Birth, particularly for people of my generation, could make the best of people squeamish.

As soon as the class finished, she was out of her seat, beelining for the door. For a woman of her age, she was impressively lithe, but after ninety minutes of watching her arranging her delicate frame on the narrow chair, I wasn't going to let her go without saying hello.

"I hope you found the class worthwhile," I called out as she zipped past me.

She hesitated then half turned back. "Er, yes. Thank you." She took another step toward the door.

"Is your daughter expecting, or another family member?"

It wasn't my style to ask such personal questions, but for some reason, I couldn't help it.

She paused again. "Neither. No one is expecting." She hesitated, perhaps unsure whether to say more. "I thought I was attending another class." She looked at the cover of the notebook in her hand. "Room C1202."

I blinked. "Toastmasters?"

A ghost of a smile appeared on her face.

A laugh escaped before I could help it. "So . . . why did you stay?"

"I'm not sure. But it sure had nothing to do with Birthing Naturally."

It was early evening. Lil and I had eaten pasta in front of a television game show that I'd pretended to follow with some interest. But my heart hurt. Not figuratively—it physically hurt. A high, twanging pain across my sternum and my left side. I was thinking about Bill again. It had been years since he was such a part of my psyche, and I hated that he still had the privilege of my brain space. More so, I hated myself for the mess I had created. I'd never regretted what I'd done. But now, with Neva's situation so closely mirroring my own, my reasons for keeping the secret all these years seemed slightly less clear.

"You all right, Floss?" Lil asked. She'd cleared away the dinner dishes and now she stood in the corner of the sitting room, unfolding the wire rack to hang the laundry. She'd also cooked the dinner. I was letting down the team. "You're holding your chest."

"Am I?" I looked at the hand hovering over my heart. "Oh. So I am."

"You're worried about something."

Lil wasn't stupid. I hadn't been myself since I'd got Neva's news, and while she'd left me to my thoughts initially, I got the feeling I'd used up my grace period. In the past few days, she'd become increasingly short with me. "I'm just . . . thinking about Neva." I tried to ignore the faded yellow envelope peeking out of the corner of my purse. "And Grace."

Lil shook out a T-shirt and hung it over the rack. "They've been taking up a lot of your thoughts lately." She picked a pair of underwear out of the basket, then paused. "Neva's pregnancy is bringing up a lot of old hurts for you." She draped the underpants over the wire and bent down to retrieve the next item. "I know virtually nothing about that part of your life. I wish you'd share with me."

She continued hanging clothes, but her comment floated there, like dust in sunlight. I felt the presence of the envelope again—the letter from Evie that I'd dug out last night when I couldn't sleep. All I'd have to do was give that letter to Lil, and she'd know everything. But something stopped me. I wanted to tell her. I knew what it was like having someone clam up when you were worried about them. Though, at least Lil saw me every day and knew I wasn't in real, physical danger. When I was worried about Elizabeth, I didn't have that luxury. After Evie's engagement party, Elizabeth all but disappeared. Plans we made were always canceled. *Bill* had had a busy week; *Bill* needed her at home. It was frustrating, particularly since I couldn't seem to get her—or Bill— out of my mind. What was it about him? I couldn't put my finger on it.

I'd hoped that as her midwife, Evie would insist that Elizabeth attend prenatal clinics. If I could just see her, I was sure the funny feeling in my belly would dissipate. But Elizabeth took responsibility for her own prenatal care. She performed her own urine tests at home and she kept a weekly record of her stomach measurements, which showed the baby was growing properly. As a midwife herself, this was perfectly safe, and it made sense, since she lived a long way out and didn't have a car. But that did nothing to reassure me.

I thought about voicing my concerns to Evie, several times, but then what were my concerns, really? That I had a bad feeling about Bill? That he tried to dance with me outside on his wedding day? They sounded pathetic at best, and at worst, like sour grapes. So I just waited for Elizabeth to get in touch with me.

A few months later, out of the blue, a dinner invitation arrived, along with a note saying that Elizabeth was sorry she hadn't kept in touch better. I accepted the invitation. I'd have preferred that she come into town so I could take her to lunch and talk to her properly, but as that didn't seem to be an option, dinner would have to do.

I made the journey to Kings Langley on my bike. Elizabeth said that their house bordered town and country, but the closer I pedaled, the more obvious it became that it was just plain country. A light rain misted down over me as I pedaled. I hadn't seen a house for over fifteen minutes when I saw the lights of the little stone cottage. A car sat out front—a black town car. Strange. Bill didn't have a car. When I reached the house, I leaned my bike against the low wall, smoothed down my pinafore, and took the path to Elizabeth's front door, taking large steps to avoid the mud between the pavers.

Bill answered the door with a cigarette and a grin. "Floss. We were getting worried. We were about to send Michael out to look for you."

Michael? I peered inside to where a young man stood. He was tall and thin, getting thinner at the top, like a sharpened pencil. His hair was brown, like his trousers, and neatly combed to the side. So *this* was the point of the dinner. My stomach, which already felt like it was being strangled with a belt, constricted further.

Bill gave me an easy hug. Easy for him. Not for me. His touch sent a strange tingle through me. I must have felt stiffer than an old corpse. He guided me through the door and straight into the kitchen, where Elizabeth stood, a clean red apron over her empire-line blouse. I was relieved to see her actually looking pregnant, even though she was carrying small, just a little mound in the front. The rest of her was normal size, perhaps even less than normal, but she'd always been slim. Her hair had been cut to chin length, and it was teased into a shiny, deep red bob that lifted at least three inches at the crown.

"Floss!" She took off her apron and hugged me. "I'm so happy you're here. I wanted to have you over sooner, but . . . well, never mind, you're here. Allow me introduce you to Michael. Michael: Floss; Floss: Michael." She flicked her wrist back and forth between us. "Michael lives on a neighboring farm—cattle—with his father and brother, and was desperate for a home-cooked meal so I insisted he join us. Single and eligible."

She lowered her voice and sang the last part, but she didn't lower her voice enough. Michael turned away, politely busying himself looking at photographs on the mantel, but his cheeks were pink, and he was clearly holding back a smile.

"Can I get you a drink, Floss?" Bill was in a jolly mood, and Elizabeth also appeared happy, high on the intoxication of matchmaking. It was hard not to get caught up in it. She ushered us to the "dining room," a small, windowless area that adjoined the kitchen and centered on a circular table. The house *was* tiny. Just a kitchen, an eating area, and another closed door, which must have been the bedroom. The bathroom, from what I could ascertain, was outside. A hard slog, I imagined, for a pregnant woman who could be up several times through the night. Odd that I hadn't heard her complain about it. Then again, I hadn't heard much from her at all these past few months.

"So, Floss," Michael said as we sat adjacent to each other at the table. "Bill tells me you're a midwife? A noble career. I'd imagine it's very fulfilling."

My eyebrows rose. I expected that a single, eligible farmer would have found midwifery a necessary but unremarkable career choice. The fact that he was interested made him rise several notches in my book. "It is," I said. "Very fulfilling. I delivered my fiftieth baby yesterday, as a matter of fact."

"Your fiftieth?" He gave me a little clap. "Well, I can't boast those kinds of numbers, but I've delivered the odd calf. Though I don't imagine it's quite the same."

I laughed. "There'd be some similarities, I suppose. But I can't say I've ever delivered a calf."

"I'll be sure to invite you along next time."

"I'll be sure to accept."

We smiled at each other. His stance—leaning forward, elbows on the table—betrayed his genuine interest. I only wished I could return it. His smile more than made up for his peculiarly shaped head.

"I see you two are getting along?" Bill said, sliding into the seat to my right.

"Just talking about our common interests," Michael said.

"Midwifery," I said. "Elizabeth used to be a midwife too," I told Michael, "before she was married."

"Is that right, Elizabeth?" Michael called out to Elizabeth in the kitchen. "You must miss it."

Elizabeth entered the room with a roast chicken on a large brown chopping board. "I do. I was just about qualified when I gave it up. Some of the best times of my life."

Bill, who sat between Elizabeth and me, raised his head. Elizabeth's face changed. It was curious. She returned to the kitchen, and a moment later she was back with the vegetables. "Anyway, I'm glad it's all behind me now," she said. Her tone was aiming for bright, but not quite getting there. "Married life is wonderful. I certainly couldn't do both." She held the knife out to Bill. "Would you like to carve, darling?"

"It seems like an awful lot of effort to go to if you quit before you're even qualified," Michael said. "Do you plan to keep practicing after you're married, Floss?"

"I hadn't thought," I answered honestly. "I suppose I would."

"Oh?" Elizabeth's voice was tight. "And how would you do that? Abandon your husband at all hours of the day and night, cycling all over town, going into strange houses like a woman of the night. And what about children? What would you do with them? Strap them to the back of the bike? It's just not feasible, Floss."

"I don't know," Michael said. "A man could cook his own dinner from time to time, surely? And going into strange houses doesn't make you a woman of the night if you're there to deliver a—"

"Elizabeth makes a good point, though," I said quickly. Something about the way she spoke made me nervous. *Woman of the night?* They weren't her words. And the stillness that had come over Bill—it worried me. "It's not always practical."

"No, it's not," Bill said. He moved to the head of the table, in front of the chicken. With a large knife, he sliced the bird in long, expert cuts. "I could hardly have Elizabeth cycling into town while she's pregnant."

"No," Elizabeth agreed. "Of course not."

For a few minutes, we ate in silence punctuated only by the occasional scrape of cutlery. The mood had taken a funny turn and I wasn't entirely sure why. So what if I planned to work after I had children? I didn't have any children, and I was fairly certain my prospects of having them were slim at best. Even if Elizabeth and Bill didn't know that, were they really so insecure about their own choices that everyone needed to agree with them?

At least Elizabeth was eating. It reassured me. She was so thin, and at this stage of pregnancy, women needed calories. She ate like she was expecting twins—triplets!—though I wasn't about to point that out.

"This is delicious, Elizabeth," I said, hoping to inject some life back into the party. "The chicken is perfect."

"You're a lucky man, Bill," Michael agreed, "a wife that can cook like this."

Bill was looking at Elizabeth. "Slow down, darling. Are you eating for two, or two hundred? You'll give yourself indigestion."

Elizabeth's smile snapped into place, frozen, if not for a slight quiver.

"Must be a boy," he continued. "That's my guess. What do you think, Floss?"

I frowned. Elizabeth's cheeks were pink. Was he trying to humiliate her?

"The gender doesn't have bearing on the amount of calories the mother needs to consume." I sat a little straighter in my chair. "Elizabeth needs to eat plenty at this stage of her pregnancy."

As usual, Bill held my gaze, but this time, it unnerved me. Perhaps I was a little sharp, but I considered it necessary. Silence fell upon the table yet again. Elizabeth wouldn't meet my eye, or Bill's. It was as though she were contemplating something very important. Finally, she married her knife and fork and rested them on her plate.

After dinner, I helped Elizabeth bring the dishes into the kitchen. While I filled the sink, she stood beside me. Right beside me. I got the feeling she was leaning on me. Physically (practically) but more so, emotionally. I was happy to prop her up. I had a strange feeling she needed it.

"So how is the pregnancy going?" I asked. I wanted to segue into Bill somehow but wasn't sure of the best way.

"Oh yes, fine."

"No issues?"

"None at all." She stepped ever-so-slightly away from me, scrubbing the same plate four times, front and back. "My blood pressure is fine, my weight and measurements are fine—"

"Actually, you look thin," I countered. "Apart from the stomach, you look like you've lost weight."

"Morning sickness. Can barely keep a thing down."

I felt my eyebrows gather. Morning sickness was rare this late in pregnancy, and besides, she seemed fine and well. "Any kicking?"

"Yes. It's kicking right now."

"May I?" I stepped forward and lifted the hem of her blouse. Elizabeth stepped back. But it was too late.

I thought I might faint. I cooled from the head down, giving me strange, falling sensation. Elizabeth tried to force down the hem of her blouse, but I held it tight. A purple, mottled bruise—red wine on cream carpet—stretched from her right hip to her navel. An angry bruise.

"It's nothing." Elizabeth forced her shirt down. She turned away from me and resumed washing dishes. "I fell on the way to the outhouse, is all. It can be awfully dark at night, and it was raining."

I stared at her.

"What? Why are you looking at me like that?"

"Have you been to the doctor?" I asked.

She waved her hand. "The baby's kicking, I told you that. You have to be tough out here, in the country. I can't be running off to the doctor with every little sniffle. And keep it to yourself. I don't want Evie worrying."

"Evie's your midwife! *You* should tell her." I lifted her shirt again and ran my fingers over the mark. "Does it hurt?"

"No. You're sweet to be concerned, but my baby is growing beautifully, and it must be tying itself in knots, the amount it's wriggling about. Don't tell Evie, Floss. Please?"

"Okay." I pressed a palm to my forehead. I could hardly force her to tell Evie, but I didn't understand her hesitation. "But you need to see a doctor."

"I can't." She took the tea towel from her shoulder and started drying dishes and returning them to their places. Still reeling, I picked up another towel and helped her.

"Well, at least come to a prenatal clinic so Evie can give you an exam."

Elizabeth crashed a stack of plates onto a high shelf. "I'm a *midwife*,

Floss. Why should I ride a bus all the way into town to be told things I already know?"

"How's it going in here, ladies?" Bill and Michael entered the room. They appeared good-humored, no trace of the awkwardness during dinner. Bill had a way of charming people, convincing them he wasn't such a bad guy. But now, I wasn't sure it was true.

Elizabeth placed the last of the cutlery into a drawer. "All done." She turned, a bright, convincing smile on her face. "Now—who's ready for dessert?"

"You're in for a treat," Bill said to Michael, all smiles. He winked at Elizabeth. "Elizabeth makes the best treacle pudding you'll ever taste. And after the dinner she's just had, I'm sure she won't be able to eat a bite. Help us, Floss."

"Better not. I have a long ride ahead of me."

"I can drive you home," Michael said. "I was going to offer earlier. I'd be happy to."

"You're very kind," I said. "But I must go."

At the time, it was all I could do to get out of there. Suddenly, standing there in that tiny house felt suffocating in a way that it hadn't when I'd arrived. What was going on with Elizabeth? I wanted so much to help her. But how could I, with her forbidding me to say anything?

With hindsight, of course, there were lots of things I could have done. But by the time I realized, it was too late.

The phone was ringing. Lil had finished hanging the washing and was sitting in front of me. She was available to talk, she *wanted* me to share this with her. She sat, ignoring the shrill, metallic ring of the phone.

I snatched it up. "Hello? Floss speaking."

"Mom, it's me."

"Grace." Lil sighed, picked up the laundry basket, and left the room. Discreetly, I picked up my purse and tucked the envelope farther inside, out of sight. "Are you all right?"

"I'm wonderful. You'll never guess what? I did a delivery with Neva last night."

"You did?"

"I was short a birth partner, so she said she'd do it. It was wonderful, Mom. I was so proud of her. Oh, and listen to this: She brought a man with her. A gorgeous man."

In the kitchen, Lil was not exactly slamming cupboard doors, but certainly closing them firmly. "She brought a man *to the birth*?"

"Yes. A pediatrician."

"Oh." I wasn't following, but from Grace's triumphant tone, I got the sense that she would fill me in.

"Something was going on between them. Something romantic. I'm sure of it."

"You think he's the father?"

"No." Her tone dipped. "No, I don't think that. At least, I don't see any reason that she'd hide it if he was. He's single. Respectable. As I said, gorgeous. It's a shame, because he was lovely. A good match for Neva."

"Why is it a shame?" I asked.

"Call me a dreamer, but I'm still hoping the baby's father will swoop in and everyone will live happily ever after. I can't help but feel that the child will be missing out, not having the opportunity to know its real father."

"Like . . . you missed out?" I spoke carefully, trying to keep the waver out of my voice.

"This is different, Mom. It's preventable. My father died—you didn't pretend he'd never existed. What Neva is doing to her baby—denying it a chance to know its father—that'd be pretty hard to forgive. And I don't want Neva to destroy her relationship with her child before it's even born."

Grace chatted awhile longer, and then we signed off. But after I hung up, the room began to blur. A throbbing pain hammered in my chest, and my hands coiled around the base of my throat, over the pain. I couldn't breathe. I tilted my head from one side to another, trying to find Lil. A sharp rattle came from somewhere—from me?—and then there it was—her face. Even amidst my alarm, the sight of her soothed me.

"Floss?" Lil's voice rang out. "Darling, what is it?"

Another great rasp came from me, stealing the last of my breath. I pointed at my chest, where the fire raged. I managed to suck in a short breath. "I think . . . I think I'm having a heart attack."

13

Neva

"Looks great, Annabelle. Does it feel better?"

It was late afternoon and I was teaching a breast-feeding clinic at the birthing center. I was exhausted. I'd finished up at Mom's place about 6 A.M. but when I'd arrived at my apartment an hour later, I found I couldn't sleep. I'd called Grace a couple of times to find out how Gillian and the baby were doing, but she must have been busy. I hadn't wanted to disturb Patrick for the second time in twenty-four hours, so I just waited for news. It was hard to focus on the task at hand, but luckily, my muscle memory for these clinics was good enough to fake it.

"It feels a million times better. Neva, you are a lifesaver."

"If it hurts, take her off immediately and relatch. It's meant to feel one hundred percent comfortable."

Around the room, all the mothers and babies were nursing

comfortably. "You're all A-plus students. Breast-feeding doesn't always come easily. It's a learned skill; every mom-and-baby unit is unique. But you've all done brilliantly. We're about done; I'm just going to grab some samples of the nipple cream I told you about. Feel free to exchange numbers while I'm gone. Other moms are invaluable when it comes to sharing knowledge."

In the corridor, I opened the cupboard where the samples were kept and began rifling through.

"There you are."

I spun around. Patrick stood by the front desk with Anne. He was dressed in suit trousers and a rumpled shirt under his white coat. He looked as tired as I felt.

"There *you* are!"

I crossed the room and, without a thought, wrapped my arms around his neck. Patrick stiffened at first. It wasn't like me to hug. But after the emotion of last night, I still didn't entirely feel like me. "How's Gillian? How's the baby?"

When I drew back, Patrick looked amused. "Wow. A hug?"

I blushed. "Hormones."

"Ah." Patrick nodded. "Gillian and the baby are both doing fine. How 'bout I update you over dinner?"

"Do they even serve food at The Hip?"

"Who said anything about The Hip?"

Anne became preoccupied with her computer screen. I frowned. Who said anything about The Hip? No one, I suppose, but . . . we only *ever* went to The Hip. In fact, other than when Patrick's father died, when I spent the day at his mother's place, I don't think I'd ever seen Patrick anywhere other than the hospital, my apartment, and The Hip.

"So . . . what time are you off?" he asked.

"Seven thirty. But—"

"Great." Patrick signed a document, closed a manila folder, and handed it to Anne. "I'll pick you up then."

He left the room and I felt my eyebrows soar. Pick me up? Usually Sean, Patrick, and I just sloped down to The Hip one by one as we came off shift and joined whoever was already perched at the bar. We left in a similar way, usually when we'd had too much to drink. No one ever picked anyone up. And, now that I thought of it, no one ever ate dinner.

"Neva." Anne's voice interrupted my thoughts.

"Yes?"

"Just had a buzz from the clinic. One of the women needs help re-attaching her baby."

"Oh." I waved at her as I hurried into the room. "Yes. Thanks, Anne."

At 7:33 P.M., I sat in a tub armchair, feeling like a schoolgirl waiting to get collected for the prom. On my lap was a canvas bag filled with empty Tupperware containers that I'd been meaning to take home for a month.

"Ready?"

Patrick had slipped in without me noticing and was standing before me in a fresh blue shirt and jeans with brown lace-up shoes that he hadn't been wearing when I saw him an hour ago. He carried no bag whatsoever—I had no idea how guys did that—and his jacket, brown leather, was tossed over one shoulder. I caught a whiff of something. Cologne.

I glanced down at my flat shoes, navy hospital pants, and white shirt. Next to Patrick, I looked like a junkyard dog. A pregnant junkyard dog. Patrick, to his credit, didn't appear outwardly disgusted, but then again, why would he? It wasn't a date. Was it?

I pushed to my feet so fast my head began to spin.

"Whoa. You're not going to faint on me, are you? I'm off shift and I usually deal with people a little smaller than you."

We stared at each other and I was struck by the unfamiliarity of Patrick. Usually I'd throw out a wry joke, but now I wasn't sure it was appropriate. The clothes, the cologne, the picking me up? I managed to roll my eyes before pushing through the door. As I skimmed past him, he took the canvas bag from my shoulder and tossed it over his own.

A couple of pretty nurses were in the elevator when it opened, and Patrick made a great show of putting his hand out to stop the door from closing on them. He couldn't help himself. One of them shot me a glare of pure envy. A flutter traveled through me from head to toe. I wasn't sure if it was a good flutter or a bad flutter.

"So, where d'you want to go?" he asked.

"I don't know. Nellie's?"

I immediately wanted to retract the words. Nellie's was casual and the food was good, but it was also located directly under my building and was staffed by middle-aged waitresses who'd seen me there alone enough to develop an obsession with my love life. Arriving with Patrick wasn't going to go unnoticed. But it was too late; he was already nodding. "Sure," Patrick said. "Nellie's, it is."

We strolled in silence. It would have been amusing if I wasn't so self-conscious. Patrick and I had never had a problem with conversation. Was he nervous too? And if he was, what did that mean? When I couldn't take it anymore, I blurted out, "I have a joke. A guy phones the local hospital and yells, 'You've got to send help. My wife's in labor!' The midwife says, 'Calm down. Is this her first child?' He replies, 'No! This is her husband.'"

This got a full guffaw from Patrick. I couldn't help feeling pleased. But when he held my gaze after his smile had slipped away, I looked away.

The bell dinged as we entered the restaurant. Judy, the worst of the waitresses (in a gossipy sense), looked up, immediately animated. By the time the door had closed, she was already elbowing one of the others. They were going to have a field day. A free booth sat in the back, and I beelined for it until a tug at my elbow stopped me in my tracks.

"Where do you think you're going without saying hello?"

I turned. "Hello, Judy."

She grinned, and her weathered face dissolved into a puzzle of lines. Although I never inquired into Judy's personal life—a kindness I wished she'd return—her lack of wedding ring indicated that she hadn't had a love life of her own, or if she had, it couldn't have worked out too well, because here she was in her blue uniform and white tennies six days a week, paying far too much attention to the lives of the customers.

"Don't go scooting back there, there's a table available here in my section." Judy gestured to a table in the middle of the restaurant. "I want to make sure you're looked after properly. I'm Judy, by the way," she said to Patrick, gesturing at her right breast, where her name was embroidered. "If you need anything at all, ask for me. I'll get y'all some water."

I slinked into the red leather booth and Patrick, after giving Judy a smile that sent her tattooed brows rocketing into her hairline, slid in opposite me.

"Sorry," I said. "Forgot to tell you about the crazies at Nellie's."

Patrick perused the menu. "I hear they have good burgers here," he said. "Should I order two?"

"If you're really hungry. Tell me about Gillian."

Patrick groaned. "Fine." He placed the menu flat in front of him. "If you're going to be all business. Gillian's daughter is completely healthy, apart from the lip and palate, and she'll be a great candidate for surgery. I gave Gillian the details of a pediatric plastic surgeon, and they can do the surgery while she's still a baby so they won't have to worry about her being teased at school or anything. It's a good result. Oh, and Gillian and David have called her Grace."

I gave a tiny gasp. "They have?"

"I should tell you, though, the doctor on duty was furious when we came in. He was ranting and raving about home births and how it was negligent to deliver this baby at home. I explained that the baby was never in any distress, but . . . he was a hater. He said he would report your mom to the Board of Nursing."

"Report her? For what?"

"Who knows? He'd probably had a long shift and was blowing off steam. I doubt he'll go through with it."

"Well, he should go right ahead if he wants. She didn't do anything wrong. The baby was delivered safely under the care of the best midwife I know *with* a pediatrician present. Good luck to him if he thinks he's got a case." Heat pulsed around my face and neck. "Who was the doctor, anyway?"

"Didn't know him. But if the Board of Nursing contacts me, I'll confirm she did everything by the book. She'll be fine." He hesitated. "I'm surprised you're so protective of your mother. Given that you can be quite . . . hard on her."

I opened my mouth to respond, and then I paused. Was I hard on her?

"At least, the way you talk about her," he continued. "You obviously have your issues."

"Well . . . it's just a matter of fairness," I said. "She wasn't negligent. In fact, it was my idea to call you and give Gillian the option of delivering at home. I don't want my mother picked on because she is in a minority group of midwives who deliver at home."

"I agree. And with any luck, she won't be. "

Judy arrived to take our orders. After she left, I folded my hands in my lap. Why was this so awkward? I'd hung out with Patrick more times than I could count. But now, when I wanted to launch into banter, my throat clamped shut like a preterm cervix. Patrick, at least, had found his tongue. He told me about a three-year-old boy who'd shoved a marble so far up his nostril that he required surgery to extract it, and a mother who'd brought her son in three times in three months for suspicious injuries, whom he'd had to report to children's services.

Once the meals were delivered, Patrick went quiet. He cut his burger in half and lifted one half to his mouth, then paused. His face was hesitant. "Anyway. I've been thinking . . ."

"About?"

"About your baby."

"You've been thinking about my baby?"

He nodded. "You said it didn't have a father. Well . . . what if you told people I was the father?"

I blinked.

"People know I stay over at your house sometimes. It would stop all the questions. I know you hate all the questions. We could say that we're a couple."

"In the nicest possible way—why would we do that? What I mean is . . . what's in it for you?"

"What?" He looked shocked. "Nothing."

"Then why? I mean . . . what would you tell your girlfriends?" I asked. "Telling a girl that you accidentally impregnated a friend can be a real mood killer. Besides, it's more complicated than you've considered. What happens down the track, after the baby is born? Are you going to tell people that you are involved in my baby's life?"

He blushed, but said nothing. It confirmed to me that he hadn't thought it through. "I don't know. We'll figure it out."

"We'll figure it out? Patrick—why would you even want to?"

He studied my face for a long while. I tried to do the same to him, but I had no idea what was going on inside that pretty head of his.

"Fine," he said. "It was just an idea."

His cheeks were still pink. I didn't get it. Anyone would have thought I'd slapped him, rather than let him off the hook.

"It's an appealing idea, I'll admit," I said. "And you're right, people would believe it. Marion would be thrilled."

He picked up his burger again. "If you change your mind, say the word."

Patrick insisted on paying, which was a little weird, but I didn't question it, lest things get weirder. He could afford it, and after all, he'd slept on my couch for several years now. He owed me. Judy and Trish smiled at Patrick with creepy enthusiasm as he approached the counter to settle the bill. When I couldn't watch anymore, I pushed through the double doors into the evening and straight into a person.

"Oh!" I exclaimed, staring into the face of Lorraine Hargreaves, chief resident of obstetrics at St Mary's. "Dr. Hargreaves. I'm so sorry."

"Lorraine," she corrected. Thankfully she didn't appear hurt. "I didn't see you there, Neva!"

Dr. Hargreaves was a formidable woman—tall, attractive, well proportioned. She bordered on intimidating, but with a few grays littering her raven hair, and a slight overbite on her front teeth, she had enough imperfections to make her approachable.

"Well, I see the rumors are true." She reached forward, letting her hand skim, but not quite touch, my belly. "Congratulations."

"Thank you."

"Best job in the world, motherhood. Even if you love your job as much as we do."

I couldn't help a smile, being part of a "we" with Dr. Lorraine Hargreaves.

"Yes," I said. My hand traveled to my belly. "Yes, I'm looking forward to it."

"You don't need an ob-gyn, I suppose?"

I laughed, imagining Grace's face. "Probably wouldn't look good for the birthing center if I got myself an ob-gyn," I said. "Besides, I couldn't afford you."

"I'm sure I could do you a deal. But you won't need me. You do a great job at your birthing center."

"Thank yo—"

"So? Who is the lucky guy?"

"Oh, um . . ." The idea of telling the chief resident of obstetrics that my baby didn't have a father was vomit inducing. "Actually . . ."

"Evening, Lorraine." Patrick appeared beside me, hand extended.

"Well, well . . . Patrick!" Dr. Hargreaves shook Patrick's hand, and whistled. "Haven't you two kept this quiet? I know a few women at the hospital who are going to have a broken heart, Patrick. And men, for that matter, Neva." She chuckled. "It's a match made in heaven, now that I think of it. I hope Patrick's been taking good care of you?"

"Oh, no, actually he's—"

"—trying but she's very independent." Patrick's warm hand enveloped mine. "Perhaps you can convince her that she should take it easy in the last trimester, avoid any situations that could make her stressed?"

I blinked at Patrick.

"I'm surprised anyone should have to tell her that. Let him help you, Neva. He obviously wants to."

Patrick's arm was strewn casually round my waist, his fingers interlaced with mine. He grinned at me and nodded imperceptibly.

"Fine." I smiled at Lorraine. "I will."

When Dr. Hargreaves was gone, I stared at Patrick.

"She's going to think we're both nuts when she finds out you're not the father of my baby, you know."

"Probably," Patrick agreed. "*If* she finds out."

"She *will* find out."

"Only if you tell her. I'm not going to."

Again, I scanned his face, looking for some way to make sense of things. I couldn't find a single, solitary reason. "Why, Patrick?"

"Are you really that dense?"

"Let's say I am."

Before he could respond, my phone alerted me of an incoming call with a short buzz. I frowned. It was very late for a call. And I didn't recognize the number.

"I'd better get this," I said. I accepted the call. "Neva Bradley."

"Hi, Neva . . . it's Lil."

"Lil." I frowned. Lil had never called me, not once in eight years. "What is it?"

"I'm sorry, I've got bad news. Your gran's in the hospital."

14

Grace

I glanced at my phone—11:01 P.M. Neva had called twice, which must have been some sort of record, although she *had* called practically every day since the day we found out she was pregnant. Today, I couldn't bring myself to call her back. I was still reeling from the last phone call I'd received, three hours ago.

I hadn't recognized the number, but that was nothing new. Clients called me at all hours, from various numbers. Sadly it meant that I was completely unprepared for what was coming.

"Is this Grace Bradley, the midwife responsible for Gillian Brennan's delivery?" asked the voice. Nothing about that question put me at ease.

"It is. Who am I speaking with?"

"My name is Marie Ableman. I am an investigator with the Board of Nursing. I am calling because a complaint has been lodged against you by a Dr. Roger White at Newport Hospital. Dr. White was the physician looking after Ms. Brennan and her baby after they were admitted to the hospital."

Wow. He'd done it. He'd made a complaint. I almost felt proud of him. Almost. It wasn't the first time I'd been abused by a doctor, of course, and I was fairly sure it wouldn't be the last.

"These home births keep me in business," he'd muttered when we met in Emergency.

"Excuse me?" I said.

"They're irresponsible, and they always end up like this, with a patient being rushed in in need of emergency treatment," he said unapologetically. "Then the doctors are left to clean up the mess."

"With due respect"—I used every ounce of restraint and professionalism I had left, for the sake of my client—"there is no *mess*. We are here to admit an infant with a cleft palate. Even if she were born here at the hospital, she'd have required the same treatment. The mother has a perineal tear—pretty standard for a vaginal birth and hardly a mess." I kept my voice civil but it dripped with thinly veiled hostility.

"Listen," Patrick said. "I'm a pediatrician at St. Mary's Hospital. I oversaw this birth, and it was quite safe. We can iron out all the details later, but our first priority is the patient and her baby. Can we all agree on that?"

"Yes," the doctor said a little gruffly. "Yes, we can." Then he pointed at me, his face a snarl. "But I want her details. I'm going to report her."

Patrick stepped between me and the doctor's finger. "Now, just a min—"

"You can have my details," I said, already in my purse, searching for my accreditation. "There you go, write it down. I have nothing to be ashamed of."

I wasn't going to be bullied. I knew these kinds of doctors. They wanted to make sure everyone knew their place. He (or she, but more often than not, it was he) was the doctor and I was the lowly midwife, the handy woman, the untrained helper. Rarely, if ever, did they recognize that I had studied for six years and completed a master's degree to become a Certified Nurse-Midwife. They never made good on their threats to make a complaint, and I doubted they ever would. Intimidating people was simply another skill they'd learned in medical school.

"What is the nature of the complaint?" I asked Ms. Ableman.

"Dr. White claims that you attempted a high-risk delivery at home with detrimental consequences for both mother and child. He reported that the baby was born disfigured and that the mother had suffered a third-degree tear that had not been tended to by the time she was admitted to his care."

"The baby was born with a cleft lip and palate," I explained. "Which, I'm sure you'll agree, has nothing to do with my competence as a midwife. The tear was left as a conscious decision not to separate mother and baby. Gillian indicated that she wouldn't allow her baby to be transferred to the hospital without her, so I thought it was best that the tear be tended to there. If you speak to Gillian, I'm sure you'll find she doesn't have any complaints about my service."

"I will be speaking to Ms. Brennan shortly, and I'll also need to question your birth assistant and anyone else present."

"Okay."

"I know this must be stressful, but do you think you could answer a few questions for me now, Mrs. Bradley? While it is all fresh in your mind?"

"I don't see any reason why not."

A mouse clicked in the background, followed by: "Now, at what time did you realize the baby had a cleft palate?"

"I wasn't sure it was a cleft palate at first." I stood and picked my way down the hall toward my office so I could check my notes. "I knew something didn't feel right. I wondered if it could be breech, but it was unlikely since the baby was head-down at our last appointment. I guess it was about eight P.M. I'll check my notes to be sure."

"I'll need a copy of your notes, but for now, tell me from memory. So, at approximately eight P.M., immediately following a vaginal exam, you suspected the baby was breech. What action did you take?"

"Well, no. I didn't 'suspect' the baby was breech, I simply thought it was a possibility. I told Gillian that I was uncertain of what I had felt, and then I asked my daughter for a second opinion."

"Your daughter? She was present at the birth?"

"She was my birth assistant. She's a Certified Nurse-Midwife at St. Mary's Birthing Center."

"St. Mary's." Her fingernails bashed against a keyboard. "Okay. What happened next?"

"My daughter performed an exam and was also uncertain of what she could feel, but she suspected it was a breech."

"And you disagreed?"

"I thought it was worthwhile looking at other possibilities before transferring her to a hospital. Gillian was very committed to having a home birth with minimal medical intervention."

"How long did you look at other possibilities?"

"A few minutes."

"What happened next?"

"We realized it was a cleft palate we were feeling. Once my daughter suggested it, we both knew immediately. We did another exam to confirm, and then we were certain."

"What time was this?"

"I don't know. Eight thirtyish?"

Fingernails clacked against the keyboard. I waited.

"And once you confirmed the baby had a cleft palate, you still felt it was appropriate to proceed with the birth at home?"

I paused. The delivery of that sentence was so laden with judgment, I couldn't help but respond defensively.

"Yes. I knew Gillian would have a hard time when she saw her daughter's face. I didn't see any reason to add the trauma of a hospital delivery to her troubles. Particularly when we had a pediatrician on-site."

"Dr. Johnson?"

"Yes." I had no idea of Patrick's surname, but Marie had clearly done her research, so that must be it.

"Now . . . Gillian was admitted to the hospital herself with a third-degree tear. Can you tell me about that?"

"A third-degree tear is one that stretches from the perineum right through to the—"

"I mean," Marie interrupted, "can you explain to me why you transferred a patient with a third-degree tear?"

"Oh, of course, I'm sorry." I played innocent. "As I said before, it was a matter of keeping mother and baby together. I knew Gillian had a tear, but she was reluctant to part with her baby. And I was inclined to agree with her. The tear wasn't life-threatening and we wanted to get the baby seen to at the hospital as soon as possible. I made a judgment call, and I'd do the same again."

I rapped my knuckles against the bedside table. I was talking braver than I felt. Had I made the right call? As I thought back to the events of the evening, I had to admit, there was room for doubt. Was it irresponsible to deliver a baby with a cleft palate at home? As for the tear, obviously it wasn't life-threatening, but there could have been complications caused by not suturing sooner rather than later. I started to feel a little sick.

"Okay, Mrs. Bradley," Marie said after an eternity. "That's all I need for now, but I may need to speak with you again. Once I have spoken with all parties, a committee from the board will review the case and make a recommendation. You will be informed of this recommendation as soon as it is made."

I found myself nodding. "I look forward to it."

"One other thing, Mrs. Bradley. Your license is suspended, pending the results of our investigation. You won't be able to deliver any babies until this matter is resolved."

I stopped nodding. "But . . . this is my business. I've committed to mothers who are due in the next few weeks, some in the next few days."

"I'm sorry, Mrs. Bradley. You'll have to tell them to make alternative arrangements."

"Like what?"

"Well, you could refer them to another midwife."

"Do you know how hard it is to get in with a private midwife in Rhode Island? If you're not booked in by the time you're six weeks pregnant, you can forget it. You think I'm going to be able to place a client who is due in a few days?"

"If they can't be placed, they'll have to go to the hospital."

I found myself unable to speak.

"And, Grace, you are not allowed to contact Gillian or her family during this time."

"Not contact Gillian? But I have to provide her postpartum care."

"You cannot, Mrs. Bradley. Not unless you want to risk losing your license permanently. She will receive postpartum care in the hospital."

"The hospital?" I scoffed. "What, maternity pads and Tylenol? She needs breast-feeding support, nutritional advice, pelvic-floor exercises. Do you think the hospital is going to provide that?"

"Mrs. Bradley—"

"No, it's fine. No deliveries. No postpartum care for Gillian. Great system you have."

"The system is here to protect people, Mrs. Bradley."

"Indeed. Doctors." I bristled. "Can I at least call Gillian to explain?"

"I'll be in touch with her. I'll explain. And I'm sure another midwife will be able to offer the services you spoke of. We'll make sure Gillian is looked after."

Ms. Ableman was playing good cop, but I wasn't buying it.

"Okay. How long can I expect to wait for your"—I curled my lip—"recommendation?"

"It should be within four weeks, depending on the speed of getting your notes and getting interviews with the other involved parties. We try to be swift—we don't want this drawn out for anyone's sake."

"That's good of you."

"Do you have any questions for me?"

How do you live with yourself? Why are you persecuting the patient who has already had to deal with having a baby with a cleft lip and palate? What right did this Dr. Whatshisface have to make a complaint about me? "No."

"Okay. Thank you for your cooperation. I'll be in touch."

Now, I sat in the blue chair, waiting for Robert to come home. He'd been working late a lot; tonight was no different. Lately, we'd been like strangers, passing like ships in the night. I got to thinking about the day we met. I was still studying midwifery and running an art class out of Mom's garage to make ends meet. Robert had been referred to the class by another student and, as an accountant, he wasn't my typical clientele. He wasn't a classic accountant; he was pretty boho, in fact. His jeans were ripped and his sideburns impressively long, and he had a psychedelic scarf tied haphazardly around his neck. It was only the bluish black dots on his cheeks and upper lip that gave him away. No one was clean-shaven back then. It was the seventies, and unless you had a corporate job, were prepubescent, or a woman, you had a mustache. I noticed Robert as I dashed from the garage back to the house for more chairs. I waved him in and when I returned, my regulars were sitting at the table, some already with lit spliffs in hand. But Robert was hovering inside the door, clearly out of place.

"You must be Robert," I said.

"Yes." He extended his hand, which was novel, as creative types tended to hug. "I'm looking for Gracie."

"You've found her," I said, suppressing a smile. Gracie? No one called me that. But I was willing to allow it. His awkwardness was charming and he was quite handsome, this accountant. Pam—the regular who had referred him—had mentioned he was handsome, but people rarely understood my type. And even if they did, Robert wasn't it. Still, I got that funny feeling in my belly, the feeling commonly described as "butterflies," though I thought it more like ripples in a pond after you throw a stone: hitting you hard in the center before gently

radiating outward to the tips of your fingers and toes. The feeling continued throughout the class, getting stronger the closer I got to Robert,
and stronger still when I leaned over him to examine his work and my
breast brushed his back. It was hard to gauge if Robert felt the same; he
was a diligent student, concentrating on his picture as though it were
a math puzzle rather than a creative expression of himself. But the fact
that he loitered after the class had ended had to be a good sign, I figured.

"Did you enjoy the class?" I asked as I washed up the paintbrushes.

"I did. Very . . . relaxing."

I covered my mouth, but a snicker came out.

"What?" he asked.

"I'm sorry, but you didn't look relaxed. In fact, you're the first person I've seen who makes life drawing class look stressful."

"Ah." He grinned. "I'm good at making things look stressful. In my
world, you get paid more for that."

"Your world sounds dreadful."

"It's not so bad right now."

Robert's gaze lingered intentionally on mine. Wow. This accountant could turn on the charm. Who'd have guessed it? I waved to the
last couple of students as they headed out.

"Maybe you'd like to stay for a while." I held his eye as I reached for
the red and black kimono that hung over the back of my chair.
"Maybe—" I held the pause as long as I could. "—you could draw me."

With hindsight, I was incredibly forward. Robert had acted like it
was no big deal, but I could see from the way his hands trembled that he
was terrified. I sat on the stool, the kimono draped over my most private
parts, my body angled to the right and my feet tucked into the lower
bar. I turned my head to face him and opened the kimono, just enough.

"Make sure you get the shape right before focusing on the detail," I told him, trailing my fingertips down the side of my breast. "Start here with the curve of the breast and the hip, then the narrowness of the head and the ankles. Use as many strokes as you need—this is art not science. The only way to do a poor female form is to fail to celebrate her curves. . . ."

I paused when I realized Robert was standing right in front of me.

"Oh." I frowned. "What?"

"You are a goddess."

A goddess. I liked the sound of that. "I don't think anyone has ever called me . . . that . . . before."

"That surprises me."

Robert's hands were no longer shaking. But mine were. When it came to men, I was used to being the pursuer. Men responded to it, yes, but the dramatic one-liners—you're a goddess, et cetera—they usually came from me. It was strange sitting in the other seat. Good strange.

"I like you," I said, as much to myself as to him. The revelation was as unexpected as it was undeniable.

"I like you, too." Robert's voice was awkward, but he may have been suppressing a smile. "Gracie."

When I heard Robert's keys in the door, I rose from my chair. I spied him at the end of the corridor, his tie pulled loose, his face concerned. "Grace. Are you okay?"

I stumbled toward him. "No. I'm not okay."

"What is it?" he asked. "What's happened?"

I let out a sob. "There's . . . there's been a complaint made against me . . . with the Board of Nursing . . . by a doctor."

Robert stepped away from me. "What?"

"It's about the baby I delivered last night. She was born with a cleft lip and palate. We delivered her here then transferred both mother and baby to the hospital. The doctor—he went ballistic. Said he would report me."

"What has he reported you for?"

"He says delivering a baby with a cleft palate was too high-risk to attempt at home, and also that I shouldn't have transferred a patient with a perineal tear."

"Did you know the baby had a cleft palate?" Robert's expression was curiously blank. His voice was low and steady, his tone unreadable.

"Once labor had started . . . yes."

"And the tear?" he asked.

"I knew about the tear, but I thought it was best for the patient and baby to—"

"Fuck, Grace!"

Robert's outburst was so unexpected, I jumped.

"This is great, this is just . . . fantastic."

"Robert, what's wrong?"

He began to pace. "Do you have any idea how much shit I am in if I lose my job? Do you? We won't even be able to make the next mortgage payment. That's what we signed up for when we moved here. Every day I go into work, wondering if today's the day I'm going to bring home my stuff in a cardboard box. I'm worrying about you and our future. Meanwhile, you're taking unnecessary risks and putting our family at risk! For what?"

Robert stopped pacing and pressed his fingertips into his eye sockets. His cheeks were red. "We need your income, Grace. It may not be huge, but we rely on it. We can't afford for you to take risks. Not right now." He let out a long sigh and looked at me. The heat in his face was gone. "I'm sorry. I shouldn't have shouted."

"It's all right," I said automatically.

"It's not. It's just . . . a rough time right now. And I need you to be at work. I don't have room in my head to deal with anything else."

"Okay."

I stood before him, shell-shocked. In our entire marriage, Robert had shouted only a handful of times. Once after I fell asleep at the wheel, driving home from a birth, and wrapped the car around a tree. (His anger was out of concern for me, rather than about the car.) Another time when Neva was nine and she ran onto the road after her Frisbee. Once when I taped *The Golden Girls* over the video of him skydiving in Australia. He was always apologetic afterwards, but this time I got the feeling that his anger remained. And I hadn't even told him the full story. I lowered my gaze and whispered: "I can't deliver any babies until after the investigation, Robert."

Robert's eyes bugged. "*What?*"

"My license is suspended. I can't do any more deliveries. So I won't be getting an income."

Robert stared at me. The disbelief in his expression was much worse than the shouting. When my phone started ringing, Robert turned on his heel.

"Robert, wait."

"I'm taking a shower," he said, without turning around. His tone indicated this conversation was over, at least for today.

My phone was still ringing. Numbly I wandered over to it, picked it up. "Uh, hello? Grace Bradley."

"Grace, it's Lil. You mom is in the hospital."

15

Floss

The hospital was quiet, apart from the usual noises. The beep and hum of lifesaving machinery. The squeak of rubber shoes. I could practically taste the disinfectant that hovered in the air. Lil was in the corner, repositioning herself every few minutes to get comfortable on the hospital chair.

Drugged up to the gills, I hovered on the brink of sleep. The edges of my mind rippled like the shallows of a pebbly stream, but in the middle, it was still and crystal clear. When I looked into it, it was Elizabeth's reflection I was seeing. But not the smiling, rosy-cheeked Elizabeth. It was the other Elizabeth. Bill's Elizabeth.

A month after my dinner at Bill and Elizabeth's house, we got the call. Elizabeth was in labor.

Evie checked the delivery bag while I got the bikes from the shed. I was accustomed to getting bikes out in the dark—women tended to go into labor at night—but navigating two bikes on the cobbled lane was a little challenging, and I dropped one out the front. It fell to the ground with an almighty clatter.

"Shhh!" Evie said, appearing on the steps with the delivery bag. "Are you trying to wake up the neighborhood?"

"Sorry." I was anxious to get there, and it showed in my shaking hands. I picked up Evie's bike and leaned it against the fence, then straddled my own. "So tell me, what did Bill say? Was she very far along?"

"It wasn't Bill." Evie's lips formed a thin, straight line as she loaded the delivery bag into the basket. "It was Elizabeth."

"On the phone? But the nearest telephone is two miles away. She couldn't have—"

"She biked it." Evie mounted her own bike. "Bill's at the pub, wetting the baby's head."

Evie sounded as though she had her own set of reservations about Bill—it was unexpected. In that split second, I considered telling Evie everything—my concerns about Elizabeth, about Bill, about what I'd seen on Elizabeth's stomach. But I didn't. If Elizabeth was in trouble, Evie would see for herself soon enough. And if she wasn't, I wouldn't have to betray Elizabeth's confidence.

We cycled, fast, into the night. It was a three quarters of an hour's ride to Elizabeth's place, and although we weren't in danger of missing the birth, I just wanted to get there.

The last stretch of the ride was paddocks. In the dark, it was downright creepy. The only lights were from the little headlights on our bikes and, when we got close enough, the flickering light shining from Elizabeth's bedroom window. When we reached her front fence,

I leapt off my bicycle and raced down the path, leaving Evie to follow with the delivery bag.

"Elizabeth?" I called, stepping through the front door.

"In here."

I dashed through the kitchen, past the tiny living room into the even tinier bedroom. It took me a minute to locate Elizabeth in the dark, but I eventually did. She was bent over at the end of the bed. "There you are!"

Elizabeth unfurled into a standing position, allowing me to see her properly by the light of the fire. Large circles shadowed her eyes, her face was gaunt, and her entire body—with the exception of her stomach— was bony.

Behind me, Evie gasped. "Elizabeth, my God. What has happened to you? You look like a skeleton."

A contraction took hold. Elizabeth breathed deeply, grasping the knobs on the chest of drawers. I stared at her, bewildered. It had only been—what?—a month since I'd last seen her? She couldn't have eaten a thing since.

When her contraction subsided, she sank to her knees, panting slightly. "Contractions are about five minutes apart"—she didn't look at either of us—"and my bag of water has broken."

Elizabeth was calm and official, more like the midwife than the woman in labor. She spoke as though she'd never heard Evie's questions— which was impossible, as we were in a room the size of a cupboard, sur-rounded by silence. At a loss, I looked to Evie.

"Elizabeth," Evie said. "If something's wrong, we need to know. It could affect your baby."

We waited but Elizabeth just pursed her lips. Her face, I noticed, had a bluish tinge, as though she were a walking, pregnant corpse. Why had I let her avoid me? If something happened to this baby, it was my fault.

"Elizabeth, please—" Evie started again, but Elizabeth held up a hand.

"I'm not talking about this, Evie, okay? Either deliver my baby or leave, and I'll manage somehow on my own."

Evie and I exchanged a glance. Thank God she was here. Normally, only one midwife attended a birth; the only reason I was here at all was because Elizabeth had asked me months ago. Even if she hadn't, I wouldn't have missed it. Perhaps it was because it was Elizabeth's, but I already felt an attachment to this child. Or, perhaps, a *responsibility to* the child.

Evie exhaled. "Have it your way. For now, we'll focus on getting this baby born. But once it's out, you *are* going to tell me what is going on. Do you hear me, Elizabeth?"

Elizabeth wasn't listening. She was already half-bent with another contraction.

Evie took me to one side. "We're going to have to assume Elizabeth is malnourished, which means breast-feeding may be difficult due to low supply. I have some evaporated milk in my delivery bag, which we can feed the baby with a syringe if necessary."

"And the baby?" I asked. "Will it be okay?"

"I'm more worried about Elizabeth, at this point. As you know, babies are very good at taking what they need while they're in utero. At the mother's expense, usually." Seeing my face, she patted my hand. "Why don't you head into the kitchen and boil some water, Floss? And while you're there, fix Elizabeth a snack. She's going to need all the energy she can get."

"Yes," I said. "Yes. Good idea."

It was just a few paces to the kitchen, but I barely made it there. My legs felt like noodles. Elizabeth was so frail, so tiny. It made no sense. Was she ill? Had they run out of money for food? I thought of the night I came for dinner, the way Elizabeth wolfed down her meal. They'd certainly had food then.

In the next room the bed rattled, sending a shudder through the entire house. It was followed by an almighty "Owwwwarggghhh." It snapped me into action.

Once I'd got the water boiling, I began opening cupboard doors. Crockery, cutlery, pots. In the freestanding larder, the shelves were clean and lined in shiny floral paper, but they were bare apart from tea and an empty sugar bowl. In less than a minute, I'd checked every cupboard except for the bottom two, which were bolted shut with a large padlock—probably where Bill kept his rifles. Nowhere was there even a morsel of food.

I poked my head back into the bedroom. "Elizabeth, where is the pantry, love?"

"It's . . . uh . . . Oh, God." Her face collapsed into itself as another contraction came on. I looked at my watch. Three and a half minutes since the last one. This labor was progressing rapidly.

"Have you done an internal?" I asked Evie.

She nodded. "Eight centimeters dialated."

Elizabeth rolled from side to side, knotted up with the pains. It wasn't going to be long now. Shiny instruments were lined up on a tray, and a clean towel warmed by the fire. The bassinet had been set up in the corner, and a wool blanket that Elizabeth had knitted hung over its edge. Evie stared off into the distance, her face a sheet of lines. I could tell she was wondering what kind of home this baby would be born into. It was hard to think about anything else.

"Why don't we try walking?" I asked Elizabeth when the pains stopped. "See if we can get this baby into a nice position?"

To this, Elizabeth agreed. We paced the floor of the bedroom for an hour. Back and forth, stopping every couple of minutes to rock through the pain. Other than the pop and crackle of the fire, the silence was absolute. Usually that was how I liked it. *Silence is the laboring mother's music.* But tonight it gave my mind too much room to think. And after an hour of it, I couldn't stand it any longer.

"Elizabeth."

Elizabeth frowned, lifted her head.

"What is wrong with you? No more excuses. You're to tell me. Right now."

She sank onto the bed and started to drop her head, but I caught her chin and held it. I could feel Evie behind me, perhaps ready to tell me that this wasn't the time, but I wasn't going to listen. I'd already waited too long.

"Nothing," Elizabeth said. "Nothing's wrong. It's my fault, really."

"What's your fault?"

"I've got fancy tastes," she said. "You used to say that yourself, Floss, remember? And Bill, he's not a rich man."

Elizabeth had a contraction, and Evie and I remained silent, waiting.

"It's hard for him," Elizabeth said when the contraction was over, "having another mouth to feed. I can hardly expect to be fed like we were at the boardinghouse. It's tough, country life."

Evie leaned forward. "But he *does* feed you?"

"Yes." There was a pause. "Yes, of course. It's just that . . . sometimes I get greedy."

Elizabeth wouldn't meet my eye. I couldn't for the life of me figure out what she meant. Elizabeth wasn't greedy. And I didn't have a clue why she'd think she was.

"What are you saying?" I asked gently.

Elizabeth looked from me to Evie and then to her lap. "Just . . . when Bill's not happy with me . . . he doesn't give me food."

The fire cracked into the silence. My mouth formed around questions that I couldn't seem to project. Perhaps because there were so many. How could a man not give his pregnant wife food? Why would he do that? How long had he been doing this? Why didn't I see it? And, most important, *Why wouldn't Bill be happy with you?*

"Does he at least give you housekeeping money?" I asked eventually. It was the only question I felt I could speak without bursting into rage or, worse, tears.

Elizabeth looked taken aback. "Of course not. We don't have that kind of money."

I could hardly believe my ears.

"What kind of money do you think he's spending at the pub, Elizabeth?" I cried, then bit back my frustration. It wasn't Elizabeth I was angry with. When I spoke again, my voice was softer. "You don't deserve this. Bill is controlling everything about you, who you see, what you eat. . . ." I trailed off when Elizabeth closed her hands around her stomach. A chill traveled down my spine. "You didn't fall, did you?"

Elizabeth kept her head down. It was all the answer I needed.

Back in my days as a student-nurse, we'd looked at a case study of a toddler who'd been starved by his mother for not behaving. When he died, at age five, he weighed less than an average one-year-old. But there was no sign of physical beating, not even a bruise. When I'd asked the matron about it, she'd said . . . *Abuse comes in many ways. The only universal thing about it is the perpetrators' need to control.*

I suddenly remembered the padlock on the larder doors. I whipped around and strode to the kitchen without a word.

"What are you doing, Floss?" Evie called after me.

An axe rested against a stack of wood next to the fireplace. I snapped it up. "Making Elizabeth a snack." The axe was small but heavy. It hit the arm of the padlock on the first go, knocking it clean off the door handle.

"Floss!"

As I suspected, the cupboards were full of food. Dry biscuits, sugar, flour, butter, eggs. There wasn't time to bake anything, so I threw a handful of crackers on a plate, slathered them in butter, and raced back to the bedroom. Elizabeth ate a couple, for my sake more than hers, I suspect. After that, I kept trying to force more on her, but she declined.

Thirty minutes later, Elizabeth felt the urge to push. At Evie's instruction, I brought in a large pail of boiled water for hand washing. I placed it on the bureau.

"Okay, Elizabeth," Evie started. "I want you to slide down so your bottom is at the end of the bed, then roll onto your side. Help her, Floss. Then, when you feel the next contraction, I want you to give me a big push. Understand?"

"I'm a midwife, Evie, I know—" The next contraction took her breath. Her face twisted.

"Good girl," Evie said. "Very nice. The head is coming."

I moved down to the end of the bed so I could see. The head *was* coming, and fast. The next contraction came, and the next after that, each time easing the head out a little more, and each time, pushing Elizabeth a little further than she could go. I'd seen a lot of exhausted mothers go through this stage of labor, but Elizabeth's condition was worrying me. A couple of times between contractions, her eyes rolled back in her head.

"It's crowning. Just hold on. Breathe!" Evie urged. "Come on, Elizabeth, breathe. Floss, I need you down here. Grab the towel and bring it here, then wash your hands." Evie had one hand on Elizabeth's knee and the other on the baby's head. "Good girl. Now put the towel down in front of me."

I grabbed the towel, then washed my hands in the hot water. I dried my hands on another towel and knelt at the end of the bed next to Evie. Elizabeth whimpered.

"You're nearly there," Evie said. "Floss, get the instruments ready—the clamp and the scalpel, please. Elizabeth, pant. You know how it's done."

I collected the clamp and the scalpel, keeping my eyes on the baby. I couldn't take my eyes off it. Even though I could see only the top of its little head, something magical was happening. Gently, the head eased out, revealing a tuft of bloody, matted hair.

"The head is out!" I exclaimed.

Evie's forehead remained lined, but her lips loosened into a slight upturn. "You are so close, Elizabeth. Your baby will be born in just a minute."

Elizabeth closed her eyes and nodded, psyching herself up. Her eyes remained closed for several minutes, long enough for me to wonder if she'd fallen asleep—or passed out. I was just rising to check her when her eyes sprang open and she moaned.

"This is it. Push," Evie encouraged. "Come on, love. That's wonderful. Here it comes."

I watched in silence as the baby turned and a little face appeared. "Oh, Elizabeth. I can see the face."

Elizabeth's face unfolded, and for a heartbeat, she looked young and healthy, the Elizabeth I knew and loved. "Really? You can see the face?"

"I can. It's a beautiful face."

Elizabeth's face crumpled again. She was struggling. Her red face shimmered with sweat. Evie appeared unflustered, going about her business, focused completely on the baby being born. I watched as she slipped her fingers around the baby's neck and guided the shoulders out, rotating as she went. The rest of the baby quickly followed, landing in the warm towel that I had laid out. Evie held the vernix-covered baby upside down by the feet. There was a tiny cry. My insides collapsed.

"Congratulations," I said as Evie passed the baby to Elizabeth. "You have a daughter."

A chorus of familiar, hushed voices roused me from sleep. "Thanks so much for calling us, Lil. How is she doing?"

It was Neva's voice I could hear, and then Lil's, reciting the prognosis from the doctor. A minor myocardial infarction. Too weary to open my eyes, I just let their words wash over me.

"What have they given her?" Grace spoke now—I recognized her bossy, professional tone. Clearly the news of my heart attack had frightened her, and she wanted to feel back in control. I heard my chart being lifted off the foot of the bed. "Aspirin, beta-blockers, nitroglycerin—"

Lil cut in. "What is nitroglycerin?"

"It's a common medicine." The male voice was unfamiliar. "It widens and opens your blood vessels, and allows blood and oxygen to reach your heart more easily. Very effective."

"Are you a doctor?" Lil asked.

"Yes, though I'm not an expert in this area. My patients are a little short in the tooth for heart attacks."

The papers ruffled again. "That's weird," Grace said. "Mom's blood type is AB positive. I didn't know she was AB positive."

My eyes flew open. Grace, Lil, and a man whom I now presumed to be Neva's pediatrician friend stood at the foot of my bed, studying my chart. Neva was by my side. Her face lit up.

"Gran," she said. "You're awake."

Grace dropped my chart back on the rail and came to my other side. "Mom. How are you feeling?"

"Absolutely fine. I told Lil not to worry you. I knew you'd just come down here."

"You had a heart attack, Gran!" Neva said. "As if we'd be anywhere else."

"You need to let us help you more, Mom," Grace said. "We can do your grocery shopping, errands, whatever you need."

"Stop your fussing," I told them. "I'm fine."

Lil watched the pediatrician intently. "Could those things— shopping, errands—have caused her heart attack?"

"I'm not her doctor, but generally speaking, light activity should *reduce* the risk of heart attack. It's more likely to be brought on by high cholesterol or poor diet. Sometimes it's just genetics or age. Sometimes stress."

Lil's ears pricked up. *Stress.*

"Sorry, Gran," Neva said. "You haven't been introduced to Patrick. He's my—"

"Boyfriend." The man sent Neva a sideways wink. "It's nice to meet you, Ms. Higgins. Sorry it's under these circumstances."

I smiled. I liked his spunk. "It's nice to meet you too, Patrick. Call me Floss."

My gaze floated back to Grace. She was holding my chart again, frowning at it. Lil's expression gave away her own worries. Both of them, I knew, had questions for me. So, probably, did Neva. I'd managed to evade them this time. But next time?

It was all starting to close in on me. And I got the feeling it was only a matter of time before my secret came out.

16

Neva

In the passenger seat of Patrick's car, my stomach wriggled like a sack of kittens. It was hard to believe that a few hours ago, he'd offered to pretend to be the father of my baby. He'd suggested we pretend to be a couple. He'd even introduced himself to Gran as my boyfriend! If it was anyone else, the intent would be clear. But Patrick, the player, couldn't be interested in me—could he?

He pulled up outside my apartment. "Here we are."

"You never answered me before," I said. My head was too full of thoughts to try to weave it more naturally into conversation. "Why would you want to do this? Pretend to be the father of my baby?"

"Would you believe I have a thing for redheads?"

I let the silence be my answer.

Patrick sighed, exasperated. "Come on, Nev."

"Come on, *what*? Tell me. If you want me to say yes, I need to know why."

"Are you really going to make me say it?"

"Say wha—?"

With a flick of his seat belt, he silenced me. He took my chin between his thumb and forefinger and bent toward me. I held still, not even breathing. His lip curved up at one side. It was the most gentle, tender smile I'd ever seen from Patrick. Perhaps the most tender smile I'd ever seen from anyone. But I only got to enjoy it for an instant before he pressed his lips to mine.

The world slipped away. His lips were soft but firm. Gently, he pulled me closer. Involuntarily, I moaned.

My approval did something to both of us. Patrick's tongue slid into my mouth, and deep inside me, a fire ignited. It was like watching a movie with a foreshadowed twist; I hadn't seen it coming, but now I couldn't believe I'd missed it. Not just the way Patrick felt about me. But the way I felt about him too.

When he broke away, I saw stars. It might have been the light, or the fact that we had just kissed, or perhaps the pregnancy hormones, but I wondered if I were dreaming. More than anything, I wanted to go back to sleep.

"Does that answer your question?"

"Uh . . . what was the question?"

"The reason I want to do this." His voice lowered to a whisper. "I think we're good for each other, Nev. I'd hoped we'd get to this point and *then* conceive a baby but . . . if the baby's been conceived and . . . you're telling me the guy's out of the picture, then . . . I'm still in. If you want me."

I blinked. It was just too impossible to be true. And yet . . .

"Are *you* in?" he asked.

"Yes." I sounded hoarse but sure. I nodded several times. "Yes. I'm in."

We stared at each other. Patrick chuckled. "Okay, then. Well, I'm going to leave you to obsess about this all night," he said. He refastened his seat belt. "I'll call you tomorrow."

"You're not going to stay?" I blurted out. Immediately, I wanted to retract it. Sort of.

Patrick looked startled.

"Um," I said. "I mean—"

He smiled. "I think I'm going to go home tonight. I'd love to stay," he said, perhaps in response to my flaming cheeks. "But after all this time, I want us to do this right."

The next day, he called during my lunch break. "Hey, there, baby momma."

I blushed, even though I was on the phone.

"You okay?" he asked.

"Yep." Actually, I was tired. I'd spent half the night tossing and turning and obsessing over the kiss, the relationship, the offer to pretend to be my baby's father. "Sorry, just a little distracted. I'm juggling two mothers in labor, early stages."

"Then I won't keep you. I just wanted to tell you that I haven't told anyone yet. About being the father of your baby. So you still have the chance to change your mind."

"Good," I said. "Because I'm still not sure it's a good idea."

"Damn." His tone was typically dry. "I really wanted to tell Marion."

I laughed and held up one finger to Ruth, my birth assistant, to let her know I'd be right in. I moved into a quiet corner and lowered my voice. "Are *you* sure about this? You've really thought it all through?"

"Yep."

I traced my finger against a groove in the wall. "You're crazy, you know that? But . . . okay. Tell Marion. Tell the world." Then another thought occurred to me. "Actually, don't tell the *whole* world. We'll tell everyone else that you are the father, but not Grace and Gran."

"Why not?"

"I . . . don't know."

But I did know. It was one thing *not* telling Grace and Gran who the father was. It was another outright lying to them. There were so many ways that Grace got under my skin, but she'd always been truthful with me. As for Gran, I doubted she'd ever told a lie in her whole life. It was something I knew I could count on with them, and I didn't want to break that circle of trust.

"I just don't think I can look them in the face and lie."

That seemed to be enough for Patrick. "Right, then. We'll tell everyone except your mom and gran. Sound good?"

I sagged. He had no idea how good.

"Oh, and Nev, about last night . . ."

The baby, or maybe something else inside me—lower down—did a somersault. "Yeah?"

"I'm hoping we can have a repeat tonight."

Twenty-four hours later, everyone—with the exception of my mother and grandmother—thought Patrick was the father of my baby. As Patrick said, everyone accepted it without question, amused that we'd finally revealed our relationship "after all this time." Marion was a little miffed that she hadn't been the one to expose the secret, but once she recovered, even she seemed pleased. Patrick accepted the pats on the back and congratulations like a proud father to be, and I smiled as the nurses tried to conceal their horror that Patrick had been snapped up. That part was fun.

As we'd told everyone we were a couple, I didn't see any way around the new sleeping arrangements at my apartment. Eloise would have thought it was strange if he'd slept on the couch. So that night, when Patrick showed up after his shift, after a brief chat with Eloise and Ted, who were snuggling on the couch, we'd both wandered stiffly to my bedroom. I used the bathroom first, and as I waited for Patrick to finish his shower, I peeled back the sheet to examine my sleepwear for the tenth time. A tank top and shorts. A negligee, even if I'd owned one, would've looked ridiculous on a woman who was seven months pregnant, but it felt a little presumptuous to wear nothing at all. I sat up. Maybe my good underwear and bra set would be better? It was pink and girly and . . . *No. Not me at all.* I lay back down.

The next time I sat up, the light was off and I could tell some hours had passed. Opposite me in bed, Patrick smiled. "Hey, there, sleepyhead."

I blinked awake. "Whoa. How long have you been staring at me?"

"I wasn't staring until you suddenly shot upright. I'm a light sleeper. Unlike you."

I yawned. "Sorry. I must have dozed off while you were in the shower."

"Pregnant women need sleep."

"True." I frowned. "You know, I'm not used to having men in my bed watching me sleep."

"You're not used to having men in your bed at all. I should know. Unless you've been sneaking them out the window—which, as a doctor, I would say is a dangerous move—on the third floor."

"So *that's* why none of them called."

I expected Patrick to laugh, but he didn't. "Is that what happened to him, then? *The* guy?"

"Yeah," I said. "That must be it."

"You're really not going to tell me who he is?"

I shook my head.

"Does *he* know?"

"No."

Patrick propped himself onto an elbow. "If it were my baby . . . I'd want to know."

"Trust me. This guy doesn't want to know."

"So he's definitely out of the picture, then?" For once, Patrick looked unsure of himself. It made my insides hurt. "He's not going to swoop in later, demanding back his fatherly rights?"

"No." My voice was confident. "Definitely not."

Finally, that megawatt smile. "Well, good. Then his loss is my gain."

The gleam in Patrick's eye was unmistakable. It made me nervous. He was in my bed. He'd have expectations. I wasn't nervous about sex . . . exactly . . . but sex with Patrick? It was thrilling and terrifying in equal parts. Thrilling because, well . . . he was Patrick. He looked the way he looked, and he was definitely very experienced. Terrifying because I was heavily pregnant and most likely not up to the job. But I was happy to try.

I reached for him under the blanket and found his naked waist, warm, flexing under my hands. Slowly, I edged toward him, sliding into his space. The baby sat between us. I leaned in, over it, and pressed my mouth to his.

"Nev."

I pulled back, my body a crescent moon mirror image of his. "Yeah."

"I know this is a bit unorthodox, me being in your bed like this. But I don't have any expectations. Fantasies, but not expectations."

"Fantasies?" I flickered my eyes to the bowling ball between us. "Even with this?"

He half smiled. "Even with that."

My head began to swirl.

"But not tonight," he said. "Tonight I thought we could just . . . talk."

"Talk?"

He nodded.

"*You* are in bed with a woman, and you want to talk."

"What is that supposed to mean?"

"It's *me*, Patrick. I know your history. Mr. Lipstick on My Shirt, Mr. Reeking of Perfume. You've been sleeping on my couch, remember?"

"Ah." He rolled onto his back, smiling, winging his arms behind his ears. "So my efforts weren't wasted."

"Your efforts?" I didn't get it.

He eyed me sideways and laughed. "Come on. Do you know how hard it is to get lipstick on your shirt collar? How many women do you know that kiss a man's neck when they're not naked? Women who still have lipstick on." I thought about it, but before I could come up with an answer, he continued. "I was trying to get a certain person's attention."

"Wha—?" I paused, taking it all in. "You mean . . . me?"

He laughed again, but now he looked a little shy. My brain continued to work overtime. "You mean . . . you were trying to get my attention by getting heavy with other women?"

"When you put it like that, it sounds a little counterproductive. But, yes."

Part of me wanted to slap him. Another part wanted to grab his half-naked body and . . . "In what world would it be productive?"

"I don't know." He smiled at the ceiling. "A lot of other women seem to find me attractive. I thought if you saw how they saw me . . ."

"So you slept with half of St. Mary's!"

"Not half."

"A quarter?"

"Two," he said.

"*Two?*"

"Two."

His face was earnest. And while Patrick was many things, he wasn't a liar. "Wow. Just two." I should have been relieved, but a strange, unpleasant feeling began to burn through me. "Which two?"

Patrick started to shake his head.

"Come on," I said. "If it's only two, you'll remember which ones. Tell me."

"I remember who they are, Nev. But I'm not telling you."

"Patrick. If we are going to be in a relationship, we have to be honest with each other, right?"

He raised his eyebrows and I cursed internally. I was hardly the advocate for open honesty. I prepared to retract the question when he spoke very, very quietly.

"Leila. And Kate."

I nodded, tried to look indifferent. I'd suspected Leila, but still, it irked me. And Kate—I didn't know her very well, but she was very nice. And pretty.

"Both were onetime things," he said.

"When?"

"Ages ago."

"When you were married to Karolina?"

"No." Patrick's response was immediate, and horrified. "I was never unfaithful to Karolina. Kate was shortly after the split, and Leila, a year ago." He searched my face. "Karolina was unfaithful to *me*. You knew that, right?"

"No. No, I didn't know that. I assumed . . . well, with all the women afterwards . . ."

"There *were* quite a few women afterwards," he admitted. "Probably not as many as you recall. But I never crossed the line while I was married. I can't believe you thought I would."

I was thrown. All the judgments I'd made about Patrick—his infidelity, his string of women—were all getting thrown out faster than I could ask him about it. Either he was a really good PR person or—or I'd gotten him all wrong. I hoped it was the latter.

"I'm not that guy, Nev," he said, and pulled me toward him. "I may be a flirt . . . but I'm not that guy."

"Well, good," I said, resting my cheek on his chest. "Then it might just work out for us after all."

17

Grace

I woke in an empty bed. It was early—not yet seven—but Robert's briefcase, which had been reclining at the foot of the bed when I got in last night, was gone. The blinds were cracked open and red-pink light filtered in, pretty but ominous. *Red sky in the morning, shepherds take warning.* Robert had been snoring when I got in, so I didn't have the chance to tell him about Mom. Then again, even if he had been awake, I might not have told him. After his outburst the other day, I felt inclined to play my cards a little closer to my chest.

At 8:53, I was still in bed. The light had faded to peach, but otherwise, not much had changed. I still had seven phone calls to make. Seven clients to disappoint. I hadn't found the right words yet. *You know how you entrusted the most important experience of your life to me? Well, I'm going to let you down at the last minute without giving you a valid alternative, because I'm being investigated for negligence.* Truthful, but I didn't like the sound of it. As the minutes ticked closer to nine, the time I'd deemed acceptable to call, my anxiety grew. So, at 8:57, when my cell phone rang, I lunged at it—a prospect of distraction—without so much as checking the screen. "Grace Bradley."

"Grace. It's Molly."

I cursed silently. Out of the seven, Molly was the one I least wanted to speak to. When I'd spoken to her last week, she told me her husband had been laid off and she was worried the stress might somehow affect the baby. We'd become close over the past months. To leave her now was unthinkable. I had a flash of pure hatred for Dr. White and his complaint.

"Molly, hello. How are—?"

"I'vebeenhavingcontractionsforaboutfourhours." Molly's words tumbled out without so much as a pause.

I shot upright. "Where are you, honey?"

"At my apartment. Is it too early for you to come over?"

It was. About a month too early.

"How far apart are contractions?"

"The last two were around three minutes apart."

My hand, which was holding the phone, began to shake. "And before that?"

"Well . . . at first they came every eight minutes. Then every five. Now they've gone down to three."

"Are they painful?"

"Oh, God. Hang on a sec, Grace. Ohhhhh." A familiar low whimper came through the phone.

"Molly, is that a contraction? Can you answer me? Can you talk through it?"

The whimper turned into a wail and then died down to nothing. "Sorry. They're getting bad. Can you come?"

Silently, I slapped a palm against my head.

"Grace? Are you there?"

"I'm here. It's just that there's something I need to tell you." I continued to slap my head. "I'm so sorry, but . . . I'm not going to be able to deliver your baby."

There was a pause. "Is this a joke?"

"I wish it was. There's been a complaint made against me. My license has been suspended until a full investigation has been done and the Board of Nursing has made a ruling. Which won't be for about a month."

"A month?" Molly's voice squeaked. "But my baby is coming. What am I supposed to do?"

"Given the fact that you're already in labor, you'll have to go to the hospital. That, as far as I can tell, is your only option." I waited, but only silence rang through the phone. "Molly? Are you there?"

I could hear her breathing, so I knew she was.

"Molly," I tried again. "I cannot tell you how sorry I am. It's just the investigation. But if you go to the hosp—"

"I watched my mother die in hospital a year ago." Her voice was calm—almost robotic. "I don't want my baby to come into the world in a place of sickness and death. That's why I came to you."

My heart sped up. Her mother. *Of course.*

"Molly. I want to deliver your baby. But if I do, I risk losing my license permanently."

"Well, I'm not going to the hos—" Molly paused to moan through another contraction. When it finished, she said, "You do what you have to do, Grace. And I'll do the same."

* * *

Fifteen minutes later, I was in Molly's bedroom. I tried to keep my mind on the task, but it kept wandering. What was I supposed to have done? Left Molly at home to deliver alone? Forced her into an ambulance to be taken to a hospital that terrified her? The way I saw it, I didn't have a lot of options. But my heart felt heavy. And weighing on my mind most wasn't the idea of the Board of Nursing finding out. It was Robert finding out.

Molly spent an hour in a squatting position, while her husband supported her weight. She was using every last bit of her energy to give the final push that would bring her baby into the world. She'd impressed me with her focus and control. Sometimes that was how things went. The calmest, most composed women came apart during labor and the timid, cautious ones rose to the challenge.

"Okay, Molly," I said, kneeling at her feet, "Let's find out if it's a boy or a girl."

When the time came, she let out a purposeful wail. I eased the baby's head out slowly. The cord was around the baby's neck, but loose, and I removed it. With the next contraction, Molly's face contorted again and she pushed her baby boy into my hands. I glanced at the clock. "Ten thirty-two A.M. A perfectly sociable time to be born."

I handed Molly her baby, and silence descended. Jimmy cried quietly. Molly stared at her baby and he stared back—an invisible cord of love connecting them. We all felt it. Magic was in the room. Magic that, perhaps, wouldn't have been there at the hospital.

"Would you like to try feeding now, Molly?" I asked. "It might help encourage the uterus to contract and expel the placenta."

Molly did want to try feeding. I had some medication that would cause the placenta to expel, but my clients generally preferred not to use it. I was inclined to agree with them. The female body was remarkable at managing this process on its own.

I covered the bed in towels, and Jimmy helped Molly lie down. The baby latched on without too much effort, and I sat back and waited for the placenta to come.

Jimmy and Molly looked spent but happy. No matter how I tried, I couldn't envisage this scene in a hospital. Molly, I knew, would have been hysterical, in an environment that terrified her, surrounded by strangers. How wrong it seemed now that I'd even considered doing that to her. Here, on her own bed, she seemed calm, tranquil, and strong. Like every new mother should.

"Okay," I said after fifteen minutes had passed. "Come on, placenta! Let's see what the holdup is."

I felt for the fundus, which was contracting, but gently, and kneaded it with my hands.

"Is everything okay?" Molly asked, looking up from her baby for the first time.

"Fine," I said. "Just giving your uterus a helping hand. Generally, I like the placenta to come out within half an hour. We still have time. Keep feeding. You're doing a great job."

The baby continued to suckle happily at the breast. Jimmy fell asleep on Molly's shoulder. But ten minutes later, the placenta still hadn't come.

"Still nothing?" Molly asked. I could feel her assessing my face for worry, so I concentrated on keeping it straight.

"Nope. Not yet."

"Are you worried?"

"No," I said carefully. "But I would like it to come sooner rather than later. If you're comfortable with it, I'd like to give you a shot, to help it expel."

She frowned, and I could see the wheels spinning in her head. I doubted she'd be opposed to the shot, but like most of my clients, she wanted to know there was a good reason for its use. "And if we don't use the shot?"

"Well, your placenta might come out on its own. Or there's a possibility that we may have to take you to the hospital. Even if I give you the shot, it won't guarantee that you don't have to go to the hospital," I added. "But I'd say the medication is your best chance. Up to you."

"Give me the shot," Molly said without hesitation.

Three minutes later, Molly had a sharp contraction, and a few minutes after that, the placenta was delivered intact.

I stayed with Molly until the early hours of the morning, then wrote up the birth—for my own records—and began to pack up my things. It was Jimmy's idea for me not to write out the birth certificate. "If we don't tell anyone you were here," he'd said, you can't get into trouble. We can just say we had the baby on our own. People do that, right? What are they called . . . free-birthers?" I told him I thought it was a wonderful idea. Too good to be true.

I left Molly a script for Tylenol 3 (the contractions caused by the shot could get quite painful) and promised to be back in a few hours. Then came the awkward part. I'd always liked the anonymity of the follow-up invoice for a few reasons. One, it felt wrong to put your hand out so soon after being part of something so intimate and special with a family. Two, it was usually the last thing on people's minds after welcoming a child into their family. But now that I was off the record, I didn't have the luxury of sending an invoice.

"Uh, Jimmy?" I hovered in the doorway. "Do you have a sec?"

Reluctantly, Jimmy left his wife and son and joined me in the hallway.

"Just about payment. Did you . . ." I couldn't seem to find the words. "Um, how did you want to . . . organize this?"

Jimmy's face pinkened. It reminded me that he'd recently been let go from his job. "Oh, yeah, um, sure. Hang on a sec."

He sloped, teenlike, into the sitting room and unzipped the computer bag that was on the round dining table. He pulled out a wallet sealed with Velcro. "How much was it again?"

I bit my lip. "Um . . . well, three thousand."

Jimmy nodded and looked back at his wallet. Already I could see that it contained nowhere near that amount. Desperately, he began to count out the notes.

"How much have you got, Jimmy?" I asked softly.

He looked up, shamefaced. I thought he was going to make something up, say it had been stolen or something, but he just sighed.

"About nine hundred. Could you take it as an installment? When I get another job, I can pay you the rest. I'm sure it won't take me long to find something."

His face was such a departure from what I'd seen a few minutes earlier. The weight of responsibility was already falling on his shoulders, and I knew too well how hard that could be for a man.

"No, Jimmy. Forget it. You need this money more than I do."

Jimmy was bewildered. "You mean . . . you don't want any money?"

The irony of what I was doing wasn't lost on me. Robert was down on me for taking unnecessary risks that could threaten my ability to support my family financially, yet here I was, taking risks for no money at all. Where would Robert's moral compass have stood on this? Was it further evidence of me putting my head in the sand, putting others ahead of our family? Perhaps. But I knew where my moral compass stood. And it was telling me this was the right thing to do.

I smiled. "You keep it. Use it to look after your wife and son."

18

Floss

People tended to show their true colors in a crisis. Running for the hills with their heads covered or diving headlong into battle to save their peers. In my case, there hadn't been a battle—except, perhaps, the one inside my chest. Nonetheless, Lil had shown her true colors. She was a hero. And I'm sure she felt like she'd been to war.

She'd spent the past week ferrying my things over to the hospital, talking to doctors, cleaning the house. She'd called Grace and Neva daily with updates. She'd made so much soup that she filled the icebox and most of the refrigerator. She couldn't have got more than a few hours' sleep each night. Now it was time for me to show her what I was made of.

She perched opposite me on the sofa. Like props, mugs of steaming tea sat in front of us but I knew we wouldn't pick them up. After what I had to say, we'd probably need something stronger. At least, Lil would.

"So," I said to her. "I suppose you want to know what has been bothering me."

"I would." Lil straightened up, her face a painful shade of earnest. "More than anything."

I sucked in a breath. "Okay," I said. "Here goes."

Kings Langley, England, 1954

Elizabeth cradled her baby in the crook of her arm. The baby was small but healthy, with a tuft of copper hair and almost-white eyelashes. Like Evie said, the baby had obviously got what she needed from Elizabeth. And despite what Elizabeth had gone through, she managed to protect her daughter.

"What are you going to call her?" I asked.

"I . . . don't know."

I cast my gaze down at the baby—pinker and more perfect than I could ever have imagined. "Well . . . . she's rosy-cheeked. How about Rosie?"

"No." Elizabeth's voice was tight. "Not Rosie. Rose is Bill's mother's name."

I raised my eyebrows. Elizabeth never spoke badly of Bill or his family. But fatigue had a way of bringing out the truth.

"I'll name her after my mother," she said. "Can you take her?" She tried to hold out the baby, but didn't have the strength to lift her. "I have to deliver the placenta."

She was right, of course. Still, I was used to new mothers fighting to keep their newborns close, in some cases even when they needed to use the ladies' room. I reached for the little bundle wrapped snugly in the towel and sat on the bed next to Elizabeth so they could still be close. I couldn't resist peeling back the towel for a better look. Her arms and legs were long and lithe like Elizabeth's, and her face was dainty. I couldn't see any immediate resemblance to Bill, a fact that pleased me no end.

I wrapped her up again and watched as the placenta expelled itself. Then, while Evie tended to a minor tear, I held the baby out to Elizabeth again. "Would you like to try feeding?" Although she was likely to have a low milk supply due to her poor nutrition, the sucking would help the uterus contract and return to normal. Information Elizabeth, of course, knew. So I was surprised when she shook her head.

"You don't want to feed?"

"No. I feel sick, Floss."

"It's probably adrenaline." I placed the back of my hand against her forehead. "You look a little pale. Why don't you let the baby snuggle against you, listen to your heartbeat—?"

"For heaven's sake, Floss, I don't want her!"

From the stool at the end of the bed, Evie raised her eyebrows, mirroring mine.

"All right, all right," Evie said. She kept her voice light, but her expression was anything but. She gestured for me to feel Elizabeth's abdomen as her own hands were covered in blood. I did.

"Feels a little boggy," I said.

Evie peeled off her gloves and rinsed her hands in the bucket of warm water by her feet, then took a seat at Elizabeth's side. I picked up the baby and moved out of the way.

"Can you look at me, love?" Evie said to Elizabeth. "Elizabeth, can you look at me?" When Elizabeth still didn't look, Evie grabbed her chin and turned it to face her. Her eyes were unfocused. "Floss, put the baby in the bassinet."

Evie didn't yell, but the urgency in her voice made the hairs at the base of my neck stand on end. She felt Elizabeth's forehead with her palm, then reached for the thermometer on the bedside table. I raced to the bassinet and set the baby down.

"Go to my bag. There's some sterile gloves in the top, put them on. I want you to very carefully check the opening to her cervix. Just do exactly as I say."

Although I was only a junior midwife, I knew enough to know that I should be worried. I somehow got my shaking fingers into the gloves and lowered myself onto the stool at the end of the bed.

"Okay," Evie said. "You're feeling for a lump, a blockage, a clot. It might be small, it might not."

Elizabeth's knees had fallen apart and I started my examination. Any concerns I had that I wouldn't know what a clot felt like were put to rest when I felt a soft mass at the entrance to the cervix. I circled the base of it. It was a clot; of that I was certain. A large one.

"Okay. I want you to pull it out." Evie's voice was calm but urgent.

"Evie—" I said, "—it's big."

"Just give it a gentle tug. If it's a clot, it will come free."

I nodded, gripping the mass between my knuckles. I winged a prayer, then tugged. There was a large spurt of bright red blood from Elizabeth's vagina—enough to soak the towel beneath her bottom. It was followed immediately by a second spurt.

"Dear Lord," I said. "She's hemorrhaging!"

"Get hold of her cervix!" Evie yelled, kneading Elizabeth's abdomen from the outside. "Hold it closed and massage. Massage, Floss! We need to get it contracting or she will bleed to death."

I did as Evie asked, forcing my gaze from Elizabeth—lying peaceful-looking on the bed—to the rivers of blood that streamed from her. Come on! I kept massaging. *Our Father, who art in heaven* . . . Beside me, Evie also prayed. We needed prayers. The flow seemed to be slowing. Usually, I would locate the nearest phone to call the flying squad, but that wasn't an option now. It was a two-mile bike ride to the nearest phone booth, and Elizabeth wouldn't last that long.

"She's contracting," Evie said, after a few—five?—silent minutes had passed. "How is the bleeding?"

"I can't see any bleeding," I said. "But my hand is in there, it's hard to tell."

"Take your hand out, Floss. I'll keep massaging from the outside. We need to know what is happening."

I hesitated. "Are you sure?"

She nodded.

"Okay." Slowly, I released the neck of the uterus, and a gush of blood followed my hand.

"So?"

"It's heavy."

Evie pushed me out of the way, reaching inside Elizabeth now with an ungloved hand. I massaged Elizabeth's abdomen. Her uterus felt spongy. Panic hit; a fist to the gut. *Contract, Elizabeth! Contract.* I kneaded the fundus aggressively. Elizabeth was drenched in sweat and pale. Too pale. She was in shock. "Evie—should I try to get the baby to suckle, do you think?" I asked. "To help the uterus contract?"

Evie was barely visible at the end of the bed, but I saw her shake her head. I could hear her panting with effort. It would be okay. It *had* to be okay.

A minute passed, then another.

We continued massaging, inside and out, in silence.

Ten minutes passed.

Evie's panting slowed, then stopped.

Fifteen minutes passed.

My breathing also quieted.

Elizabeth was still, like she was asleep.

The silence was eerie. I watched what I could see of Evie's face, waiting for direction. Her frown, etched so deeply into her forehead before, had disappeared, replaced by a . . . a different expression.

"Evie?" I asked. There was a wobble in my voice that, for some reason, I wanted to conceal. As if its presence were admitting something I wasn't ready to admit. "What . . . what do you want me to do?"

Evie met my eye over Elizabeth's belly. Her expression was frighteningly blank.

"Nothing, Floss. I don't want you to do anything." Her eyes closed. "She's gone."

19

Neva

I was awake most of the night. After Patrick drifted off to sleep, I wondered about what he'd said. Was it possible that the father could swoop in and demand fatherly rights? I'd said no definitively when Patrick asked, but . . . if he were to find out . . . perhaps that was exactly what he'd do? Perhaps *that* was the reason I was keeping this secret? If so, my secret, like a rolling snowball, now had the power to hurt Patrick too.

When I arrived at the birthing center the next morning, Anne took one look at me and ordered me into one of the birthing suites for a nap. No one was in labor and she wanted to make sure I was rested enough to do a delivery if someone did come in. Usually I would have protested, but not today. The appeal of catching a few winks was too hard to resist.

When I woke, the sun was high in the sky. A chorus of high-pitched giggles rang in the hallway and then the door opened and

Patrick appeared beside the bed. He kissed my mouth. "Good morning, princess."

"Don't let the princesses in the hallway hear you call me that."

"Ah, but you're the crown princess." He kissed my nose. "Can I get in?"

I ignored the stirring in my loins that screamed yes, Yes, YES, and instead arranged my features in what I hoped was a skeptical expression. "Are you a mother in labor?"

"You guys get into bed with the clients? How unprofessional. Not to mention unhygienic."

I chuckled. "Oh, I have a joke."

"Hit me."

"What's the difference between a pregnant woman and a model? Nothing, if the pregnant woman's boyfriend knows what's good for him."

Patrick smiled softly. "But you're more beautiful than a model, pregnant or not."

I couldn't help but laugh. Hopeless charmer.

"So . . . is this where we're going to have this baby, then?" Patrick swaggered over to the chair and picked up a pillow, inspecting it playfully.

"Not necessarily this room, but yes. I like it here."

"Me too." Patrick nodded. "Oh, I almost forgot! I had a phone call from the Board of Nursing this morning. About your mother."

"You did?" With everything else going on I'd forgotten about the investigation. "What did you say?"

"I told her what happened. That the baby and the mother were never in any danger and that Gillian was in as good hands with your mother as she would have been with any ob-gyn."

"You said that?"

"It's true. Hopefully that will be the end of it. What a waste of tax-payers' money, investigating someone like your mother when there are all sorts of cowboys around claiming to be medical professionals."

His face was completely earnest. It occurred to me that he was ex-actly the kind of person I wanted to spend my life with. "You are a good guy, you know that?"

"Don't tell anyone. Speaking of your mom, is she going to deliver the baby?"

I snorted. "What do you think?"

"Then who *is*?" He sprawled onto the bed on his stomach and rested his chin in his hands. "I guess I should know this."

"Susan," I said.

He cocked an eyebrow. "Do you want me to be there?"

I hesitated. I'd assumed it was a given that Patrick would be there. It hadn't occurred to me to even ask. "Oh, um . . . well it'd be good to have a pediatrician in the room. And people will expect it. You being the father and all." I watched for a reaction, but Patrick remained infu-riatingly blank. "Do you *want* to be there?"

He crossed his arms, making a great show of thinking it over. "I think I would, yes. I can hand you ice chips and mop your forehead, that sort of thing."

I suppressed a smile. "Good, then."

Patrick rolled onto his side, his hand skimming the length of my belly, back and forth. He frowned, then pressed down sharply just above my pubic bone.

"Um, ow!" I half laughed, half gasped. "What are you doing?"

Patrick ignored me, feeling along the curve of my stomach, pressing down now on the highest part of the mound. "Did you know the baby was breech?"

"It's not." I smacked his hand playfully and replaced it with my own, feeling what he had felt. I located the head and pressed down. "See. The head."

"Hey—I'm not an ob-gyn, but from the lie, I'd say it was back here, legs here, head here"—he pointed to the pelvis—"breech here."

"Um, I think I would have noticed if my baby was breech." I lay flat and felt my stomach properly. Back, legs, head . . . bottom . . . I paused, felt again.

Patrick winced. "Told you."

I felt again. He was right. Right down at the bottom of my pelvis were the soft edges of the buttocks.

"It could still turn," he said.

"Maybe, but . . ." I felt it a third time. "It's unlikely at this stage. Guess I won't be delivering at the birthing center after all."

I tried to roll into a sitting position, but got only halfway up before I started to fall back onto the bed. Patrick gave me a push. "Hey. You okay?"

"Not much I can do about it, is there? I guess I'll need a C-section." I shimmied to my feet.

"We don't know that for sure." Patrick also stood. "Why don't we go see Sean, see what he says?"

"No. It's fine. A C-section is fine."

"Seriously? You're so dedicated to natural birthing—"

"Are you trying to upset me?" I smiled.

Patrick continued to frown. "Why don't I take you home? You must be tired."

"Thanks, but I'm on until five P.M. And since I've slept most of the morning, I'd better get busy."

"There's no one in labor."

"We do other things besides deliver babies, Patrick." Again, I smiled to show I was being lighthearted. I didn't want Patrick worrying about me. He was doing enough. "I've got postnatal rounds. You go. It's your day off."

"You sure?"

"I'm sure. I'll see you later."

Patrick leaned over and kissed my cheek. "Later." He ducked and planted a kiss on my stomach. "See you later too."

I smiled until he was out of the room, and for a good minute after he left. But once I was sure he was definitely gone, I sank back onto the bed.

My baby was breech.

All the images I'd had of myself pacing the floor, sitting on a birthing ball, lying in the tub, panting and pushing my baby out—it juxtaposed starkly against the image of lying flat on my back, having my baby extracted from me like a tumor. All the women I'd seen turned into warriors before my eyes—it would never be me.

It didn't escape my consciousness that I was being a hypocrite. All those women I'd reassured on the operating table that the magic of motherhood had nothing to do with how the baby came out? At the time, I'd believed that was true. In theory, I still believed it. But now that I was charged with the same outcome myself, I felt a little cheated.

Abruptly, I stood. I slipped into my shoes and told Anne to call me if anyone came in. Then I hurried toward the hospital maternity ward. Sean was at the nurses' station, leaning over the desk and telling a joke or story that, judging from the stifled laughs from other staff, was either inappropriate or about one of the patients. Marion stood nearby, her lips pursed. Her frustration at not being able to get into Sean's inner circle had clearly morphed into intense dislike. I'd seen it happen before, with other doctors, but I doubted Sean would care. I waited until the punch line had been delivered, then tapped Sean's shoulder.

"Hey," I said. "Do you have a minute?"

"Sure thing." Sean was unnaturally cheery. "What's up?"

I was about to ask him the same thing when I noticed his wife, Laura, standing beside him.

"Oh, Laura. Hi." I swallowed.

"Hi, there. Neva, right?"

Neva. She knew my name.

I nodded. "How are you doing?"

"I'm pretty great, thanks for asking."

She looked pretty great too, considering. Her hair was a couple of inches long and done in a messy pixie style. She wore a full face of over-the-top makeup, which included blue eye shadow that somehow, really worked on her. "We've just been to see the doc."

"Is everything—?"

"Wonderful!" she said. "The tumor is barely visible, can you believe it?"

I couldn't believe it. "You must be ecstatic. Are you going out to celebrate?"

"No, headed home like a boring married couple," Laura said, but the way she smiled at Sean made them seem more like loved-up teenagers. "Did you need Sean?"

"It can wait."

"No, no." She grabbed Sean by the elbow and shoved him toward me. "Please. Talk."

I swallowed the enormous lump in my throat. No wonder she'd been the one to turn Sean from a womanizer into a one-woman man.

"I'll wait downstairs," she said to Sean. "And I'll see you soon, Neva."

"Thanks, Laura. And, um, great news."

Laura wandered down the hallway breezily. After her appointment, it seemed, she didn't have a care in the world. Sean and I waited until the elevator doors closed and she disappeared from sight.

"Sorry to interrupt," I said. "I just wanted to run something by you."

We stepped into an alcove. Sean's face was apprehensive. I hadn't spoken to him properly since he found out I was pregnant. I suppose I couldn't really blame him for being nervous. I decided to cut to the chase.

"My baby is breech."

He managed to look relieved and concerned at the same time. "Oh, Nev. I'm sorry."

"So I guess that means you don't know of any new and hugely effective procedures to turn babies this late in pregnancy?" I forced a laugh.

"I wish." He looked genuinely sad for me. "You can always try, but—" He touched the top of my belly and pressed down. "—I don't like your chances."

"And I don't suppose you know anyone who would deliver a breech baby vaginally?"

He raised his eyebrows. "Surely you wouldn't want to try?"

"No, I guess not." I sighed, deflated.

"Are you okay?"

"Yeah."

"You and Patrick all ready for the baby?"

I nodded.

"Good."

We both shuffled a little.

"It's funny," Sean said. "Patrick never mentioned that you two were seeing each other. Back then, I mean."

I tried to look Sean in the eye, but he evaded my stare. "Does Patrick tell you everything?" I asked.

"No." His gaze shifted to my belly. I didn't breathe. "So you're definitely sure about your dates, then?"

"Yes. Definitely—"

Before I could register what was happening, I was in Sean's arms. He squeezed me, too tight, one arm around my waist, the other pressing my head to his chest. I smiled at his obvious relief and allowed him to hold me briefly. When he started to loosen his grip, I stepped away.

"That's great. It's . . . really exciting for you and Patrick. You'll make great parents. I always knew he was in love with you."

"You . . . *did?*"

"I have eyes. Most people thought you were in love with him too." He laughed. "Obviously they were right. Anyway, it's great that you guys have finally got it together."

I felt my cheeks warm. Was it possible that Patrick and I had both been into each other all this time? How had I not seen it? Particularly when *Sean* had?

"Well, I'd better run," he said. "Laura's waiting."

"Go, go," I said. I gave him a push, then followed him out of the alcove. Marion stood nearby, watching Sean hurry toward the elevator, then her eyes snapped back to me. It might have been my imagination—or perhaps the fact that I'd had very little sleep—but I could have sworn she was giving me a dirty look.

20

Grace

I'd delivered four babies since my license was suspended. Robert knew nothing of it. Each mother had been given the facts, and each of them decided to take her chances with me as their midwife. Three out of the four had even paid me.

I'd managed to explain my absences to Robert with tales of early morning yoga and helping take care of Mom, but as it happened, he wasn't asking many questions anyway. He'd been working long hours and when he was at home, he was distracted. I didn't blame him. He'd been carrying the burden of our family's financial pressure alone for months. Not anymore. All my payments had been collected in cash and were stashed in my office in a large yellow envelope. With the tax that I'd saved, it'd be enough to make our first few mortgage payments, if it came to that.

Tonight Robert was his usual reticent self. He sat next to me on the couch, staring at sitcom after mindless sitcom. When I couldn't stand the silence anymore, I said, "How are things at work, Rob?"

He blinked as though he'd been asleep or forgotten I was there. Then he did that long sigh-through-the-nose thing. "Oh . . . you know. Could be better."

"I'm here if you want to talk."

He smiled. It reminded me that it had been a while since I'd seen that smile. "Wow," he said.

"Wow, what?"

"Wow . . . that's very non-Grace of you. In a good way. It actually sounds like something Floss would say."

"Oh." I frowned. "What would I say?"

Robert curled his hands around an invisible neck in front of him. "What is going on with you? I demand you tell me this instant or I will snoop through your phone and wallet, looking for clues!" He adopted an affected, womanly voice that most certainly did not sound like me.

"Oh, yeah? Well, how about you?" I slumped back on the couch and stared at the television. I made my voice deep and bored-sounding. "Work's really intense." I grunted. "You wouldn't understand."

Robert burst out laughing. "Have I been that terrible?"

"Yes." I smiled. "But I forgive you."

Robert's face took on a somber hue. "Today we all had to fill out a document that asked what we actually do. Basically, making it easy for them to see who is expendable and who isn't."

"I'm sorry."

He waved his hand. "Not your fault. . . . What about you?" he asked. "When is the investigation over?"

"A week or two, I think."

He smiled. "You're handling this like a trouper, you know that, Grace?"

I thought of the four deliveries I'd done since I was put on notice. "Thank you."

"You're welcome." He picked up the remote control and shut off the television. "Ready for bed?"

Outside, the sky wasn't even completely dark. I glanced at the clock above the television and frowned. "It's eight fifteen."

"I know."

"Oh."

We smiled at each other. Then the phone rang.

"I'll get rid of them," Robert said, heading for the phone. He winked as he lifted the receiver to his ear. "Hello? Yes, she's right here." He held the phone out to me. "It's Gillian."

"Oh. Thanks." I stood and took the phone. "Gillian? Is everything okay? How is the baby?"

"She's fine." Gillian's voice was steady but small. "She's doing really well actually. We have a meeting next week with a plastic surgeon that Dr. Johnson recommended to discuss her first surgery. Everyone's been really optimistic that it will be repaired by the time she starts school."

I hadn't realized how stiff my body had been until it started to soften. "That's . . . that's . . . wonderful, Gillian. I don't know what to say. It's fantastic."

"It *is* fantastic. Look, I know we're not supposed to be communicating."

"No we're not," I said, remembering at the same time as she said it. "But I'm glad you called. I've been thinking about you."

"And I've been thinking about you. I can't believe you're being investigated. And, I'm really sorry, but I think I've made it worse."

The boulder in my stomach, which had disappeared for the last few, jokey minutes with Robert, came back instantly. "What do you mean?"

"The investigator contacted me and I told her the complaint was ridiculous, and that you didn't do anything wrong. I answered all her questions, but . . . I think she is going to twist what I said."

"What did you say?"

"That you didn't inform me of the risks of waiting to suture a third-degree tear. I did say that I would have insisted on going with my baby anyway, and that it wouldn't have mattered if you did inform me. But the investigator, she zeroed in on the fact that you didn't inform me and kept asking questions about that. I should've just said that you did inform me. I wish I had. I just froze when she asked me, and then I . . . I thought she would know if I was lying. You didn't inform me, did you? Perhaps I forgot?"

"No, I didn't." Robert, who was still standing there, pointed his thumb over his shoulder toward the bedroom, and I nodded. "The investigator is right, I should have," I said to Gillian. "And you were right not to lie. That might have made things worse. I appreciate you calling to tell me, and I'm sorry you've had to be involved in any of this."

"But will you get into trouble? I feel terrible."

"If I do get into trouble, it will be my fault, not yours. Really, Gillian, you shouldn't worry about this. You've given your statement honestly which is exactly what you should have done. You need to focus your energies on your darling daughter. Leave this investigation business to me."

"You really are an angel, you know that? I don't know how you can be so strong through all of this. You're amazing."

"No, *you* are amazing. As for me, if the Board of Nursing finds me to have been negligent, it won't be because of something you said. It will be because of something I did. And I'll have to face the consequences."

"Well, no matter what they find, I'll be calling you to deliver my next baby."

I smiled. "Thank you, Gill. You take care."

"You too."

I ended the call and slumped into the chair. And with Robert waiting for me in the bedroom, I finally felt some empathy for him. Turns out life could be quite the libido killer.

21

Floss

"Breech? You're sure, dear?"

When Neva arrived on my doorstep with groceries, I'd had a feeling something was up. Her hair, which was normally smooth and restrained in a ponytail, was wild and stringy. At first I'd thought it was Grace standing there. Her face had been flushed, and it looked like she'd been crying. Now, with her legs crossed underneath her on my sofa, the tears flowed freely.

"Completely sure." A new tear slipped down her cheek and she flicked it away. "Sorry, I don't know what's wrong with me."

"Don't apologize, dear."

". . . the ridiculous thing is, I didn't even notice it was breech. It was Patrick who pointed it out. Patrick is the guy you met at the hospital," she said before I could ask. "He's the one who is pretending to be the father of the baby."

I repeated the sentence in my head to be sure I'd heard correctly. "*Pretending* to be the father?"

Neva nodded.

"I see." I tried to keep my face neutral. Any reaction too large had a way of frightening my granddaughter into silence, and she clearly needed to talk this through. "And why is he doing that?"

"He offered, to help with the questions. We're kind of seeing each other."

I waited, but Neva didn't say anything more. "Patrick must care about you a lot to pretend to be the baby's father," I said gently. "Are his feelings reciprocated?"

"Yes, but . . ." She trailed away.

"But what, dear?"

"I just don't see how it can last. He's not the baby's father. And sooner or later, he's going to want to know who is."

"You wouldn't consider telling him?"

"I can't. He'd leave me."

Behind Neva, Lil trailed the hall, a garbage bag in her hand. I met her eye briefly. Last night, once I'd finished recounting my own secret, Lil had thanked me for telling her then excused herself for bed. This morning, she'd bustled around, preoccupied with all the jobs in the house that suddenly needed doing. I left her to it. She needed time to process.

"You never know," I said. "People can surprise you."

"Not this time."

Neva sank farther into the couch, almost as though she wanted to disappear into it. I knew better than to push her. "Well, it's up to you, of course."

"I wish he was the actual father, Gran."

"But he's not," I said. "No point in wishing things are different than they are." Neva nodded, staring at her lap. "For what it's worth, though," I added, "I think biology is an amazing but largely irrelevant part of being a parent."

"You do?"

I nodded. "In *fact*, I think choosing to be there for a child, despite the fact that you aren't biologically related to it, makes it even more special."

Slowly, a smile appeared. "You're so wise, you know that?"

"Not wise. Just old."

She heaved herself out of the chair and kissed my cheek. "I have to go."

Neva saw herself out, and the room was quiet again, apart from Lil shuffling around in another room. After a minute or two, she came in and lowered herself onto the opposite sofa. "Is Neva gone?"

I nodded. "She's found out her baby is breech."

"Breech?"

"Upside down. She'll probably have to have a C-section. Not the end of the world, but a disappointment for Neva." I exhaled. "She also has some other personal problems. Poor love has got herself into quite the tangle with this baby/father business."

"Were you able to offer her some advice?"

"I'm hardly one to be giving advice on secrets, Lil. Besides, it's complicated. Now that she has Patrick, she has so much to lose."

"There's always something to lose when it comes to revealing a truth," Lil said. "But there's also something to be gained."

Before me, Lil had only loved once before, a woman name Rosita.

Rosita was married to a man with whom she shared four children, and she told Lil that when her youngest son turned eighteen, she would leave. As the time grew close, Lil searched for rental properties and found a cottage in Jamestown—two bedrooms, in case any of the children wanted to come and stay. But Rosita's youngest son's birthday came and went, and still, Rosita only came for day visits to the cottage. They'd cook meals together, go grocery shopping. Take strolls along the beach. Then, at night, Rosita went home again to her husband.

One sunny afternoon as they strolled along the pier, they bumped into a man. He was gray-haired, probably in his early fifties. A friend of Rosita's husband. When he saw Rosita, Lil saw a glimmer of recognition. At the same time, Rosita took a subtle step away from Lil. "Rosita," the man said. "Fancy seeing you in Conanicut Island! Is Vince with you?"

There was a brief shaking of hands, and then Rosita twisted on the spot. "Oh," she said. "Yes, this is Lil. An old school friend."

Lil hadn't expected to be introduced as Rosita's lover. But the way Rosita tied herself in knots spoke volumes. That was the day Lil realized their relationship would always be a secret. And after a lifetime of hiding who she was, she wasn't prepared to live with secrets anymore.

I knew all this. So Lil's clasped hands and settled jaw shouldn't have been a surprise.

"What are we talking about, Lil?" I asked.

"We're talking about secrets. Sometimes people keep them for so long, they forget the reason they're even doing it. Or the reason changes or becomes distorted."

I still didn't know exactly what Lil was getting at. "Meaning?"

"Meaning Grace is an adult now. She can handle this."

"I'm not sure about that."

"She can," Lil said. "People handle a lot worse every day. But I'm not sure *you* can handle keeping this secret. You just had a heart attack, Floss. If you don't tell Grace the truth, I'm afraid—" She paused, cleared her throat. "I'm afraid it's going to kill you."

"No. You don't understand, Lil. You couldn't *possibly* understand. Unless you have children of your own, you can't understand the need to protect them before all else. Before even yourself."

Lil winced a little, and I was stung by my own words. But rather than running away or crying, she sat a little taller. It was as if I had further confirmed her resolve.

"Why don't you be honest, at least with me?" she said. "This isn't about Grace handling it or not handling it. This is about *you*. What *you're* afraid to lose. You are afraid, not for Grace's welfare, but for your own. You're afraid that if you tell her this, she won't consider you her mother anymore."

"No. That's not it."

"I may not be a mother," Lil continued, "but I know what it's like to keep a secret. I spent the best part of a lifetime denying who I was. And it wasn't until I admitted the truth that I ever felt any peace. I want that peace for you, Floss. You need to tell Grace the truth."

22

Neva

As I was stopped at the traffic lights on the way back home, I slid my phone out of my pocket. A little envelope flashed on the screen. I smiled when I heard Patrick's voice.

"Nev, it's me. I was thinking of dropping by. Thought maybe we could . . . I don't know . . . watch a movie and fall asleep on the couch together, what do you think? Call me back."

My heart skipped as I pressed delete. The idea of Patrick and me falling asleep on the couch together sounded like something I could get used to. Something I wanted to get used to. I thought about what Gran had said. Could I tell Patrick? Was it possible that he would understand? Or would I be forcing our relationship into an early grave?

I waited for the next message.

"Yes, hello. This is a message for Neva Bradley. My name is Marie

Ableman from the Board of Nursing. It's six fifteen P.M. Can you please call me when you get this message? 555-4102."

Pulling over, I lowered the phone and stared at the screen. The Board of Nursing? Calling to get some incriminating evidence on my mother? The time on my phone said 9:35 P.M. Too late to call. Though . . . if she was investigating my mother, perhaps I didn't care about Marie Whatshername's personal time. The phone rang four times before someone answered.

"Hello?" It was a woman's voice—the voice from the message. She sounded curious, annoyed, and very much off duty.

"This is Neva Bradley. I'm sorry it's late, but I just received your message."

"Oh, yes, Ms. Bradley, thanks for calling back." The voice immediately took on a new, polite tone. She exhaled, getting her work hat on. "Yes, as you may know, I am investigating a complaint made against Grace Bradley in the delivery of Gillian Brennan's baby. I understand you were assisting with this birth."

"I was."

"I'd like to ask you some questions about it. It will only take a few minutes."

For some reason, I pulled myself tall in my seat. "Go right ahead."

It did only take a few minutes. I answered Marie's questions honestly, if a little stiffly. I didn't need to lie. Mom had not acted negligently. But I would have lied if I had to. Without hesitation. And I was certain she would have done the same for me.

"In your opinion, was Mrs. Bradley irresponsible at any time during labor and delivery?" Marie asked, winding up her questions.

"She was not. She acted in the best interests of her client and the baby at all times."

"Thank you, Ms. Bradley. You've been very helpful. I'll let you go."

"Wait. What happens now?"

"I have a few more people to speak with yet," Marie said. "Then the notes will be reviewed by a subcommittee and a recommendation made to the Board of Nursing on a course of action."

"What kind of course of action?"

"It really depends. If no evidence is found to support the complaint, we will recommend the case be closed."

"And if *evidence* is found? Not that it will be."

"If Mrs. Bradley is found to have been negligent, it is possible that she could be fined or even lose her license." Marie's voice softened. "But as I said, I still have a few more people to speak with. Let's not get ahead of ourselves."

Infuriatingly, Marie was calm, impartial, and fair—not at all the villain I'd thought she would be. She was just doing her job. I wanted to believe from her tone that Mom would be given a fair hearing, that was all I could really ask for. Because if she did get a fair hearing, there was no doubt in my mind that the case would be closed.

"Okay. Thanks."

I hung up the phone. Even though I believed Mom would be vindicated, I felt a little sick. Mom losing her license was too wrong to comprehend. Like a world-class sprinter losing their legs. Or an opera singer losing her voice. It wouldn't just be her who would lose. The world would.

I pulled up in front of my apartment. As I took the stairs, I rang

Patrick. In my building, another phone was ringing. I shoved a finger in one ear, anticipating his voice. It rang again, and then he answered.

"Hello, gorgeous."

"Hello," I said, feeling shy. I took the last three steps to my door and found it ajar. "Hey, can I call you back? The door to my apartment is open, and I need to check that there isn't an intruder." I laughed. "If there is, he'll be disappointed with our abysmal lack of technology and easy-to-move goods."

The door peeled open, and Patrick appeared in the doorway. He pressed the phone to his ear and raised his other hand, palm toward me. "Please don't call the police."

I crossed my arms. "Give me one good reason why I shouldn't."

"I'll put back your 1990s VCR and your collection of Spice Girls CDs."

"Even *Greatest Hits?*"

He pouted. "Fine."

It probably wasn't romantic, but I loved being with Patrick like this. Other than my Dad and Gran, he was the only one I felt completely comfortable with. It had to be a good omen for us. He stood aside and I entered the apartment.

"It's a good thing you decided to let me keep my 1990s VCR," I said. "How else would we watch a movie and then fall asleep on the couch?"

"Ah, you got my message."

He shut the door and turned to face me. In a gray T-shirt and jeans, he was deliciously rumpled and weary-looking. His gorgeous looks gave me a burst of courage, and I sidled up to him and touched his chest. "I did. But I have a better idea."

The oven beeped, and Patrick retreated toward the kitchen. "Oh yeah?" he called over his shoulder. "If your idea is nachos, I'm way ahead of you."

"Uh . . ." I followed him to the kitchen and lingered in the doorway. "Nachos are good. But that wasn't my idea."

Patrick's head was in the oven. "What was your idea?"

"It was . . . something else."

I let that sink in. Then Patrick unfolded into a standing position. I knew I was blushing, but I forced myself to hold his gaze.

His brow was furrowed. "But . . . nachos are terrible cold."

I blinked.

"Kidding!" He crossed the kitchen in two large steps. "I mean, they *are*. But I don't care. Sorry." As he talked, he covered my face in kisses. I accepted them, and his apology. "Let's eat the nachos later," he said, his lips pressed against mine. "Let's eat them . . . never."

He marched me backwards toward my bedroom, all the while mumbling about the insignificance of nachos, about how, actually, he didn't really even like nachos. In fact, apart from the fact that they'd kept him alive throughout college, he hated them. I laughed between kisses as we made our way through my kitchen and living room. We stopped when the backs of my knees hit the bed.

"Enough about nachos," I ordered.

His smile fell away, replaced by a serious, intense expression. "What nachos?"

I reached for the top button of his shirt and flicked it open. I undid another, then another, releasing each button until the shirt slid off his shoulders and onto the floor. Carefully, we unfurled on the bed. And after what felt like an eternity, he kissed me.

It continued like a dream. On and on, we kissed, hands trailing, mouths exploring. I lay back as he kissed my nipples, rubbing and caressing and even nipping me gently with his teeth. I felt a rush of adrenaline, and I began to get excited about what would happen when he went farther down.

As if reading my mind, his mouth descended farther, obscured completely by my belly. I stared at the ceiling and then . . . *ahhh* . . . . his mouth was warm and wet as it rolled over me. I lifted my hips to meet him and threw my head back. *Oh. God.*

Abruptly his mouth pulled away and cold air hit where his warm mouth had been. I whimpered, about to protest, when all at once his hands were on my waist, lifting me, turning me. Then I was on my knees and his lips were on my back.

"Is this okay?" he asked.

"Yes," I breathed. *God, yes.*

When he entered me, we both gasped. And for a heartbeat, we remained just like that, with Patrick deep inside me. Finally, he took me by the hips and began to move.

I pushed back against him as he filled me. Again. And again. To his moans, I started to let go. I felt confident. Sexy. Safe. And, maybe for the first time in my life, like I was in the exactly right place.

The next month passed like a movie montage: little snapshots whizzing by so fast that all I registered was the happiness, rather than the individual moments. I could almost hear the background music, something soft and beautiful like Sarah McLachlan. Patrick and I were a couple. We were expecting a baby.

Eloise moved in with Ted at the end of November, and though Patrick didn't officially live at my place, he pretty much did. Eloise's room was now the baby's room, which meant it housed the boxes of stuff we'd bought at IKEA but still hadn't opened—a crib, a changing table, a bassinet. Patrick bought a stroller online that, according to him, was top-of-the-line, but when it arrived neither of us could figure out how to assemble it, so that had gone into the room too, still in the box. If Patrick wondered who the baby's actual father was, he never brought it up. So I decided I wouldn't either. Patrick was the father, and that was that.

In the meantime, I was getting on with business. I'd made an appointment to see the ob-gyn and I was meeting Patrick there in twenty minutes. I trudged through the snow, my boots crunching in the ice that was forming on the sidewalk. Setting up the appointment had been almost as tumultuous as the snow.

"I've made an appointment with Dr. Hargreaves on Friday morning for my scan," I'd said to Patrick between bites of toast a couple of mornings earlier. "Nine A.M. Can you make it?"

"Lorraine Hargreaves? *Chief Resident* Lorraine Hargreaves? You know how to hobnob with the important people, Nev."

"She offered, remember?"

"So she did." Patrick nodded, duly impressed. "Of course I'll be there. Hopefully she'll give us some good news. Maybe she can turn the baby?"

"Unlikely. I already went over it with Sean. He felt the position, said it didn't look good."

Patrick blinked at me several times before he could respond. "Sean *examined* you?"

"No." I grabbed a piece of his toast, took a bite. "He just felt my stomach. In the hallway."

There was a long, uneasy silence.

"What?" I asked.

"Nothing. I just . . . don't want Sean touching you."

"Why?"

"Because. It's . . . weird. And he'll never let me hear the end of it." He picked up his coffee and stared into it.

"Are you okay, Patrick?"

"Sure." With his eyes still downcast, he gave me a halfhearted smile. "Fine."

We finished our breakfast and went on with our respective days, but the exchange left me feeling wary. If Patrick felt that strongly about Sean examining me, how would he feel if he knew what we had actually done together? I knew on some level it suited Patrick to keep his head in the sand, to keep pretending my baby was the result of the Immaculate Conception rather than the child of another man. But how long could that last? It felt like we were skating around a precarious section of ice, and as soon as either of us stopped concentrating on avoiding it, we were both going to fall straight in.

Now I pulled up the hood of my jacket. It was wicked cold. I tugged at the middle of my puffer coat, but it was no use, it wouldn't close. My belly was officially enormous. Fall had been kind this year, but today it was as though Mother Nature had looked at the calendar and, realizing she'd overslept, was overcompensating.

I hurried through the sliding doors of the hospital and, feeling the rush of warmth from the heaters, lowered my hood. Eloise crossed the foyer, and I lifted my hand to wave but she didn't see me. Patrick stood at the information desk, chatting to, by the looks of it, the parents of a patient. His green scrubs exposed a deep V of olive skin and chest hair, partially covered by an orange lanyard holding his hospital accreditation. He looked tired after an all-night shift in Emergency, but he smiled at the couple and ruffled the hair of a little boy who wore his arm in a sling. I stood just inside the door and waited, rubbing my hands together to get some feeling back.

When Patrick noticed me, he excused himself and came over. His smile told me the strange conversation about Sean had been forgotten. For now.

"Hi." His lips brushed against mine.

"Long night?" he asked.

He shrugged, sliding my coat off my arms and tossing it over his arm. He took my hand as we began to walk. I eyed his unusually large smile.

"What?" I asked.

"I'm excited about seeing the baby."

"Oh, yeah." I grinned. "Me too."

He led me down through the hospital, a maze of halls that even after all these years could get me lost. On the way, we passed several acquaintances of Patrick's, who nodded at him but seemed to avoid my gaze entirely. Before I could analyze it too much, we arrived in front of a white door with a glass panel and a sign that said DR. LORRAINE HAR-GREAVES, followed by a lot of letters. We slipped in.

"Neva Bradley and Patrick Johnson," Patrick said. "We have an appointment."

"So you do," Dr. Hargreaves said, appearing at the desk alongside a heavily pregnant woman and a man who I assumed was the father of her baby. Though one never really should assume. "Go straight in," she said, gesturing to the room she had just exited, before chatting to her receptionist about billing for the couple who were leaving. Patrick and I skulked into her office and sat down. Dr. Hargreaves joined us a little while later.

"Breech, huh?" she said, after a quick look at her notes. "Shame. You could always try a vaginal birth next time, though."

"Maybe," I said. I didn't want to get upset about it. Not in front of Dr. Hargreaves. "We'll see."

"Would you like to find out the gender today?"

"No," Patrick said immediately, although we hadn't discussed it. He turned to me as an afterthought. "I mean . . . we don't, do we?"

I grinned. "I guess we don't."

"Good," Dr. Hargreaves said. "I like surprises. Now, let's take a look. Up on the table, Neva."

I felt a smidge of excitement; Patrick was rubbing off on me. With his help I climbed onto the table and sat still as Dr. Hargreaves took my blood pressure. Then I lay on my back and pulled my T-shirt up to my bra-line. Patrick held my hand, his gaze already focused on the monitor.

"I'll measure you first." Dr. Hargreaves reached into her pocket for a tape measure and stretched it across my belly from pelvis to ribs. She clicked her tongue. "Good size for thirty-six weeks," she said mostly to herself. "Got your height, Patrick."

Patrick's smile froze.

"Now, just a little bit cold, Neva." She squirted some clear, sticky liquid onto my stomach. "Let's take a look."

She lowered the device onto my belly and the beating heart immediately came into focus. Patrick clutched my hand.

"There it is." Dr. Hargreaves continued to swirl the device around.

"Head, bottom—the wrong way around—and there's the heart, the brain." Patrick, I noticed, was smiling at the monitor. "Right arm, left arm, right leg, left leg. I'll avoid this area since you don't want to know the sex."

I found myself smiling too. When I found out I was pregnant, I hadn't expected to have this. A loving man, a father-to-be, by my side. And although I'd never allowed myself to go there, the idea of doing this alone was suddenly unimaginably sad.

"Good-looking little thing, I think," Dr. Hargreaves said. "Right then, you can hop down."

She wiped my stomach with a sheet of paper towel. When we were all back at her desk, she opened a new document on her computer.

"Okay, I have a few questions for each of you. Any hereditary conditions I should know about? Heart defects, spina bifida, blood disorders, Downs?"

"Nope," I said.

"And in your family, Patrick?"

"Uh, no. Not that I know of."

Patrick shook his head a little too fast, almost like a twitch. Dr. Hargreaves didn't seem to notice, but I did.

"And you've been taking your prenatal vitamins since the beginning, Neva?"

I nodded.

"Good. Then this is going to be pretty straightforward. Now, we can do the C-section this side of Christmas, if you like. That's only a week early. Give you a nice little Christmas present."

Scheduling a date and time wasn't something I'd expected to do for my labor. But before I could feel too sorry for myself, Patrick broke into the most adorable grin. "The best Christmas present ever."

"Fine. You can book in the date with Amelia on the way out. Is there anything else? Any concerns?"

We bumbled through the rest of the pleasantries, and then Patrick walked me to the birthing center for my shift.

Halfway there, he stopped. "Nev, I've been thinking."

I resisted making a joke about it hurting his head, as his expression was somber. "Go on."

"All those hereditary conditions Lorraine asked about today—that's important information. I deal with kids all the time who are born with genetic disorders. It's horrible, especially if it comes as a surprise. Having that information in advance is invaluable—for early treatment, for readiness, for planning."

"This baby won't have any genetic conditions."

"Are you sure?" Patrick was tight in the jaw. "Do you know the father well?"

"Yes. I know him very well."

He paled. I took his hand.

"You're the father, Patrick. In every way that counts."

It wasn't the answer he was looking for. Or maybe it was. I got the feeling that, over the past few weeks, Patrick had gotten as attached to my secret as I had. The idea that there was no father would be much easier to accept than the idea of an unknown man lurking out there, liable to burst in at any minute and turn our lives upside down.

Resignedly, he kissed the side of my head and we continued along the corridor. Perhaps it was a victory, but it didn't feel like one. It wouldn't be long before the subject came up again. And eventually, we were both going to have to admit the truth.

23

Grace

Neva and Mom sat on kitchen stools as I tossed flounder fillets in bread crumbs. I'd been looking forward to hosting our monthly dinner. Robert had been verging on mute for days—so consumed by his work—and I'd hoped I'd get a chance for some real conversation tonight. No such luck. Mom and Neva stared at the wall beyond the peas they shelled, barely answering the questions they were asked. They must have eaten a slice of the same silent-pie Robert was eating.

I thought about divulging my secret to them, that I was actually delivering babies while the investigation was going on, but I decided against it. I was actually quite enjoying my double life. Somehow, it felt like my way of giving the finger to that smug doctor who'd issued the complaint. The only difficult part was the technicalities. Two nights earlier I'd received a text from a mother in labor. At two in the morning. Robert roused as I started to get dressed, and I'd had to pretend I was sleepwalking. A few minutes later, once he'd fallen back into a deep sleep, I'd seized the keys and left the house in my pajamas.

Only occasionally, when I really allowed myself to think about it, did I worry about the consequences that would come about if I were caught. By the Board of Nursing. By Robert. But whenever those thoughts popped into my head, I chased them out again. *Positive thinking, Grace. Positive thinking.*

"Having any food aversions, darling?" I asked Neva, trying to get some conversation out of my unusually quiet daughter. "When I was pregnant with you, the mere sight of a mushroom was enough to send me running to the bathroom."

Neva shrugged. "I've gone off tuna, I guess."

"Oh." I paused, my hands still buried in fish and bread crumbs. "Are you okay with flounder?"

"Should be. Though I won't know for sure until you put it in front of me."

I chuckled, trying to catch Mom's eye. Any woman who'd been pregnant could sympathize with that. "Did you get any food aversions when you were pregnant, Mom?"

Mom focused steadily on her sleeve, picking off some lint. "I suppose I did."

"What about cravings?" I asked. "When I was pregnant with Neva, I could have eaten fried rice all day long."

"Oh, I don't know . . . It was a long time ago, dear."

It was odd, how hazy she was sometimes. Even though she was eighty-three, I'd have thought these kinds of things would be burned into her mind.

The doorbell chimed as we were about to sit down. "Neva," I said, "your father's eating in front of the hockey game. Can you take him his dinner in the den? Be nice—he's in a mood."

I dried my hands on a tea towel as I made my way to the door. Behind it stood a small woman with a cap of short, blond-gray hair. She held the neck of her navy anorak with one hand against the wind.

"Can I help you?"

"Hello. I'm Marie Ableman. From the Board of Nursing." Marie clutched the coat as a gush of wind ripped past. She shuddered.

"Oh. Uh . . . Come in." I held the door open and she came into the foyer. "I wasn't expecting you, was I?"

"No. I was going to call you tomorrow, but I thought it might be a good idea to speak in person. I hope you don't mind me stopping by."

"No, I guess not."

But I did mind. Good news was given via the fastest possible means, be it a phone call or an e-mail. Bad news was given in person. At least, that was how I figured it.

"The investigation is still under way," she said, possibly in response to my face. "We still need to speak to a few more people yet."

"Okay."

"The reason I'm here is about this." She reached into her pocket and unfolded a piece of paper. A photocopy of a prescription. "I was concerned to find that you had prescribed Tylenol 3 for this woman the day that her son was born. I was even more concerned when I saw that she was a former client of yours. And then, when I found that no medical professional had signed her birth certificate, I became a little suspicious."

Marie had the stance of someone who was trying to be fair. It was a stance I was sure she used regularly, in her particular role. "Believe it or not, Mrs. Bradley, I am on your side. I am a nurse myself. I know it is a difficult, sometimes thankless, profession. I don't believe you were intentionally negligent, or that you tried to hurt Gillian or her baby. I'm sure you did what you thought was best. But I now have reason to believe that you are delivering babies while your case is being reviewed, which is something you were expressly told not to do. I want to help you, but if this is the case, my hands are tied."

I felt the heat in my cheeks. I'd been caught. In some ways it was a relief. This secret was weighing on me, perhaps heavier than I'd allowed to myself to believe. Part of me wanted to share the load. "Marie, I'm sorry—"

"It's not the case," Neva said from the doorway. She stood beside Mom. It was funny, they were two tiny women, but suddenly, together, they seemed so large.

"What's not the case?" Marie asked.

"The prescription. That's not Grace's signature. It's mine. I'm Grace's daughter, Neva."

"*You* wrote a Tylenol 3 prescription for Molly Harris, your mother's former client?" Marie asked.

"Yes. And I delivered her baby. I offered to take over all Grace's clients while this investigation was going on. That way, at least Grace could attend and they could have some continuity of care."

"So . . . this . . . is your signature?" Marie said.

Neva stepped forward, barely glancing at the paper. "Yes."

Marie looked back at the paper, and Neva also looked. The paper clearly said G. Bradley, but to Neva's credit, she didn't miss a beat. "I'd just attended a fifteen-hour labor. You want to argue over my penmanship?"

I became aware of Mom advancing until the three of us—Mom, Neva, and I—stood, shoulder to shoulder in a row. Marie looked from one to the next to the next, then shook her head. She knew she was right. But she couldn't prove it.

"No. I don't want to argue anything. I'm here because I want people to have access to a good standard of nursing. Believe it or not, I don't always think doctors are the best judge of that. But I need you to work with me." She looked at Neva. "So, if you do deliver any more of your mom's client's babies, please make sure you sign the birth certificate. All right?"

Neva nodded. "Yes. I will. Sorry about that."

"And try to get your initial right on the prescription."

A trace of red appeared on Neva's cheeks.

"I'll get the door," I said as Marie reached for the handle.

"It's fine, Mrs. Bradley. I'll let myself out."

We all watched her leave. After the door had snapped shut, I turned to face my daughter. "Thank you, darling. Thank you so much."

"I don't know what you are up to, Grace," Neva said, shaking her head, "but a little prior warning might have been helpful. By the way, what's with the easy-to-read signature? God, couldn't you be more like a—?"

"Doctor!" we all said in unison, then laughed, a little giddy with our small victory.

"Come on." I linked arms with Mom and Neva. "I guess I owe you an explanation. I'll fill you in over dinner." We turned toward the dining room.

"Perhaps you'd do me the courtesy of filling me in too?"

I froze, then lifted my eyes to the top of the stairs, where Robert was standing. And, all at once, my giddiness bubbled away to nothing.

24

Neva

When I arrived for my shift at the birthing center, I was already tense. Patrick had been strangely unavailable for a few days. He'd said he was exhausted from his week on night shift, and that was probably all it was, but . . . I missed him.

It might have been everything that was going on with my family that was putting me on edge. After overhearing what Marie Ableman from the Board of Nursing had to say, Dad was furious with Grace. Gran and I had tried not to listen, but they were yelling pretty loud. At one point, I got up to go and set Dad straight. He was laying it on too thick—what she did was stupid, but ultimately a kind act. But Gran stopped me. People a lot weaker than Mom handled worse every day, she told me—it made them stronger.

Something was up with her too, but I had no idea what.

In any case, all I wanted to do on this shift was kick back with Susan and bring a life into the world. It was probably what I needed to restore my equilibrium. But I'd forgotten Susan was on vacation. And I was rostered on with Iris.

Iris was my least favorite birth assistant. While she was patient and undeniably good with the clients, she had an irritating habit of talking to everyone like they were preschoolers, and today she'd taken to talking to me only indirectly, using the mother in labor as a medium.

"Just breathe through the contraction," she was saying to Brianna. "Good girl. When this one's over Neva might suggest a nice bath to ease the pain. She's in charge."

Brianna was on her hands and knees on the floor, clearly approaching transition. Her husband, George, was beside her, rubbing her back and generally looking out of his depth. I scanned the birth notes and saw that she was six centimeters dilated at the last examination and her water hadn't broken. A bath wasn't a bad idea.

"How about a nice bath?" I said brightly when the contraction finished. If Iris heard the humor in my voice, she didn't respond to it.

"Wonderful idea," she said, not meeting my eye. "I'll go get it started."

Iris disappeared into the bathroom and I frowned after her. She seemed preoccupied herself. Had I done something to upset her?

"Neva," Brianna said, stealing my attention. "It hurts."

"This is the hardest part," I said, squatting beside her. "Just a little bit longer and we are going to meet your little one. In the meantime, the water will help ease some of the pain. Did you bring your iPod with the playlist you talked about? A lot of women find music helpful at this point."

George was already searching in Brianna's bag for the iPod, clearly grateful for something to do. I decided he could be useful. "How about I show George some of the pressure points in your feet? Some of them are known to reduce pain significantly."

"Bath's ready," Iris said, returning. "George, you come and sit at the end of the tub if you're going to rub Briann's feet."

"Brian*a*," I whispered to Iris with a conspiratorial wink that she ignored. Weird. Something was definitely up with her. She was normally patronizing, but it wasn't like her to be rude.

"Uh . . . okay, let's get this show on the road," I said. "George, why don't you help Brianna get undressed? I'm just going to get a few things ready out here."

Once Brianna was undressed, Iris wordlessly scooted her out of the room and into the tub. In the delivery room, I turned on the baby warmer and went about preparing my instruments.

"Brianna wants to put her iPod on surround sound," Iris said, alerting me to her presence behind me. "Do you know where the speakers are?"

"They're in the cupboard with the towels. Wait," I said. "Is everything okay?"

"Of course. Why wouldn't it be?"

"I don't know. You just seem upset with me."

"Not upset." She frowned, clearly contemplating whether to say more. "Just surprised. I'll admit, I thought better of you."

"Iris, will you please just come out with it?"

"Fine," she said. "I heard about you and Sean. Having an affair behind Patrick's back."

My mouth fell open but it took me a moment to formulate words. *"What?"*

Iris folded her arms. "So it's not true?"

"Of course it's not true! Who told you that?"

"My sources are pretty credible."

"Iris, are we in the playground? What are people saying about me and Sean?"

She pinched her lips together. "That your baby is his. That you two had an affair, and now you are pretending the baby is Patrick's."

I was trying to grasp the magnitude of what she'd said when George appeared in the doorway and cleared his throat.

"Um, excuse me, ladies. Brianna wants to start pushing."

My sneakers squeaked against the linoleum floors. I hadn't moved this fast since before I was pregnant. By the time I arrived at the elevator, I was jogging.

When the elevator door opened, three nurses I recognized were inside. A brief glance told me they had heard the rumor too. They were probably delighted. Patrick Johnson would be available again soon. One of them would probably love to be the one to tell him. Thank God he wasn't rostered on until tonight.

I exited on the maternity floor. I scanned the halls and looked into each room I passed. Maybe Sean was on nights too? I was about to ask at the desk, when I heard his voice. I spun, and there he was, talking to a couple who carried their baby in a car seat, clearly about to be discharged.

"Better start saving for college," he was saying. "And remember, we have a no-return policy on babies. Even with a receipt."

The couple laughed and waved to Sean. As they walked away, Sean noticed me. "Hey, Nev. What's up?"

"There is a rumor going around that we are having an affair."

"Excuse me?"

"Iris told me this morning. Apparently, I've cheated on Patrick with you and the baby is yours."

"That's ridiculous." Outwardly, Sean spoke in the arrogant, self-assured way that he had perfected, but I could tell he was nervous. "Who started the rumor?"

"Iris wouldn't tell me. But I think a lot of people have heard it. I've been getting funny looks around the hospital for days."

"Shit." He raked a hand through his hair. "Have you been talking to the girls down at the birthing center?"

I didn't dignify that with an answer, and Sean didn't wait for one.

"Well, no one will believe it," he said. "It's gossip, pure and simple. We should just ignore it. Gossip dies down eventually. Especially when it's not true."

"It isn't entirely false, Sean."

"It is," Sean snapped, then lowered his voice. "It *is* entirely false. We are *not* having an affair."

I took his arm and pulled him into the stairwell. I didn't need Sean adding to the problem by participating in what might be misconstrued as a lovers' quarrel.

He threw off my arm as soon as we arrived in the stairwell and started pacing. "Sorry, I'm just pissed. People start these rumors for fun; they don't realize they are messing with my life. Imagine if Laura heard this."

"And what about Patrick?" Sean could be such a selfish jerk, thinking only about how things affected him. "This affects me too, you know."

Sean wasn't listening. "Laura had just been diagnosed with a brain tumor, for fuck's sake. I won't lose her now because of one reckless night that only happened because you were blind drunk and I was out of my mind with worry!"

I shushed him, but the night was already flooding my mind. It was strangely vivid, given the fact that I was flat-out drunk. I could still see his face, staring trancelike at the wall in the staff room where, after a tip off from the nurses, I found him. He'd just been given the news about Laura's tumor, and the prognosis wasn't good. His stillness indicated he'd been that way for a while.

Laura was spending the night at the hospital before going in for surgery, so I called Patrick, and we took Sean to The Hip for a drink. We thought a drink might loosen him up, allow him to talk, but when we got there, he just stared into space for hours. There was a vacantness to him that I'd never seen—not when his father died, not when he'd delivered his first stillborn baby. Sean and I drank beer after beer, wine after wine. It was the only time in my life that I'd ever felt really good about getting hammered, like drinking my weight in alcohol was showing solidarity to Sean. Patrick, who was working nights, remained sober.

At closing time, Patrick went back to the hospital to start his night shift. I said I'd put Sean in a cab, but when we got onto the street, Sean suddenly started to talk. It spewed from him—how sick she was, how powerless he felt. After an hour of listening in the cold night air, I brought him back to my apartment. I made him up a bed on the couch and tucked him into it.

"You're a good friend, Nev," he slurred.

I nodded and continued tucking. Somehow wrapping him up tight felt like it would be a comfort—like swaddling to a newborn. Or maybe I was just too drunk to know what else to do.

"Could you stay with me awhile?" he asked. "I don't want to be alone."

"I'll sleep here in the recliner," I said, feeling glad I didn't have to make the journey back to my room. My head felt so heavy, I didn't think I'd make it there. "Just wake me if you want to talk."

Sean opened the sheet that I'd just wrapped around him. "Could you sleep here?"

Sean looked pale, wide eyed, like a little boy. So at odds with the arrogant, self-assured man I knew. The couch looked more inviting than the recliner, so sleepily, I rolled in beside him so my back pressed against his front. I think I heard the words thank you before Sean's warm, heavy arm lulled me to sleep.

When I woke, it was with strange urgency. It was still dark and I could hear whimpering. Awkwardly, I rolled over and frowned into the darkness.

"Sean, are you okay?"

"No," he sobbed. "God, why is this *happening?*"

"I don't know," I said, patting his shoulder. I willed my brain to snap into gear so I could find some words of wisdom to help my friend. But my words sounded as foggy as I felt. A favorite saying of Grace's popped into my mind: *Words are a poor man's touch.* And touch, even in my state, I could probably manage.

It took some shuffling, but I managed to get my arms around Sean's neck. He pressed his face into my chest. He cried a bit longer, and just as I was drifting into a light sleep, he spoke.

"Nev?"

"Mmm?" When I ducked my head to look at him he came at me like a hurricane: lips, hands, everything. At first I was stunned, and then . . . something else. As he rolled me onto my back, the pull of attraction was immediate, and fierce. Shapes floated before my eyes. And before I knew it, his body was heavy on mine.

In the back of my mind, I knew something wasn't right. But with our arms and legs snaking through the darkness, I couldn't figure out what it was. It was like admiring beautiful, ornate coral while the rain rapped against the surface of the water eight feet above—I suspected something was up there, but with everything else I had going on, I didn't bother to look.

Sean was gone the next morning, and I was glad. Waking up alone gave credence to my theory that the whole thing was a dream.

I didn't see Sean for two weeks after that. After Laura's surgery, he took time off to care for her. Without him around, I was able to pretend it never happened. And when he returned, that was exactly how we acted. It wasn't until he found out about my pregnancy that he even acknowledged the night had ever happened. But now, we had to acknowledge it.

"You won't lose her, Sean. No one knows about that night, at least I haven't told anyone. This rumor is probably based on someone seeing us together at the pub downstairs or whispering a joke in the hall or . . ." I trailed off.

"What?" Sean asked.

"Marion." I swore under my breath. "Remember that day I came up here and told you my baby was breech? You hugged me. And after you left I saw Marion watching us. She's obviously read more into it, and she's not a huge fan of yours—"

"And she's hardly averse to a good rumor. Shit!" Sean reached for the door handle. "I'm going to put a stop to it now. Don't follow me, for fuck's sake! The last thing we need is people seeing us emerge from a stairwell together."

There was a whoosh of air; then Sean was gone. Headed to extinguish the problem. As for his tone, I couldn't care less. As long as he was taking care of Marion, he could speak to me however he wanted. I reached for the handrail; then my breath stole away.

"Patrick."

He stood on the landing below, a pillow wedged under his arm. He stared at the stairs ahead of him. "I brought this in for you. In case you decided to have another nap at the birthing center." He lifted his eyes. They were vacant, cold. "You and Sean? Seriously?"

I wanted to run to him, to throw myself at his mercy, but I was eight months pregnant, so instead I carefully made my way down the stairs. On the final step, I reached for his arm. To his credit, he let me hold him until I had both feet on the flat surface. Then he dropped me like a hot stone.

"Let me make this clear," I said. "There is no 'me and Sean.' It was a rumor started by Marion, we think. We are *not* having an affair."

"But you did sleep together?"

I stared at him, and with no other choice, nodded.

"And this"—he poked my stomach gently with his finger—"is *his* baby?" He watched me, waiting for confirmation.

"Yes."

"When?"

Now I was the one to drop my gaze.

"*When*, Neva?"

"Remember the night Sean told us about Laura's tumor?" As much as I didn't want to, I met his eye. Patrick's face was completely frozen—not a flicker of an eyelid or twitch of a lip. I forced myself to continue. "He didn't want to be alone. I said he could come back to my apartment and—"

"I get the picture."

"No. You don't."

Patrick began to pace. I stared at him. The angle of his jaw and the curve of his forearm. It was hard to believe that, only a few minutes before, this beautiful human being was mine. He wanted to share a life with me and my baby. I felt faint.

"Neva?"

I became aware of his face, close to mine. "Yes?"

"Are you okay?"

"Fine. Just . . ." The walls swayed slightly. ". . . a little dizzy."

"Sit down," he said.

I started to shake my head, but Patrick's arm went around my back and he lowered me onto the linoleum floor. "Just take a breath."

"I never meant for any of this," I said as he propped me against the wall. "The last thing I wanted was to hurt you."

He sat beside me. "I know."

He sounded resigned. I wanted to say something more, but there were no words. I settled for sitting beside him. After what I'd just told him, I wasn't sure if I'd have the chance to sit beside him again.

A few minutes later, the door swung open and a nurse I vaguely recognized appeared at the top of the stairs. "Do you need help here?"

"Yes, please, Rose." As if awakened from a dream, Patrick sprang to standing. "Neva's not feeling well. She's thirty-six weeks pregnant, registered to deliver at St. Mary's Birthing Center. I'd like you to check her heart rate and blood pressure for me."

The nurse started down the stairs. "Yes, Dr. Johnson."

Patrick pulled me to standing. "If everything looks okay, could you please order her a taxi?" He looked at me. "I don't want you walking home in this weather, okay?"

At first I didn't understand what he was saying. Then, I did. "You're not coming?"

Patrick shook his head. "I'll call the hospital when I get home, make sure you're all right."

I nodded. Somehow I even managed to choke out a thank you.

The nurse linked her arm through mine. "I'll take good care of her. Shall I send the results to the birthing center, Dr. Johnson?"

"Thanks, Rose." He looked at me. "Will you be okay, Neva?"

I pretended I didn't hear, and let Rose guide me up the stairs. I'd never been good at good-byes. And no matter what had passed between us, I still didn't want him to see me cry.

25

Grace

I got home just in the nick of time. The snow was coming down and the roads were slippery—not a good day to be driving. As I pulled up, the radio announced there had been an accident on the Beavertail Road and it was closed in both directions. I'd have worried that a client would go into labor tonight, but as I was no longer taking clients in secret, I had no other clients.

I'd never seen Robert quite so upset. The way he'd looked at me—it was a hundred times worse than when I'd told him about the investigation. He'd used all the worst words—betrayal, dishonesty, disappointment. Initially I'd stayed quiet. After all, I'd earned it. But when he kept it up, banging on about how selfish I was, I got my back up.

"Hang on a second!" I yelled. "I may have done the wrong thing, but what about you? You've been moping around here for weeks. *Poor me, I might lose my job. Poor me, people got fired today.* How about: *Lucky me, I still have my job. Lucky me, I didn't get fired today!* And did it ever occur to you that I was doing this so I could support my family? I have an envelope full of cash in the study—"

"Wonderful, so now we are tax evaders too? Fantastic, Grace. You're right. I should be thrilled."

Eventually we'd reached a stalemate and gone to bed in separate rooms. We'd hardly spoken since, and I was still pissed off. Now, warm air hit my cheeks as I opened the front door to the house. A good, warm mug of soup was what I needed. Peeling off my scarf, hat, and gloves I hurried toward the kitchen. I was about to pass the sitting room when I heard Neva's voice. I held back, out of sight. I hadn't noticed her car. She sounded like she was crying.

"Are you sure it's over?" Robert asked.

Neva must have nodded.

"Then he's an idiot. An idiot and certainly not a gentleman. Abandoning you when you're about to have a baby. What have you done to deserve that?"

I crept a few steps forward and pressed my ear to the wall.

"I slept with a married man, Dad. A man who was going through something awful with his wife."

I clapped a hand over my mouth. But Robert, in usual Robert fashion, didn't react.

"She's made a full recovery—his wife—and she knows nothing about me. The whole thing was a horrible mistake."

I wanted to run in there, to wrap my arms around her, but something stopped me. Robert was with her.

"Well . . . you know what, sweetie? If there's something I've learned from being married to your mother, it's that mistakes, misjudgments, failures—sometimes they're the best part of life. In fact, as far as mistakes go, I'd say this one is the best you've ever made. Creating a life. Giving me a grandchild."

Neva laughed and sniffed. "You sound like Mom."

"She's rubbed off on me after all these years. As for Patrick . . . well, I'm guessing he'll need some time. He might come back. You never know."

"I doubt it. Why would he?"

"You can flagellate yourself if you want, justify all the reasons he won't come back to you, the reasons he *shouldn't*. But you know what? It won't affect the outcome. You're better to focus on what you do have, which is a baby, due very soon. A baby who, even without a father, has been blessed in the parent department."

I peered around the corner. Robert had his arm around Neva, and her head rested on his shoulder. I took a step back, then another, retracing my steps out the front door and onto the street.

I powered along the unplowed roads for what felt like hours. The ground was carpeted white, apart from patches where reeds peeked through, too frozen even to sway in the wind. Suddenly it was all so clear. Why Neva didn't come to me. Why she was so much more open with her father. I'd come into our relationship with so many strings attached. *Love me. Share with me. Validate me.* And when she didn't, I pushed her even harder. Even further away. The truth was, she could never have filled me. She wasn't the one who'd left the hole. It was my father.

As I walked, I watched two cars skid in the snow, and passed a third lodged in a fence. I kept walking. I didn't know where I was headed, but after an hour or so, I found myself outside Mom's house. It was where I usually ended up when things got tough.

I let myself in and strode toward the sitting room, then skidded to a stop. Neva sat by Mom's side, cradling a mug of coffee. Tearstains swam on her creamy skin. "Neva!"

I don't know why I was surprised. I'd been walking for a long time—there had been plenty of time for her to leave her father and come to see her Gran. A part of me was hurt that she hadn't factored me into the visiting schedule, but I immediately took that thought back. This wasn't about me; it was about Neva. And there would be no strings attached. Not anymore.

"Grace!" she said. "I've been looking for you everywhere."

"You were?" My cheeks heated. Although I knew it shouldn't matter, I warmed through at this fact.

"I'll make more coffee," Mom said, rising slowly from the armchair. I moved to Neva's side, and she fell into my arms.

"Shhhh," I said. "It's okay, darling. It's okay."

She cried until my chest was wet. It was strange, rocking my twenty-nine-year-old daughter in my arms. Strange and sort of beautiful. She told me it was over between her and Patrick. She told me it was all her fault. She told me about the ob-gyn and his wife with cancer. Unlike Robert, I didn't have any words of wisdom, only sympathy. Sympathy and sadness that, unlike when she was a little girl, I couldn't magic her pain away with a kiss and an ice cream.

Mom arrived back with coffee a short time later.

"Okay," Neva said. "I'm going to the bathroom and then I'm going to come back and get myself together. Okay?"

I nodded, pressing confidence into my face. "Okay."

Neva heaved herself to standing. She moved slowly, carefully, her knees buckling under the weight of her belly. It had grown since the last time I saw it, and now it was hard to believe she had a month to go. As she lumbered toward the door, a shudder skittered through her.

"You okay, darling?"

She nodded with a slight wince. "Fine. A few Braxton Hicks, that's all."

She toddled out, and when she was gone, I raised my eyebrows at Mom, a question of sorts.

"She's got herself into quite the situation," Mom said. There was something playful in her expression. "Reminds me of someone else I know."

I laughed. "She reminds you of me? Ha."

"More and more lately."

"Don't let her hear you say that."

"Too late. I heard."

Neva stood in the entrance to the sitting room, her legs slightly apart. A wet stain darkened the leg of her sweatpants. "My water just broke."

I leapt to my feet. It was a month early, not dangerously early, but early. I eyed the patch again. Was it possible that it was something else? Many women had trouble with their pelvic floor in the late stages of pregnancy, perhaps—

"I felt the pop, and there was a good volume of liquid, so yes, I'm certain," she said. "And it was followed immediately by a contraction I couldn't talk through."

Mom, sensing the urgency, rose to her feet.

"And you said you'd been having some Braxton Hicks?" I asked. "How often and for how long?"

Before she could answer, Neva doubled over, breathing the slow familiar pant of a woman in progressed labor. Mom and I exchanged a horrified look.

"They were irregular until about an hour ago," she said once the contraction ceased. "Since then, I don't know. About every five minutes or so? I wasn't paying close attention. I didn't think it was labor."

I concentrated on keeping my face calm, but I was already a step ahead, and my observations were grim. The snow outside was approaching knee-deep. The only road to the hospital was closed. And even though I could deliver a baby at home with my eyes closed, this baby was four weeks premature. My own clients who went into labor this early would be referred to a hospital.

Neva moved about the room, robotically collecting her phone, her coat, her keys.

"What are you doing, darling?"

"I'm getting my stuff together. We need to get to the hospital." Another contraction started. Her face contorted.

"Beavertail Road is closed, Neva. Besides, it's carnage out there. I wouldn't put my worst enemy on that road."

"Well, what do you suggest?" she said once another contraction had ceased. "That we deliver a breech baby right here?"

My blood iced in my veins. Somehow, with everything else going on, I'd forgotten Neva's baby was breech. Now that fact pinned me to the spot. If anything went wrong, the baby, and Neva, would—

"I'll call the ambulance!" I yelled. "Mom, can you examine her? I need to know the baby's position, dilation, everything."

I snatched the receiver off the cradle and stabbed the numbers into the phone. The few seconds it took to connect felt like an eternity. All I could hear was my heartbeat. I began to pace.

"Emergency Services, how may I direct your call?"

I stopped short. "I need an ambulance. My daughter is in labor with a breech baby—thirty-six weeks gestation. Her water has broken and her contractions are rapidly becoming more painful and frequent. She needs to go to the hospital, but the road is closed and we're stuck here."

"Where are you located, ma'am?"

"Conanicut Island. Southern tip, near Hull Cove."

Long nails tapped against a keyboard.

"She's five centimeters dilated, Grace," Mom called from the other room.

"And your daughter is in labor?" the woman on the phone asked. "How far progressed—is she pushing?"

"No! She's not pushing. She's five centimeters dilated, and the last two contractions were about three minutes apart. Her water has broken. It's a breech baby," I repeated. "It needs to be delivered in a hospital."

"And she's full term?"

I bit back my urge to scream. "No. She's thirty-six weeks gestation."

"Okay." *Tap. Tap. Tap.* "Hold the line please, ma'am."

I began pacing again. In the sitting room, Neva lay on a pillow on the floor, battling through another contraction. Mom knelt beside her, a tough position for a woman in her eighties, but she looked at ease. Almost like it was no big deal, delivering a breech baby at home. . . .

Of course. I'd completely forgotten. Mom *had* delivered breech babies during her midwifery training in England, in circumstances far more challenging than these. It was some comfort, but still I didn't plan for us to be delivering it here tonight.

"Are you there, ma'am?"

"Yes."

"I have requested a helicopter for your daughter, but there are a number of emergencies this evening with this weather, and it might not be soon enough. I will get an ob-gyn on standby to talk you through it over the phone, just in case. In the meantime, I'm going to need your full name, address, and two contact phone numbers."

Neva started moaning again. I felt ill to my core. It couldn't have been longer than two minutes since the last contraction. This baby was coming, and fast. And they were going to give me an ob-gyn *over the phone*?

"I need someone *here*. I need medical equipment. I've never delivered a breech baby."

There was a pause. "Have you ever delivered a baby?"

I screamed internally. "Of course! I'm a midwife. I've delivered hundreds of babies. But this is my daughter's baby. Its breech and four weeks premature. We cannot deliver it here. We need an ambulance!"

"Just calm down, ma'am." *Tap. Tap. Tap. Tap.* "I need you to stay in control, for your daughter's sake. I've requested a helicopter ambulance, but we need to plan for the worst-case scenario. If you are an experienced midwife, the worst-case scenario isn't as bad as it could be."

I dropped my head into my hand. This wasn't happening. This. Was. Not. Happening. Not Neva. I'd take the charge against me from the Board of Nursing. I'd settle for a boring, sexless marriage with a husband who hated my guts. I'd forfeit any notion of a close relationship with Neva forever. I'd forget about her baby's father. But I wouldn't lose my daughter.

A high-pitched, broken wail pulled me from my thoughts and sent me running to the sitting room. Neva was on her hands and knees on the floor, stripped from the waist down. Her face was mangled in pain. Mom knelt beside her.

"They're sending a helicopter ambulance as soon as they can," I said.

"They're not going to make it, Grace," Mom said. "The baby is coming now."

26

Floss

The announcement that the baby was on its way came as a shock, even though I was the one who announced it. Several seconds of silence followed, and it probably would have continued if Neva hadn't whimpered, snapping us all into gear.

"Now?" Grace asked. Her face was even more ashen than usual. "No. Surely not."

"The baby is coming," I said. "And it's a footling."

Grace dropped the phone and raced over to where I knelt. She gasped when she saw the baby emerging. It wasn't a breech we were seeing; it was a foot. Things had just got a little more complicated. "Shit!"

"You're going to have to deliver the baby, dear," I said.

"I can't. You've delivered a breech before—"

"Never a footling. And I haven't delivered a child in twenty years, Grace."

"I need to push," Neva said between deep breaths. She looked over her shoulder at Grace desperately. "Grace, can I push?"

Grace and I exchanged a look. Neva had decided who was delivering her baby.

"Um." Already, sweat poured from Grace. She closed her eyes, exhaled, and nodded. When she opened her eyes again, her expression was purposeful. "Soon, darling. Just pant, exactly as you're doing." She turned toward the stairs and hollered, "Lil!"

Lil appeared at the top of the stairs. "Did you call?"

"Yes, love," I said. "Can you come down here, please?"

"We need your help," Grace said as Lil descended the stairs. "Neva is going to have her baby right here, any time now. There's no time to get to a hospital, and the road is closed anyway. I need you to go to my place. You'll find my delivery bag on the bench in my birthing room. It's sterile and ready to go. I also want you to grab the forceps from the counter. My keys are on the coffee table. Hurry. We have minutes, not hours."

Grace's voice was calm, but the urgency registered on Lil's face. She nodded. Despite her age, despite the weather outside, despite what was going on between us, she didn't so much as hesitate. I had never loved her more ferociously. "I'll be as fast as I can."

Grace knelt down. "Mom, I'm going to need you to walk me through this, step-by-step. Speak to me like I'm a student; assume I know nothing. I'm not taking any chances with this delivery."

"All right," I said. "We'll need towels, a knife, and something for clamping in case Lil doesn't get here in time. Neva, try not to push, dear. I'll be right back."

I hurried toward the bathroom for towels as another contraction gripped Neva. My heart thundered. A footling delivered at home? Even back in England, I'd have called the flying squad for this. And this wasn't just any client. This was my granddaughter.

On my way back, I turned up the heat. It was important the room was nice and warm. If the baby's startle reflex was activated by the cold, it could start to breathe in utero and inhale amniotic fluid, something we wanted to avoid at all costs. I'd learned that particular fact over fifty years ago, during midwifery training. What other midwifery training would I need to draw on today? Would it all come back to me when I needed it?

By the time I returned, the baby's left leg had emerged as far as the knee. Grace looked like she was using every last ounce of energy to stay calm. "Mom, I need instructions. What do I do?"

I touched Grace's shoulders. "The most important thing is that as long as delivery continues spontaneously, you need to keep your hands off. If you pull, even a little, you can interfere with flexion of the head or stop it rotating effectively. Worse, it can cause nuchal arms, where the baby wraps its arms around its neck, making it impossible to deliver vaginally. So do not touch the baby at all. Understand?"

Grace nodded, but her jaw was tight. I understood. It felt unnatural to see the baby coming and not be able to touch it. It must have felt even more unnatural when the baby was your grandchild. Silently we watched as the tiny leg emerged from Neva. Grace's hands hovered a few centimeters back from the baby. "Now what?" she said. "I really do nothing?"

"Nothing," I confirmed. "Just wait."

The leg continued to come. I felt a little sick. I'd delivered a breech before, but never a footling. It was what we referred to while studying as a complicated delivery. Far from ideal under these circumstances. If things didn't go to plan . . . well . . . I couldn't think about that. The baby rotated as it descended, and Grace and I watched silently as the left buttock appeared, then the right. Then—pop—both legs were out. So far, so good.

"When you see the umbilical cord, pull down a small loop to prevent traction on the cord later in the delivery," I told Grace.

Grace did as I asked. The baby was out as far as the torso. But the most difficult part was still to come.

"With the next contraction, I want you to push, Neva," I said. "Hard as you can."

Neva nodded, gripping the couch. And when the next contraction came, she pushed. I held my breath and, I'm sure, so did Grace. The contraction finished. Two more contractions came and went. Neva pushed and pushed. Still the shoulders did not appear. I cursed under my breath.

"The shoulders aren't delivering spontaneously, so you'll need to assist," I said to Grace. Any hope for a smooth, straightforward birth was gone. Now I just prayed for a safe birth. "The anterior arm can be delivered by sliding two fingers over the baby's back," I said, "along the humerus to the elbow. Then you can sweep the arm around in front of the baby's face and chest. Do the same for the other arm."

If Grace was feeling anxious, it didn't show. I marveled as she delivered the arms. It was a tricky technique, but it was as though she'd done it a hundred times before.

"Good," I said. "Very good." Now the entire baby was out, apart from the head. "Okay, Grace. Is the head engaged?"

Sweat drenched her face. "I . . . I don't know."

"Can you see the baby's hairline?"

Grace looked. "No. I can't."

I looked at the baby, its little torso supported by her right hand. "Let go of the baby."

Grace looked at me like I was crazy.

"Let it go," I repeated. "If you let the body hang, the weight will pull the baby down and, with any luck, engage the head."

Tentatively Grace let go of the baby, leaving it to dangle from Neva. Grace's body became still. I doubted she was breathing.

"Good," I said. "With the next contraction, Neva, I want you to bear down with all your might, okay?"

Neva nodded, gripping the sofa. Another contraction came and went. I willed Lil to get back. Things were moving fast, and if anything went wrong, we'd desperately need those instruments.

"Okay, Grace," I said, turning back. "Is the head engaged now?"

Grace looked, then shook her head. I squeezed my hand into a fist.

"What is it?" she asked.

I hesitated before speaking. "I'm just a little concerned about the biparietal diameter of the head."

I didn't need to say any more. If the baby's head was too large to pass through Neva's pelvis, she would need a C-section. Without one, Neva and the baby would die. Grace knew that. Unfortunately, Neva did too.

"No!" Neva cried. "My baby—"

"—will be fine, darling," Grace said simply. "And so will you. I'll make sure of it."

Neva calmed immediately. Strangely, so did I. There was something about Grace. She *seemed* in control. Grace, who lived for adrenaline, was, as it turned out, wonderfully cool under pressure.

"Mom," Grace said to me. "What are our options?"

I stared at the wall. I'd been asking myself the same question. "If the head is stuck, we might be able to turn it in a way that will allow it to pass through the pelvis." I thought about it some more. Yes, it could work. The risk of a serious tear to Neva was increased, but we didn't have a lot of choice. "This is important, so I need you to listen carefully: We need to turn Neva over so I can apply pressure to her abdomen when she starts to push."

Neva was already turning from all fours into a reclining sitting position. Grace helped her. I said a silent prayer.

"Now, Grace. Let the baby straddle your right hand . . . Yes, like that. Now, I want you to slide your middle finger into the baby's mouth and your other fingers over the baby's shoulders. Perfect. Now, with your other hand, press against the back of the baby's head. I'll apply pressure on the outside of her belly at the same time. All right?"

The door clattered shut and Lil appeared beside me with the delivery bag. I opened it and lay out the clamp, the cord, the gloves. I got everything unpacked just in time for the next contraction.

"Okay, Grace—push the head up slightly, rotate, and then pull down. Understand?" I looked at Neva. "Push, dear. Push as hard as you possibly can."

Neva touched her chin to her chest and squeezed. At the same time, I pressed hard on the outside of her belly. The bones in her neck stood out like kindling.

"It's coming," Grace said, her voice barely a whisper. "The head. It's coming."

It was only then I realized my cheeks and blouse were sodden with tears. I felt movement under my hand as the baby's head moved down. Grace lifted the baby's torso as the head emerged. The baby was out.

Grace placed the baby straight into her mother's arms. The raven-haired babe let out a soft mew. "Congratulations, dear," I said to Neva as an overwhelming sense of déjà vu swept over me. "You have a daughter."

27

Neva

The first thing I recognized when I opened my eyes was the nursing chair in the corner. I was in a maternity suite at St. Mary's Hospital. The second thing I recognized was the person sleeping in the nursing chair. Patrick.

"Hey."

My greeting came out as a hoarse whisper, but he sprang to life immediately. He came to my side and pressed the buzzer by my bed. "Hey." He cleared his throat. "How do you feel?"

I looked past him and scanned the room for a bassinet. "Where's my baby?"

"She's in the nursery with your mom and Gran. She's fine. Your mom hasn't put her down since she was born. We were much more worried about you. You had a third-degree tear and lost a lot of blood. You were pretty out of it when they brought you in."

My eyes found Patrick's. "She's fine? You're sure?"

"I examined her myself. She's six pounds two ounces. Completely healthy."

Patrick was doing his confident pediatrician thing. I'd seen him do it with hundreds of parents over the years, and it never failed to put them at ease. It was even working on me. A little.

Two nurses I didn't recognize appeared in my room. "We've paged Dr. Hargreaves. How do you feel, Neva?"

"Fine. I want to see my baby."

"Leila is getting her," said the nurse, slipping a blood pressure cuff over my hand and dragging it up my arm. "In the meantime, let's have a look at you."

The mention of Leila's name made me look at Patrick. It might have been my imagination, but he looked like he wanted to smile. He took a seat on the side of my bed while the nurse took my temperature and read my blood pressure. When it was time to check my bleeding, the nurse glanced at Patrick, clearly expecting him to excuse himself. He didn't. I tried not to read too much into it, but my heart sang.

"Six pounds two ounces?" I asked as the nurses did their thing under the sheet.

"Yep," he said. "She's a good size."

I paused. "Full term?"

He nodded slowly and I could see he had already done the math. "Possibly even overdue." He remained silent while I took that in. "She's beautiful," he continued. "Looks like you, except her hair is black and her skin is olive. She looks sort of . . . Spanish or Greek or something."

"Italian," I whispered.

"Yes."

I stared at the sheet in front of me, so plain and blank, yet suddenly swirling.

"Anyway, I'm glad you're okay," he continued. "I was worried there for a minute. Your mother is a hero, doing a vaginal footing delivery at home. Someone suggested she should be nominated for an award."

This snapped me out of it. "They did?"

"Mmm hmm. Look, I'm sorry about—"

"Here she is!" In the doorway, Leila stood behind a bassinet. Through the clear plastic I could see a mess of black hair and a pile of pink and white striped blankets.

"Someone has been eager to see her mommy," she said. She reached into the bassinet and cradled the tiny bundle under her bottom and head. She came around the bed. "Congratulations. She's a beauty."

Leila's voice was like elevator music—I could hear it, but it was irrelevant, barely noticeable. All my attention was concentrated on the person in her arms. My daughter. She was more perfect than I could have imagined. I reached for her. In my arms, she weighed almost nothing, like a cloud of cotton candy or a bunch of daisies. I opened my mouth to tell her something, anything. But there were no words.

I was right, I realized. When I reassured mothers that it didn't matter how the baby came out, I was right. Right now, I didn't care if this baby had been beamed down to me from outer space. The special moment had happened. She was mine. And I was hers.

"She's got your chin," Patrick said.

"You think?" I puckered my chin. "I've never paid much attention to my chin. Is it a good chin?"

He smiled with something resembling fondness. "It's a very good chin."

"It's a *perfect* chin."

Grace stood in the doorway, an award-winning grin on her face. She was still dressed in the clothes she'd been wearing last night—the paisley skirt now had a sizable bloodstain on the left side. A fluorescent pink elastic dangled from a few strands of hair. She'd been through hell. Without warning, fat tears began to slide down my cheeks.

Grace crossed the room in three large steps. "Don't you cry or you'll make me cry," she said. In fact, a few tears had already escaped. "It's a happy day. I'm a nana."

We beamed at each other through tears, then dropped our eyes to the baby.

"Does she have a name?" Grace asked.

"Not yet. I only had a boy's name picked out."

"What was the boy's name?"

"Robert. Robbie."

"Your father would have loved that. But ladies are his lot in life, it seems. So no girls' names, then?"

"Nope."

In truth, I'd pretty much decided on Florence a few months back. It had occurred to me that Mom might have been offended being overlooked, but at the time I hadn't cared. Now I did.

"We'll think of something," I said, and then I noticed that Patrick had slipped out of the room. "I mean . . . I'll think of something."

"He's probably just gone to the bathroom, darling."

I looked back at Grace and saw understanding in her eyes. She nodded encouragingly. But I didn't share her optimism.

"Neva," Grace asked. "I want to ask you something. Why didn't you tell me? About the pregnancy and the father? I understand why you wouldn't tell Patrick, or people at the hospital. But why not me? You know I wouldn't have judged you, don't you?"

"Yes," I said. "I do know that."

"Then . . . why? You don't have to answer—"

"No. It's okay." I closed my eyes and exhaled. "It might sound strange, but . . . I felt like if I talked about it, it wouldn't be mine anymore. I'd barely got my head around it myself, and I knew if I shared it, you'd want to be involved. But this wasn't something I wanted to share. I thought that if I didn't keep it close, I'd lose it. Not the baby but . . . my way. And I wasn't willing to do that. Not with my baby."

I opened my eyes, steeling myself for the look of hurt on Grace's face. But it wasn't hurt I found. It was something resembling . . . pride.

"Does that make sense?" I asked.

She cupped her hand over mine. "Nothing has ever made more sense. Protecting your baby, listening to your instincts—that's what being a mother is all about. Sounds to me like you're going to be a good one."

"Mom, don't make me cry again."

It was the first time in years that I had called her Mom. It felt surprisingly right.

Suddenly I remembered that I hadn't told her the full story. "But, Mom, the baby was full term. Which means Sean isn't the father. The father is a guy I went on one date with, a month before anything happened with Sean. Not married. An accountant. An Italian guy who wears sensible shoes. A guy who now has a serious girlfriend."

I waited for Mom to scream, pursue me for more information, or do something outrageous. But she didn't. She just waited.

"So I need to tell him about her," I said.

"You mean now?"

I nodded. "It's already far too late."

"Okay." Grace stood. I couldn't believe this restrained, accepting woman was my mother. "Do you have his number?"

"Yes."

"I'll get your phone." She crossed the room to retrieve my phone from my purse, then brought it back to me. She took a few steps toward the door, then turned back. "You know . . . children are accepting little people. Much more than adults. Some have two mommies or two daddies. They have step and half and adopted siblings. They don't question it. The biological parents are important, of course. But the more people to love a child, the better, I say." She held my gaze. "He hasn't left your side, you know. Patrick, I mean. He wanted to be here when you woke up."

It took me a moment to process what she was saying. By the time I did, she had already left the room.

28

Grace

After leaving Neva's room, I roamed the hallways in search of a coffee machine. As I passed the nursery, I couldn't resist having a peek. Fathers and grandparents lined the halls, pointing at their babies from behind glass. I felt a stab of sadness. The father of my granddaughter wasn't doing that. He probably didn't even know about her yet.

I was about to turn into the waiting room opposite the nursery when I noticed Patrick among those peering at the babies. I sidled up behind him and touched his shoulder.

"Grace," he said. "Hello again."

"Are you going in?" I asked.

"No. Just doing the rounds. I'd better get back." He lifted his bag over his head so it hung across his torso. I opened my mouth to speak, but he beat me to it. "Congratulations. You have a beautiful daughter."

At first, I assumed he'd meant to say "granddaughter." But after I thought about it a little, I wasn't so sure. He was clearly in love with my daughter. And though Neva was much harder to read than Patrick, she obviously loved him too. I felt an overwhelming urge to grab Patrick and frog-march him into her room. I'd force them to admit how they felt about each other, and they'd all live happily ever after. But I resisted. It was their lives. They'd have to figure it out for themselves.

I watched until Patrick disappeared from sight. Then, while I waited for the coffees, I texted Robert.

Mommy and baby reunited. All is well. G x

After we'd gotten the all clear that Neva and the baby were okay, I'd sent him to Neva's apartment to get her some things and then to Walmart to get Onesies and sleep suits for the baby. Those little instructions were the most communication we'd had in days. Weeks. It made me sad. We had just become grandparents. More than anything, I wanted to share it with him. I stared at my phone, debating whether to call him, but ultimately, I decided not to. I dropped my phone back in my purse and grabbed the coffees.

Mom was in the family lounge, which was empty apart from a young woman who was reading a tatty picture book to a toddler. Mom turned the pages of the magazine in her lap while staring out the window. She rose to her feet when I entered. "How is she?"

"Still resting," I said, handing her the coffee.

She sat again. "And the baby?"

"Precious." I sat beside her and we both sipped our coffees. "More precious than you can possibly imagine. Neva's calling the baby's father now, to tell him about her."

Mom raised her eyebrows, but I just shrugged. I didn't have the strength to go into it now. But when her eyes lingered on my face, I saw that she wasn't asking for information. She was contemplating speaking herself.

"What is it, Mom?"

"I'm just thinking . . . perhaps I should follow the bravery of my granddaughter and admit some truths myself."

"Truths?" I laughed. "When have you not told the truth?"

I expected her to smile, but her face remained straight.

"Mom?"

"Grace," she said. "This is going to be a lot to take in. But there are some things you need to know about your father." She took a deep, raspy breath. "And about your mother."

29

Floss

Kings Langley, England, 1954

The fire had burned to embers and the room was almost as dark as the fields outside. Elizabeth lay still, her cool face cupped in my hands. It was like a horrible dream that wouldn't end. Evie held Elizabeth's wrist loosely, but I knew it had been a while since she'd felt a pulse. Still I couldn't help but feel that any second now Elizabeth's hand would move, or her eyes would jolt open. She'd been alive a few minutes ago. She'd *created* a life a few minutes ago. It couldn't end like this.

"She can't be gone." I looked desperately at Evie. "She *can't*."

Evie let go of Elizabeth's wrist. "It's been six minutes, Floss. Six minutes with no heartbeat."

She stood and walked to the window. Outside, there was not a light to be seen. There wasn't a sound in miles, apart from the crackle of the fire.

"One of us will have to ride to the phone box," she said.

Her words, flat and final, pushed me over the edge.

"No. No! It's not over."

"It is," Evie said simply, and I knew it was. No matter how I wanted to deny it, it was over.

"Who do we call?" I asked, wiping a tear from my cheek. "Sister Eileen? The police?"

"Both. And Bill."

Just the sound of his name caused a physical reaction in me. My heart felt like it was being flung against my rib cage. My chest strained like an overfilled balloon.

"Damn that man. *Damn* him to hell!"

In the bassinet, the baby began to fuss and without a thought, I snatched her up and held her to my chest. Elizabeth lay lifeless on the bed. My friend—the striking, flame-haired beauty—was gone. So skinny and pale, with a huge boggy mound on her stomach. I wanted to bathe her, comb her hair, wrap her in a warm blanket. But this wasn't what Elizabeth needed from me. She needed something much more important.

"What about Grace?" I asked.

Evie continued to stare out the window. "Grace?"

I looked down at the bundle in my arms. "The baby. Elizabeth said she wanted to name her after her mother."

Evie nodded. "Well, what happens to her is for Bill to decide."

"Like hell it is."

Now Evie did look at me.

"I'm not handing this child over to that man, Evie. Not over my dead body."

"What choice do we have?" When I didn't respond, a slight crease came to Evie's brow. "What are you suggesting, Floss?"

I wasn't sure what I was suggesting. But a second later, I was saying, "We'll tell him that the baby died as well."

Evie looked me straight in the eye. "You're talking madness. Pure madness." But her slow, careful tone gave away her true feelings. She wasn't so sure it was madness.

"I'll take her, right now, on the bike." I was talking so fast, I tripped over the words. "You've got the birth documents there—write my name down as the mother. I'll leave town tonight, go to a new village, a new country if I have to. I'll say I had her out of wedlock, or that I'm a widow. I'll raise her as my own."

"Floss—"

"I've decided. Don't try to talk me out of it."

Evie went quiet. I returned the baby to the bassinet and with shaking arms, gathered up my things. The evaporated milk, the syringe, one diaper. I felt Evie's eyes, but I didn't look. I couldn't do anything except what I needed to do. With my hands on the wool blanket that Elizabeth had knitted, I paused.

"Take it."

The voice was so soft, I wasn't sure I'd actually heard it. Slowly, I lifted my eyes to Evie's.

"Take it," she repeated. "By the time he gets home, hopefully Bill will be far too drunk to notice it's missing. You've got a long ride ahead. You'll want to make sure she's warm."

Evie and I locked eyes.

"You're right," I said, taking the blanket. "Elizabeth told me once that he often remembers nothing from when he drinks. He probably won't even remember that it existed." I finished piling everything into my bag. When I looked up, Evie was staring at me. "What is it?"

"Elizabeth said that? That Bill blacks out?"

I nodded.

Evie seemed strangely contemplative. I wasn't sure what she was thinking. She wandered over to her bag and pulled out some paperwork, then moved to the kitchen table. I picked Grace up out of her bassinet and went to stand beside her.

"Birth certificate," she said, scribbling on the page. "It's dated two weeks ago, so people don't question why you're out and about with a newborn."

She seemed calm, in control. Much more than I was. She held out the page.

"What are you going to do, Evie?" I asked.

Evie's eyes drifted over to Elizabeth, then down to the baby that was snuggled peacefully against me. "Same as you. I'm going to make sure Bill never gets his hands on that baby."

It took over an hour to tell Grace everything, and while I did, she just listened, never once interrupting, flying off the handle, or dissolving into dramatic, disillusioned tears. I wished she *would* do that, or at least do something familiar to reassure me that she was actually still my daughter. Even though she wasn't.

"So what did you do?" she asked. "Once you left the house?" Her words felt distant, as though they didn't belong to her.

"I wrapped you up, wedged you in the basket of my bike and cycled faster than I ever had in my life. I reached the boardinghouse before sunrise, packed my things in the dark, and took the first train to London."

"And then?"

"I went to my parents' house. I told them you were born out of wedlock. They were Irish Catholic, and I knew it was about the only thing I could've said to get my father to cough up the money for the passage to America. An unwed daughter with a baby would've been a disaster. I stayed with them for two weeks, long enough to get a passport for you and me, and then they deposited me on the ship. And that was that."

Grace was silent for a long time, perhaps longer than she'd ever been in my company. As she sat, her fingers trailed up and down her legs, dragging the fabric of her long skirt with them.

"Why didn't Evie take the baby? Take . . . me."

The question baffled me. In all these years, the idea had never occurred to me.

"I'm not sure. Evie was engaged, I suppose. She couldn't just turn up overnight with a baby. But I was single. I was able to move far away. No one knew I'd even been at Elizabeth's house that night. Evie was her midwife, I'd just gone as a favor to Elizabeth. I suppose it made sense." I frowned, trying to think about it more. "It sounds strange, I suppose, but I think . . . in both of our minds . . . the second Elizabeth died, you became mine."

There was a tiny lift in Grace. So tiny, most wouldn't even have noticed. I liked to think it was something that only a mother would notice.

"What happened when my father got home and found his wife dead and his baby missing?"

"For a long time, I didn't know," I admitted. "It took me two years before I dared to write to Evie. Six weeks later, she wrote back."

"And?"

The letter was still in the front pocket of my purse and I plucked it out. "I think this contains the answers you're looking for, dear."

Over the years, I'd become pretty good at knowing what my daughter was thinking. But as Grace looked from the letter to me, then back again, the skill deserted me. I watched as she opened it. Though I knew its contents by heart, I read along over her shoulder.

Dearest Floss,

After two years I had all but given up hope of hearing from you again. I was overjoyed to receive your letter, and to hear that you and Grace are healthy and well. I was also glad to hear that you're still practicing midwifery. I wasn't sure I'd continue myself after that night. I thought that with each new mother I'd see Elizabeth, and with each new baby, Grace. I blamed myself for Elizabeth's death for a long time. But there's something about what we do, isn't there? Something about new life that helps to heal old wounds. I hope you've found it to be the comfort that I have these past years.

I hounded your poor mother for months after you left. The hardest part of not knowing was not being able to picture you and Grace. Were you walking along a beach somewhere? Rocking on a porch swing? Trudging through the snow? I realize, of course, that

I'm not the only one with gaps in my knowledge. I'm sure you've wondered many times what happened after you pedaled away into the night with Grace. And as much as I am loath to revisit it, even in my memory, I believe it is necessary so all of us can finally close this chapter.

After you left, I bathed Elizabeth. I combed her hair and changed her linen. Perhaps it was silly, but after what Bill had put her through in life, I wanted her to have some dignity in death. A car pulled up just after sunup. The publican was driving Bill, and I could hear the singing from inside. I made sure my bicycle was out front, where it could be seen, then I slipped out the back door. Once Bill was inside and the car had disappeared over the hill, I cycled the two miles to the pay phone.

I told Sister Eileen that Elizabeth delivered a healthy baby girl before she died, and that I'd left her in the arms of her father. I also told her Bill was drunk and upset, and I was concerned for her welfare. Sister Eileen, Dr. Gregory, and Sergeant Lynch picked me up at that phone box fifteen minutes later. When we arrived at the house, Bill was nowhere to be seen. A search went out immediately, and he was found before breakfast, passed out, on the side of the road near Wharton's Creek. Everyone assumed that he'd drowned the baby in his grief. I think Bill himself assumed that, as he didn't dispute my version of events. For once, those blackouts that terrified Elizabeth served some good.

Bill was charged, but not convicted. Without a body or a witness, there wasn't enough evidence. But everyone thought he'd done it. He had to leave town. Beating up on your wife was one thing, but drowning a baby daughter was more than a little place like Kings Langley could handle. I like to think that Bill got his dues, but who knows? The most important thing was that he didn't get Grace.

It's funny, I've probably watched over a hundred women become mothers over the years. But you should know that none stand out as much as the moment I watched you become one. The way you stared at her? The way you instinctively held her to your heart? Perhaps it's an odd thing to say, but . . . it almost feels like she was yours all along.

Thinking of you both always,
Your friend,
Evie

"Is he—" Grace's voice caught, but she cleared her throat and tried again. "—is Bill still alive?"

"No, dear. Evie wrote a few years ago to tell me he'd passed away."

Grace nodded. Her face was dry. Blank. I could just about handle any emotion from her—and I'd seen many over the years—but no emotion was another story.

"Why didn't you tell me?" she asked.

There were several answers. I worried for her safety. I didn't want her near him. I feared the legal consequences of what I'd done. But none of them were the truth. "I was afraid if I told you, you wouldn't think of me as your mother anymore."

I felt foolish enough just saying it, but waiting for her to reassure me felt more foolish. *You're my mother,* I wanted her to say. *You'll always be my mother.* But she didn't reassure me. She didn't say anything. I wanted to hang my head, to cover my face with my hands. But I forced myself to hold her gaze. This wasn't about my need to be validated as a mother. It was about Grace.

"Am I . . . like him?" she asked. "Bill?"

"No. You're like Elizabeth." I forced myself to say the words. "You're very much like your mother."

"I am?"

I nodded. "In looks and in personality. Elizabeth was great fun. Loving. Adventurous. A midwife too. She was the one who gave you and Neva your beautiful hair color."

Grace glanced up abruptly, catching her reflection in the window. She turned her head from side to side. It was almost as if she was seeing herself for the first time.

Her lips upturned slightly. Not a smile exactly. But not that lost, empty look I'd seen on her face a moment earlier. It made me wonder if Lil was right. Perhaps it wasn't the lack of a father that had damaged Grace. Perhaps it had been the secret all along.

30

Neva

Mark was in the doorway. He looked the same. Tall. Dark. Clean-cut. Still, I nearly didn't recognize him, his expression was so cold and disbelieving.

"Come in," I said when he made no move to enter.

He surveyed the room. Mark wasn't stupid. I was sitting up in bed, propped up by several pillows. My daughter lay in my arms. It didn't take a genius to figure out that you didn't call an insignificant ex-lover to come and visit you and your newborn in the hospital if you didn't have a bombshell to drop.

He walked inside cautiously, as if any step might set off a grenade. His eyes found the baby. "Is it a boy or a girl?"

"A girl."

"And she's mine?"

"Yes."

He cursed quietly and twisted away from me. "*Why* didn't you tell me?"

"I didn't think she was yours. But she arrived last night . . . and she's full term. Full lung capacity, a good size. Black hair." I paused. "So she's yours."

He took a couple of steps toward the door, then abruptly turned back. "So . . . you're not on the pill?"

"I have this condition, polycystic ovaries, so the chances of getting pregnant spontaneously are slim. It was just . . ." Looking down at my daughter, I couldn't use the word "unlucky." Instead I let my voice trail off. Mark didn't seem to notice.

"But you're a *midwife*," he cried. "How can you miscalculate a date by a month?"

"Because of my condition, I rarely get periods. I went on the baby's measurements. . . . Turns out she was small."

Mark looked desperate. He strode to the fogged-up window, placed both hands on the sill. "What about the other guy? Has he been given the good news, that he's off the hook in daddy duties?"

"I never told him. He was married and . . . it was complicated. I didn't think he needed to know."

"Lucky him," Mark said. He remained that way, at the window, for several seconds, breathing audibly. Then he whipped around to face me. "Imogen and I got engaged last week, did you know that?" He barely paused before continuing. "Anyway, how do I know you're not lying now?"

It was a valid question. After everything I'd put him through, why should he take my word for it? He didn't know me well, and what he did know of me was that I was a liar, a liar who'd turned his world upside down. "I guess we'll have to look into a paternity test," I said.

He nodded. "I guess we will."

We remained in silence for several minutes. I wanted to talk to Mark, to beg for forgiveness, to throw myself on his mercy. But this wasn't about me.

"Can I hold her?" he asked.

Instinctively, my arms tightened around her. But with a little effort, I loosened them again. Mark was her father; he had a right to hold her. In fact, he had many more rights, and I'd denied them all so far. Yet, here he stood before me, waiting patiently for my agreement. "Yes," I said. "Of course you can."

I held her out and he froze, as though he couldn't believe I'd said yes. But when he took her, he cradled her with the utmost care, barely moving an inch. He reminded me of a child carrying a mug of hot coffee.

"She looks like my mother," he said quietly.

"She does?"

He nodded. "She passed away two months ago."

I closed my eyes. Another person who'd suffered because of my decision. Deep inside, I felt a quiet resolve build. "What was her name? Your mother?"

"It was . . . Mietta."

"Mietta," I repeated. "I love it."

Mark's eyes met mine briefly. Then he dropped his gaze back to the baby. "Is that your name?" he asked her. "Mietta?"

"If it's all right with you, I'd like to call her Mietta Grace," I said. "Then she'll be named after both her grandmothers."

He nodded. "It's all right with me."

We remained that way, staring at our daughter until someone cleared their throat.

Mark and I looked up simultaneously. Patrick was standing in the doorway. He was wearing his hospital accreditation on his lanyard, probably for ease of getting around the nursery. Security was tight in maternity wards.

"Sorry," he said. "I didn't know you had company."

"It's all right, Doctor," Mark said. "I'm not going anywhere, so you may as well examine her now."

Mark looked back at Mietta, so he missed the slap of pink that hit Patrick's cheeks.

"Oh . . . ," I said. "No . . . this isn't the doctor—well, he *is* a doctor, but he's actually, he's . . ." I twisted my mouth around, trying to find the right thing to say.

"Patrick Johnson," he said, extending his hand. His eyes flickered to mine, then returned to Mark. "And you are . . . ?"

Mark slid the baby up his arm, freeing one hand with which to shake Patrick's. He smiled, oblivious.

"Mark Bartolucci. I'm the baby's father."

I'd never seen Patrick at a loss for words before. Perhaps from his experience dealing with anxious parents, he'd learned to be quick to smile or make a joke or just come up with the right thing to say at the right time. That skill deserted him now.

Mark, by now, looked wary. He was starting to get the picture.

"Mark, can you give us a minute, please?" I asked.

I thought Mark was going to refuse, which would have been under-standable, considering he had just been introduced to the daughter he knew nothing about. But eventually he handed Mietta back to me.

"Actually, I'm going to go, Neva. I have to talk to . . . family and things. I'll call you tomorrow and we can, um, make a plan."

Vaguely I wondered what on earth that plan would look like, but I didn't want to be bothered with those details now. "Okay," I said. "I'll speak to you then."

He jerked forward and planted an awkward kiss on Mietta's head, then hovered there for a couple of beats, smelling her, maybe. "See you soon," he whispered.

"So that's the guy?" Patrick said, once Mark had left. "Seems nice enough."

"He's engaged," I said, though I don't know why.

Patrick sighed. "So what happens now?"

The plan Patrick and I had to share the child care while both working part-time seemed too perfect to have ever been real.

"Go back to my apartment, I guess. Start my life with my daughter."

He nodded. I wanted him to say that he'd be there. That all the plans we'd made still stood, and this was just the beginning for us. He didn't.

"You'll be a great moth—"

"Patrick?" The words leapt out of my mouth before I could process them.

"Yes?"

I choked on my tongue. What did I want to say? Stay? Let's go back to the way things were? I know what I did was unforgivable, but . . . can you forgive me?

"Can you stay awhile?"

When it boiled down to it, it was the only thing I felt I could ask him. He might say no, but that, I could cope with. I couldn't cope with him saying no to a life with me and my daughter.

A reluctant smile crept across his face. "Yes. I can stay awhile."

31

Grace

It was a day for letters.

When I arrived home from the hospital, a letter awaited me on the hall table. I didn't need my glasses to recognize the stationery—it was from the Board of Nursing. I waited for the rush of joy or fear. Anticipation. Trepidation. Nothing came. It was hard to believe that just a day ago, my whole life was pinned on the contents of this letter. Now, I still wanted to practice midwifery again; I wanted it badly. But somehow the letter in my purse had put it all in perspective.

In the sitting room, I fell into an armchair and tore my thumbnail along the top of the envelope. The font was small, and a large blue signature was scrawled at the bottom. I lowered my reading glasses from my head, and read from the top.

Dear Mrs. Bradley,

With regards to the complaint filed against you for negligence in the management of labor for Mrs. G. Brennan, we are writing to advise that we have thoroughly investigated the claim, and spoken to all parties involved in the matter. We are pleased to inform you that we have found no evidence to support the allegations; therefore, this case has been closed. Your record is clear of any charges.

Sincerely,
Marie Ableman
Board of Nursing

I reread the letter. That was it. One typed paragraph, and it was over. I wasn't going to lose my license. It was good news, yet for some reason, it felt anticlimactic. Perhaps it was because so many questions remained. Would Robert forgive me? Would we find our way back to each other after everything that had happened?

"Grace." Robert appeared in the doorway. "You're home. I didn't hear you come in."

"Seriously? It feels like my legs are made of lead."

He eyed the letter in my hand.

"Oh," I said. "The Board of Nursing let me off. I'm not guilty."

Robert slapped the arm of the couch and cheered. Then he looked at me. "That's it? That's how you make the announcement? No megaphone? No squealing?"

"Do I look like I have the energy to squeal?"

He sat in the chair opposite me. "Well, this is fantastic."

"Mmm-hmm. Seems to be a day for news."

"What does that mean?"

"Long story."

Robert, bless his heart, seemed to accept that. In his polo shirt and jeans, he looked young and carefree. I did a double take. Polo shirt? Jeans? It was a Tuesday. "Robert, why aren't you at work?"

He sank further into his chair. "I got a letter of my own yesterday. Said I didn't need to go to work today. Or any day."

I shot upright.

"Don't get upset," he said. "It's not the end of the world. It's a *job*. Not as important as our daughter. Or our granddaughter." He leaned forward and put his hand over mine. "Or you."

"But—"

"Grace, you blew me away yesterday. I used to chuckle when you called your job magic. But you saved our daughter's and our granddaughter's lives. That *is* magic. I get how you can't stop doing it." He smiled at me so softly, it gave me tingles. "What I do? It's not magic. It's just numbers."

"But it's important. Robert, we need the money. We can't survive on magic."

"I got a couple of months' salary in my severance package. And if I don't find something else, we'll sell the house." He shrugged, as indifferent as I'd seen him in years. "It's just a house."

I blinked. Was this the same man who'd hardly eaten or slept for weeks, worrying about his job and the future? Was he putting up a brave front for my sake?

"Are you sure you're okay, Rob?"

"Actually it's a relief," he said. "When something is forced upon you, you have no choice but to deal with it. The uncertainty—the *not* knowing—was much worse."

I laughed. "Funnily enough, I know *exactly* what you mean."

32

Floss

In some ways, telling Neva was harder than telling Grace. She broke down in tears, which perhaps was to be expected, but I didn't expect it of Neva. Some of it may have been to do with her hormones, but I suspected it was more than that. I was coming to realize that Grace was a lot stronger than I'd given her credit for. And Neva, perhaps, was more fragile.

I remained by her side until she fell asleep, but as the sky began to darken, I thought of Lil. I was desperate for her, desperate to tell her I had a great-granddaughter, desperate to tell her I'd told Grace the truth. I wrote a note to Neva, telling her to call any time, day or night, and planted a kiss on her forehead. Then I slipped out.

Back home, I had only just turned the key in the lock when the door opened. Lil stood behind it in her house slippers with a tea towel draped over her shoulder.

"You're home!" she said. "Come in, come in." I followed her into the foyer. "You must be starving."

She disappeared into the kitchen before I could say a word. I noticed two places were set at the dining table. The sight of it warmed my heart. And although I wasn't in the least bit hungry, I'd have happily eaten an entire horse if that's what Lil produced.

"Salad," she said when she returned, setting a glass bowl in the center of the table. "I thought you'd probably want something light."

Lil smiled and a small part of my heart, a broken part, snapped back against the whole—a perfect fit. "You thought right, dear."

We sat in comfortable silence, our smiles speaking the words we couldn't. I had no secrets anymore. At eighty-three, I finally understood what it was to have peace. I wanted to bottle it—swaddle it—and share it with the world. I no longer had anything to fear.

As we finished our salad, the doorbell rang. A few moments later, Grace appeared at the head of the table.

"Grace!" I wiped the corners of my mouth on a napkin. "Hello."

"Can I have a word, Mom?"

I glanced at Lil. She was already standing up and clearing the dishes away. "Of course," I said. "Come into the sitting room."

We sat down on opposite ends of the couch. The act of sitting there with my daughter, so comfortable only a day ago, now felt awkward.

"I want to thank you for telling me the truth," she started.

I tensed. I knew what was coming. She'd want to know more about Bill. More about Elizabeth. She'd want family trees, photographs. And why shouldn't she? She had a family history to reconstruct. The least I could do was to help her.

"—but if it's all right with you, I'd like to pretend you didn't."

I stared at her. "I'm sorry?"

"It's an amazing story. But what you did for me just proves that, if you weren't my mother to begin with, you are now. I'd have liked to know Elizabeth, but . . . I can't say I'm unhappy with how things worked out. Sometimes things happen exactly the way they are supposed to."

"Grace—" I struggled to take a breath. "Really? I thought when I told you this, you'd be determined to take off for England, to . . . I don't know . . . find answers. I'd understand if you did. Are you sure you don't want to?"

"I'll never say never," she said. "But right now I'm pretty happy with the status quo. I have a good relationship with my daughter. I have a precious new granddaughter. I have a wonderful husband. And—" Her smile was almost shy. "—I have a mother who literally went to hell and back to protect me."

Grace was crying and, I realized, so was I. I exhaled. "If you're sure. But if you change your mind, and I can help you, just let me know."

I glanced at the archway a split second before Lil appeared in it. After all our time together, I could anticipate her movements.

"I'm going to head on up to bed and give you two some privacy," she said. "Nice to see you, Grace."

"No," I said, struggling to my feet. "Don't go. I'd really like it if you stayed."

Lil looked at Grace, who now was also on her feet. She nodded vigorously. "Yes, Lil. Please stay."

"No. You two need time. You don't need me hanging around——"

"Nonsense," Grace said. She hooked Lil's arm in her own and brought her back to the sofa. Lil's cheeks, I noticed, pinkened a little. "You're family. And we don't have any secrets from family."

"No, we don't," I said, taking Lil's other hand. "Not anymore."

33

Neva

Before I was released from the hospital, Mark visited again, this time with Imogen. I was surprised—and at first, resistant—when he asked if he could bring her to the hospital. The idea of someone else touching my daughter, holding her—it felt too soon. But it wasn't about me. Mark had every right to introduce his daughter to his fiancée. More importantly, Mietta had the right to know them.

"She looks like Mom, don't you think?" Mark asked Imogen.

Imogen frowned, shaking her long hair back off her face. "Yeah. I guess so."

They'd been in my room for half an hour, and Imogen still hadn't looked me in the face. I got the feeling she thought that if she ignored me heartily enough, I might actually disappear. I couldn't blame her. Until today, I hadn't given too much thought to how this whole situation would affect Imogen. Now I did. Her whole world as she knew it had been turned upside down. But she was here. And she was doing her best.

"Would you like to hold her?" Mark asked Imogen.

Imogen shook her head. "No. I shouldn't."

"It's fine with me," I said, a little reluctantly.

Mark brought the baby closer. "Go on. Hold her."

Her gaze hovered on Mietta for a moment. Then she said, "Fine. Why not?"

Imogen got herself settled in the hospital armchair, then looked at Mark, palms upturned. "Okay," she said. "I'm ready."

I fought my instinct to give instructions. *Be gentle. Support her head.* They were competent adults. For someone who didn't have any children (that I knew of) Imogen was actually remarkably comfortable. Maternal, even. It was bittersweet. I hated having another mother figure holding my daughter. But at the same time, I was grateful Imogen's feelings for me didn't seem to extend to Mietta. I actually got the feeling from the way she smiled at her that, if I were out of the picture, Mietta might even be welcomed.

"I'm sorry, Imogen," I heard myself say. "I know how difficult this must be for you. And it's not fair. None of this is your fault."

"I realize that." She still didn't look at me. "It's *your* fault."

It was a figurative slap in the face, and I accepted it. "Yes."

That must have appeased her a little, because after a short silence, she sighed. "But she's Mark's daughter, so I have to make the best of it." She looked at Mark, standing beside her chair. "That's what you do when you love someone. You stick by them, even when life throws you . . . other people's babies."

Imogen and Mark smiled at each other. I got the feeling that her little speech was for his benefit rather than mine. But I was glad I'd heard it too. It made me think about Patrick and the way that, despite what life had thrown at us, he had stuck by me.

I was getting released. For the first time in days, I was dressed and wearing shoes. I sat in the hospital nursing chair with Mietta in my arms, sucking in her sweet scent. My parka was draped over my arm.

"Knock, knock." A wheelchair nosed around the door, pushed by Susan. She parked it beside the bed and sidled up, her twinkling eyes defying her no-nonsense expression. "Ah. Look at the wee thing." She broke into a full smile. "She's a beauty."

"Thanks, Suse."

"Mom and Dad on their way?"

"Nope," I said. "It's just us. I'm going back to my apartment."

Mom had asked me to come back home for a while, but I don't think she expected me to agree. I had to do this on my own. At least, that was what I'd told her. But I was talking a lot braver than I felt. It was probably just the hormones, but I'd been on the verge of tears all morning.

A frown etched into Susan's forehead. "By yourself? How are you going to get home?"

"Cab." I waved my hand to stop her worrying. "We'll be fine."

"No such thing. You can't take your baby home to your apartment alone in a cab. Let me get my coa—"

"It's okay, Susan. I'm here."

In the doorway, in her turtleneck sweater and jeans, was Mom. It wasn't the dramatic entrance I was used to—it was much more like the way I would arrive, without fanfare. She carried no balloons or flowers or banners. Her clothes were plain and her hair pulled back off her face. I barely recognized her.

"Mom."

"I know you wanted to do this yourself, but—"

The tears I'd held at bay for hours finally pushed over my lids. "I'm so glad you're here."

"Well, hallelujah!" Susan smiled as she snapped down the sides of the wheelchair. She muttered something about being glad she didn't have to go out in this weather, and then reached for Mietta. "May I?" I nodded and she took the baby and handed her to Mom. "Hold your granddaughter for me, would you? There's a love."

While Susan helped me into the wheelchair—a requirement of discharge that I really didn't need—I couldn't stop staring at Mom and Mietta. Mom held her close to her face and stared, right in her eyes. I'd seen Mom with babies before—she loved them. But this was different. They were connected by so much more than a gaze. I would have said it was a biological pull, but now, thinking of Gran, I wasn't so sure.

Susan gathered up my things and I signed a hundred documents before we started to roll. In the hallway, Mom started to talk.

"Now, I hope you don't mind, darling, but your father is at your apartment."

"Oh?"

"Yes, well . . . there were a few things in the baby's room that needed doing. I know you're independent, but I couldn't let you go home to a house without a crib or a—"

"It's okay, Mom. Thank you."

"Thank your father. The stroller was a little tricky, but I think he figured it out."

Without warning, my eyes filled again. I looked at my lap. "Good. That's . . . great."

Susan started a low cough, and the chair rolled to a halt.

"Hello, Dr. Johnson."

I lifted my head. Patrick stood in front of me in green scrubs and a white jacket. He'd been by to visit me every day during my stay. He'd even held Mietta a few times. We hadn't discussed "us" during the visits, though. I wasn't ready for my last ray of hope to be extinguished, so I didn't bring it up. Patrick probably didn't bring it up, because there was nothing to say. Still, I enjoyed the visits. And I would miss them.

"Going-home day?"

I nodded. "I can't believe it."

"And how's this little one doing?" He bent, pushing back Mietta's blanket to look her over in a way that I knew was instinct for him, a pediatrician. "You look pretty good to me."

He smiled as he closed the blanket up again. I fought the urge to cry.

"Dad got that stroller set up," I said. Why, I had no idea. Perhaps just to fill the silence.

"He did?" Patrick frowned. He didn't like being beaten.

Beside me, Mom and Susan hovered awkwardly. The silence drifted on. I could feel their eyes, waiting for me to wind up the conversation. I didn't. But Patrick didn't either.

"Well, then," Susan said eventually. Her tone indicated that she thought we were both a little loopy. "I guess we'd better—" I felt my chair start to roll.

"I have a present for Mietta," Patrick said, as if he'd just remembered, or perhaps, just decided to tell me. Susan stopped pushing. "Maybe I could come by sometime and give it to her? Once you've had a chance to get settled."

"Yes," I said. "We would love that."

"Good. I would too." He bent forward, filling my airspace with his scent, and planted a brusque kiss on my cheek. "I guess I'll see you soon."

I nodded. "Yes. I guess you will."

Mom and Dad stayed the first night at my apartment.

Like so many of the mothers I'd cared for over the years, I didn't sleep a wink. Every time my lids became heavy, fear clamped around my heart. If I didn't watch her constantly, would she remember to breathe? What if she spit up and then choked on it? What if? What if? What if?

At some point, I couldn't fight it anymore. Just one second, I'd rest my eyes. Just . . . one . . . second . . .

At 3 A.M., I jerked upright, frantically taking in my surroundings. Where was I? I was home. With my baby. I snapped my head up and looked over the rim of her bassinet. It was empty.

I shot through the house so fast that I got dizzy. Mom was asleep in my bed. No Mietta. I dashed up the hall into the sitting room and stabbed at the light switch. As the room illuminated, Dad thrust out a hand, shielding the light from his eyes. He sat in the recliner. Mietta was cradled against his chest.

"Dad." I held my chest. "You gave me a heart attack." I switched off the light and turned on the small lamp.

"Sorry, darling. She was fussing a bit, and you were asleep—so I just brought her out here. She's fine now."

I looked her over. She did look positively blissed out. Dad's hand covered her bottom, and he stroked her back with two fingers. He'd probably held me that same way once.

"Do you want me to take her?" I asked.

"No. You sleep. We're having some Papa-and-me time."

I smiled. "Papa, is it?"

"Oh, I don't know. Grampy? Gramps? Poppa? I don't care."

He kissed the top of her head. My smile widened. My daughter would have a Papa. It was a relationship I had no frame of reference for, but I had a feeling it would be an important one.

"Now, off with you," he said sleepily. "Mietta and I have some bonding to do."

I skulked back to my bed. In the next room, Mom was already snoring. My daughter was asleep in the living room. And, with my dad watching over us all, my eyelids fluttered closed.

The next week passed in a blur, and I didn't go out of the house once. Mom and Dad went home. I had mixed feelings about them leaving, and it was hard watching them go, but once they left and it was just me and Mietta, I felt a strange sort of content. Patrick called, a couple of times, but he had a knack for calling when I was asleep or in the shower. Once, he left a voice message, saying he hoped we were doing okay and was looking forward to seeing us soon. Another time, he texted, asking to see a photo. I thought these were good signs, but I didn't want to read too much into them. I was in self-preservation mode.

Mietta and I camped out on my bed: sleeping, breast-feeding, and snuggling. The hormones must have buoyed my mood, because although I still thought about Patrick, and I still desperately hoped that we might have a chance together, I knew my world wouldn't fall apart if things didn't work out. No, I held my world—my tiny, pink world—next to my heart, virtually at all times. I'd always thought the idea of being attached to your baby at all times, as Mom advocated, was a little much. Sleeping in the same room, carrying them strapped to your chest—I thought it was her hippie mumbo jumbo on crack. But during the week that my daughter had been in the world, I'd realized both of us were happier that way. Turned out Mom knew more than I gave her credit for. About a lot of things.

Dad, who was unemployed, came by every day—even more than Mom—to see his granddaughter. Gran and Lil had visited twice, once with roast chicken. I wanted to enjoy living in my bubble for a little longer, but I knew I would have to go outside soon. Anne had called and said everyone at the birthing center was champing at the bit to meet Mietta. And it hadn't escaped me that it might be a chance to run into Patrick. Even if things could never be as they were, I missed him. I had the feeling that glimpsing him—in the real world—would give me a good indication of how the land lay.

On the eighth day, I pushed Mietta to the birthing center in her new stroller. It felt good to be outside. It was a brilliant, blue-skied day. The snow had turned to mush at our feet, but my heavy-duty stroller made easy work of it. The week indoors had done nothing for my complexion.

I'd slapped some pink on my cheeks and brushed my hair and squeezed into jeans and a bright blue knitted poncho. It was amazing the lift dressing up gave me. Even Mietta seemed happier to see me. I hoped she wasn't going to be the only one.

I decided to head to the birthing center through the hospital, even though it had a street entrance. I told myself it was to get out of the slush, but I wasn't kidding anyone, even myself. I knew whom I was hoping to see. The halls were pretty quiet. I passed a few familiar faces, I even waved to a few folks, but no Patrick. Then, as I turned the final corner, I heard my name.

Sean beamed at me. "Wow! You look fantastic." He hugged me. "And look at this. A beautiful baby girl."

Sean and I smiled into the stroller, and though it was probably gas, Mietta smiled back.

"There you go, she's got good taste. Already recognizes a handsome man when she sees one."

"She just thinks you're funny-looking, Sean."

"By the way," he said, his selective hearing as good as ever. "I heard about the birth. Your mom is an absolute hero."

I couldn't hide my smile. "She sure is."

"What a coup for midwifery, eh? Dr. Hargreaves is really excited about it—she wants your mom to come and speak to the Obstetrics department."

"Really? I'm sure she'd be happy to do that." It was the understatement of the century. Grace telling doctors how to suck eggs? It would be the highlight of her life.

"I bet her business is booming. It was all over the newspapers: 'Breech Baby Delivered Amid Conanicut Island Blizzard.' What a headline."

"I don't know if her business is booming. We haven't talked about it. All we've talked about is the baby since she was born."

He smiled. I smiled.

A doctor across the foyer caught Sean's eye, and he held up one finger. "Well look, I have to run. Glad I got to meet your darling daughter." Offhandedly, he pecked my cheek. "You girls take care of each other."

"We will. Bye, Sean."

I hadn't expected all the fanfare at the birthing center. Anne had made chocolate-chip muffins, and a few of the midwives who weren't even on shift had come in. Only one woman was in labor, and it was the early stages, so we managed to have a little party in the foyer.

"Tell us about the birth," Anne said between fielding calls. "We're dying to hear!"

I retold the story of Mietta's birth several times to gasps and covered mouths, and funnily, quite enjoyed being the center of attention. Particularly on this subject, which I found quite interesting. Since Mietta's birth, I'd read everything I could find on vaginal footing births and was constantly on YouTube, watching it happen. If I could have a successful safe vaginal footing delivery, I was determined to find out if others could too.

Mietta was passed around from person to person. It was quite nice having my arms free for a while. Talking to adults was also a nice change of pace. I chatted happily but kept my eyes trained on the door.

Susan sat by my side the whole time, and every now and again, I reached out and gave her hand a squeeze.

The party crumbled when two clients arrived in progressed labor.

"We must do this again soon," Anne said when the phone rang for the fifteenth time. She scrambled back to her desk. I took my cue, bundling Mietta back into her winter suit. While I waited for her to hang up so I could say good-bye, I felt—actually felt—Patrick arrive.

He wore a gray winter coat over a T-shirt and jeans. A leather bag crossed over one shoulder. His lips were curled into a preliminary smile. "Hi."

Anne hung up the phone, still scribbling a message. "Okay. Do you need help getting out, Neva?"

"It's okay, Anne. I'll help her."

Anne's head snapped up. When she located Patrick, she inhaled sharply.

"Thank you for the party," I said, before she could speak. "I won't hang around. I see you're busy."

I held Mietta out for her to kiss, which she did, studying my face. I worked to keep it carefully neutral and avoided her stare. I felt like my feet might rise right up off the floor at any moment, and one pointed look from Anne, I knew, would be enough to send me into a full-blown panic.

Patrick commandeered the stroller and snaked it one-handedly out the door. I followed him down the hallway and through the automatic doors into the cold, sunny day. Once we got there, though, I had no idea what to say.

"I have a joke—" I started, but Patrick cut in.

"Sorry," he said, "I just want to say this first. I'm sorry about how I reacted. When you told me about Sean."

I opened my mouth.

"I was jealous," he said louder, making it clear he was going to finish. "But I shouldn't have left you on the stairs like that. I shouldn't have let you believe that it would change things between us." He blinked, frowned; then his face morphed into a soft smile. "Why are you crying?"

I reached up and touched my wet cheek. I *was* crying. "Because I love you. And I couldn't have blamed you if you'd changed your mind—"

"I didn't change my mind. Just so we're clear on that. And"—he blushed—"I love you, too."

A tear dripped off my chin. I laughed. I was crying. I was professing my love for a man on the street. All the things I'd known to be true about myself were fast proving to be lies.

Patrick grinned. "Oh, I nearly forgot. Here. I've been meaning to give you this." He fished a package, wrapped in white paper covered in yellow rattles, from his bag. "For Mietta. I bought it a while back. Before . . . well, you know. But I thought you still might like it."

I wiped my cheek and took the gift. "Should I . . . open it now?"

"Yeah. Why not?"

As I slipped my hands out of my gloves, I saw they were shaking. I started to pick at the tape on one end and then decided to take a leaf out of my mother's book and tear it off in one go. Patrick laughed. The sound of it unraveled something in me, something that had been wrapped too tight for too long.

A book with a pale green cover stared back at me. BABY'S FIRST YEAR.

I opened the cover. The brightly colored pastel pages reminded me of the paint swatches Patrick and I had picked out for the nursery a lifetime ago. "Thank you," I said. "We don't have one of these."

"Well, now you do."

I turned the page. At first it looked blank, but then I noticed the scrawly, doctorly pencil marks along the right-hand side. MOMMY'S NAME IS *Neva*. DADDY'S NAME IS *Patrick*.

I glanced up. Patrick blushed. "I filled it in before she was born, obviously, but you can change it to Mark's name if you want."

His face was carefully neutral, his hands dug into pockets, shoulders sloped down. A strange stillness came over him. I couldn't even see the rise and fall of his breath.

"Well . . . there's a bit of space here," I said slowly, looking back at the book. Maybe we can leave it and . . . just add Mark's name?"

Patrick's chest began to move again. "Sure. We could do that . . . if you want."

Now we both smiled shyly. My insides tickled—that feeling when you've won a race and you're just waiting for it to be announced to the crowd. We rocked back and forth a few times, grinning stupidly.

"So . . . ," I started. "Gran and Lil are coming over later. They'd love to watch Mietta for a few hours. We could . . . I don't know . . . go for coffee or something—"

"Actually, I was hoping the *three* of us could go for coffee," he said. "You, Mietta, and me?" His lips curled into a sexy half smile. How did he always know the exact thing to say?

"Nellie's?" I said.

He nodded. "Nellie's." He started to push the stroller he had failed to assemble. "So what was the joke?"

"Ah yes," I said. "Two babies were sitting in their cribs when one called over to the other: 'Are you a little girl or a little boy?' 'I don't know,' replied the other baby. 'What do you mean, you don't know?' asked the first. 'I mean I don't know how to tell the difference.' 'Well, I do,' said the first baby, chuckling. 'I'll climb into your crib and find out.' So he carefully maneuvered himself into the other baby's crib, then disappeared beneath the blanket. After a couple of minutes, he resurfaced with a big grin on his face. 'You're a little girl and I'm a little boy,' he said proudly. 'You're so clever,' cooed the baby girl. 'But how can you tell?' 'It's easy,' replied the baby boy. 'You've got pink booties and I've got blue ones.'"

I grinned at Patrick expectantly. "Good, right?"

"No." But he chuckled. "Terrible."

He kept walking, and I fell into step beside him. "Come on. Like you can talk."

With one hand on the stroller and the other slung low around my waist, Patrick maneuvered us through the snow toward Nellie's. The sun was at our backs, and the light slid over our shoulders and onto Mietta's face. Before I could reach for the hood, Patrick quickened his step, putting himself between her and the sun. It was an instinct, a reflex. Something a father would do.

Gran was right. When it came to family, biology was only part of it. Patrick and I, Mark and Imogen, Mom and Dad, Gran and Lil— we'd give Mietta a wonderful family.

Together, the three of us turned the corner, toward Nellie's. Toward home.

1. Grace's response to Neva's refusal to reveal the identity of her baby's father is complex: "Despite my shock and frustration, a pleasant surge of adrenaline rushed through me....Neva was rebelling. And despite my desperation to know the parentage of my grandchild-to-be, I was excited." What does Grace mean by this? Why does she feel this way? How do we see the relationship between Grace and Neva change as the story progresses?

2. As Floss tells the story that she has been hiding bit by bit throughout the novel, did you have any guesses as to what the secret would ultimately be? How did your predictions change as the story was revealed? Did the truth surprise you, or were you able to figure it out?

3. Did you have any guesses as to who the father of Neva's baby was? Were you surprised when he was finally revealed?

4. Reflect on the structure of the novel. How does having all three women's viewpoints give us a complex, richer picture of the women's individual stories? How do Floss's flashbacks to her past give us insight into their present situation?

5. We are able to observe as Grace weighs her options for how to proceed during the home birth that results in her suspension. Do you think she did the right thing during the birth? What would you have done in her position? Did your opinion of what she did remain the same or change after the conversation she had with the investigator from the Board of Nursing?

6. What did you think of Grace's decision to continue to deliver babies secretly during her suspension? What was your response to Robert's reaction when he found out?

7. Grace expresses strong views on the differences between delivering a baby in a hospital versus in a birthing center versus at home. What are the differences? What are her arguments for home birth? Do you agree or disagree with her?

St. Martin's
Griffin

8. Did you learn anything new about midwifery, birthing, or pregnancy in general while reading this novel? What surprised you most about the birthing scenes?

9. When Neva watches Grace hold Mietta as they are about to leave the hospital, she observes that "They were connected by so much more than a gaze. I would have said it was a biological pull, but now, thinking of Gran, I wasn't so sure." In your opinion, what is it that defines a family? What creates a familial bond?

10. Throughout the novel, we see characters forced to confront unexpected situations and grapple with how to handle and react to them, knowing that their reactions will not only greatly affect themselves but also the other people involved. Put yourself in the position of different characters, such as Mark, Imogen, Patrick, Sean, Floss, and Neva. How would you react if you were faced with their situations? Were there certain characters that you felt especially sympathetic toward? Were there others with whom you disagreed?

Turn the page for a sneak peek at
Sally Hepworth's next novel

The Things We Keep

Available January 2016

1

Anna

Fifteen months ago . . .

No one trusts anything I say. If I point out, for example, that the toast is burning or that it's time for the six o'clock news, people marvel. How about that? It *is* time for the six o'clock news. Well done, Anna. Maybe if I were eighty-eight instead of thirty-eight, I wouldn't care. Then again, maybe I would. As a new resident of Rosalind House, an assisted-living facility for senior citizens, I'm having a new appreciation for the hardships of the elderly.

"Anna, this is Bert," someone says as a man slopes by on his walker. I've been introduced to half a dozen people who look more or less like Bert: old, ashen, hunched-over. We're on wicker lawn chairs in the streaming sunshine, and I know Jack brought me out here to make us both feel better. *Yes, you're checking into an old folks' home, but look, it has a garden!*

I wave to Bert, but my gaze is fixed across the lawn, where my five-year-old nephew, Ethan, is having coins pulled out of his ears by a man in a navy and red striped dressing gown. My mood lifts. Ethan always jokes that he's my favorite nephew, and even though I deny it in public, it's true. He's the youngest of Jack's boys, and definitely the best one.

Once, when he was four, I took him for a spin on my motorcycle. I didn't even bother asking Brayden or Hank; I knew they'd just say it was dangerous and then tattle to their mother. As far as I know, Ethan never tattled. Brayden and Hank know what's wrong with me—I can tell from the way they constantly glance at their mother when they talk to me. But Ethan either doesn't know or doesn't care. I really don't mind which one.

"And this is Clara."

Clara wanders toward us with remarkable speed (compared to the others). She's probably in her eighties—but portly, more robust looking than the rest. With a cloud of fluffy yellow-gray hair, she reminds me of a newborn chick.

"I've been looking forward to meetin' you," she says, then gives me a whiskery kiss. A burst of fragrance fills my airspace. Normally I don't like to be kissed, yet from her, the gesture feels oddly natural. And these days, I make a point of respecting people who are natural around me. "If you need anything at all, you let me know, honey," she says, then wanders off toward a huge oak tree. When she gets there, she kisses the man in the navy and red striped dressing gown full on the mouth in a way that feels vaguely territorial, like she's staking her claim.

Beside me, Jack is talking to Eric, the center's manager—a paunchy, red-faced man with a thick Tom Selleck mustache and a titter of a laugh that, by rights, should belong to a female in her eighties. Every time I hear it (which is a lot, he seems to chortle at the end of every sentence), I jerk around, looking for a ladies' auxiliary group giggling over its knitting. He and Jack talk, and I listen without really hearing. "We do a lot of activities . . . we'll keep her active . . . twenty-four-hour care and security . . . experience with dementia . . . the best possible place for her . . ."

Blah, blah, blah. Eric has a certain desperate-to-please manner about him that, a few years ago, Jack and I would have exchanged a look over, but today Jack is eating it up. He's happily oblivious to Eric's false laugh, his too-tight chinos, his gaze that wanders to the right (and vaguely near my chest), every few moments. Eric's only redeeming quality so far is that when we arrived, he asked my advice on an old knee injury that had been giving him some trouble (probably because he hoped I'd offer to give it a rub). He needed a doctor, not a paramedic, and I explained this, but I appreciated him asking. These days, the most interesting conversations I have are about my favorite color or type of food. I like it when people remember that I'm a *person*, not just a person with Alzheimer's.

Jack seems to have forgotten that. Ever since I went to live with him and Helen, he's stopped being my brother and started being my dad, which is beyond annoying. He thinks I don't hear when he and Helen whisper about me in the kitchen. That I don't notice them exchanging a look whenever I offer to walk the boys to school. That I don't see Helen trailing after me in the car, making sure I don't become disoriented on the way there.

Jack's been through this before—we both have—and I know he considers himself an expert. I have to keep reminding him that he's an attorney, not a neurologist. Anyway, the situations are different. Mom was in denial about her disease. She fought to hang on to her independence right up to the point when she burned down the family home. But I have no plans to fight the inevitable. It's why I've checked myself into residential care.

The upside of this place, if I'm choosing to be positive, is that not everyone is nuts. Jack and I looked at a few of those dementia-specific units, and they were like Zombie City, full of crazies and folks doing the seven-mile stare. This place, at least, is also for the general aging community—the ones who need their meals cooked and laundry done—kind of a hotel for the elderly (the wealthy elderly, judging by the zeros on the check Jack wrote this morning).

Still, I'm not exactly thrilled to be here. It was bad enough when Jack sent me to "day care." Seriously, that's what it's called. A day program for people *like me*. Also for people *not* like me, because with only 5 percent of Alzheimer's cases occurring in people under the age of sixty-five, there aren't a lot of people *like me*. That's what makes this situation all the more unusual. I'm not checking into just *any* residential care facility—no sirree. We've traveled all the way to Short Hills, New Jersey, from Philadelphia so I can live in a facility with someone *like me*. A guy, also with younger-onset dementia, someone Jack heard about through the Dementia Support Network. Since learning about the guy, Jack has been hell-bent on getting me into the very same care facility as him. It's like he thinks having two young people in a place filled with oldies makes it spring break instead of residential care.

"Would you like to meet Luke, Anna?" Eric asks, and Jack nods enthusiastically. Luke must be *the guy*. I wonder if he's going to rappel down from a tree or something. His entrance will have to be pretty impressive if they think it's going to make a difference to my mood.

"I just want to go to my room," I say.

Jack and Eric glance at each other, and I feel the wind leave their sails.

"Sure," Jack says. "Do you want me to take you there?"

"Nope. I'm good." I stand. I don't want to look at Jack, but he stands, too, gets right in my face so I can't look anywhere else. His eyes are full and wet, and I catch a glimpse of the softhearted man he used to be before his brushes with dementia and abandonment hardened him up.

"Anna," he says, "I know you're scared."

"Scared?" I snort, but then my vision starts to blur. I *am* scared. One thing about being a twin is that you get used to having, someone right by your side whenever you want them. But in a moment, Jack's going to leave. And I'm going to be alone.

"Get lost, would you?" I tell Jack finally. "I have a pedicure booked in half an hour. This place has a health spa, right?"

Jack laughs a little, shooing a drop from his cheek. When we were younger Jack sported a golden tan, but now his skin is vaguely gray, almost as white as my own. I suspect this has something to do with me. "Ethan! Come and say good-bye to Anna."

Ethan thunders across the lawn to us and tosses himself into my arms. He strangles me in a hug. "Bye, Anna Banana."

When he pulls away, I take a long hard look at the large white bandage covering his left cheek and try to remember the angry red burns and welts underneath. I *need* to remember them. They're the reason I'm here.

The first time I knew something was wrong with me, I was at the mall. I was lugging my bags toward the exit when I realized I had no idea where I'd parked my car. The parking lot was seven stories high. In the elevator, I stared at the buttons. None seemed any more likely than the other.

Eventually I made my way to the security booth. The man behind the desk laughed and said it happened all the time. He picked up his walkie-talkie and asked for the license plate number. When I looked blank, he smiled. "Make and model?"

It was such an easy question. But the more I tried to find the answer, the more it blacked out. Like a photograph with a question mark over the face, a criminal with his jacket over his head—something was there, but my brain wouldn't let me see.

The man's smile faded. "The color?"

All I could do was shrug. I waited for him to say *this* happened all the time. He didn't.

I caught the bus home.

If I'd been tested for the mutated gene, as Jack was, I'd have known for sure it was coming. But finding out you're going to be struck down in your prime didn't fit into my life's plan.

After that, things started happening all the time. Usually, I could explain the incidents away. Sure, I forgot a lot of appointments, but I *was* a busy paramedic. Getting lost on the way home from work was a little stressful, but directions had never been my strong suit. Unfortunately, there were things that were harder to explain. Like the time I smashed my car window with a ski pole when I couldn't get the keys to open the door (and then found out the car belonged to the family across the road). And the time I showed up to work on my rostered day off (for the fourth time in a row).

It was the time I forgot the word "twin" when introducing Jack to my buddy Tyrone, from work, that I really started to worry. It was a year after the parking lot incident. I remember staring at Jack, wondering if there was indeed a word for what we were. I searched the dark, dusty corners of my brain, but it was useless. Eventually I called him a person who my mother carried in her uterus at the same time as me. I know, I remember "uterus" but not "twin." Tyrone laughed; he'd always thought I was nutty. But Jack didn't laugh. And I knew the jig was up.

I quit my job that day. If I couldn't remember the word "twin," what would happen when I couldn't remember how to resuscitate someone or when I decided it was a good idea to move a patient with a possible neck injury? I had a feeling I'd already been off my game. And when I know something's going to happen, I don't see the point in dragging it out.

The same theory applies to life. Life's going slowly in one direction. I can stay in the slow lane, just keeping rollin' on down that hill, gathering moss and cobwebs until finally, when I come to a stop, I'm so covered in crap, I'm unrecognizable. That's what Mom did. That's what most people do. But that's never been my style.

At Rosalind House, there are a lot of drugs. Enough that everyone has their own basket. Every morning and afternoon, the nurse rolls her table-on-wheels through the halls with the baskets, a veritable candy woman of pharmaceuticals. In my basket is Aricept, a round peach-colored tablet responsible for slowing the breakdown of a compound that transmits messages between the nerve cells. Also in the basket is vitamin E, clear and yellow, long and thin. Lastly there is Celexa, a powerful antidepressant responsible for making all of this feel like no big deal. That's the one I know *for sure* isn't working.

I don't get dressed until my second week at Rosalind House.

When I do, I wonder why I bothered. All I do here is lie in bed, scribble in my journal, and stare out the window. Any visitors I might have had (Jack notwithstanding) have been told, at my request, that I'm at a facility on the other side of the country (Hey, I'm not likely to remember them anyway, and I need a "pity visit" like a hole in the head). Eric, the manager guy, stops by continually, trying to cajole me into bingo. (Yeah. Like that's gonna happen.) Various nurses and staff have popped in. But I've been out of my room only once, and when I did leave it, I got so twisted around that I couldn't find my way back. As far as blips went, this one wasn't so bad. At least I knew I was at Rosalind House. I knew I *had* a room. But the only thing my little trip out of my room taught me is that I'm in the right place. Residential care.

Today, outside my window, a handsome gardener prunes the boxwood. It's warm out, and he's stripped to a thin white T-shirt, which allows me to enjoy his ripped physique. A few years ago, I'd have leaned out and asked for a sprig of something, or even asked if he needed any help. (When I was a kid, Jack and I used to spend a lot of time in the garden with Mom, planting and weeding and mulching.) But now I can't even be bothered to return the gardener's smile. I'm too busy thinking about Ethan. About *the incident*.

It happened at night. I get restless at night, one of many joyous side effects of "the disease." I was in the living room, trying to figure out how to use the Xbox when I heard his little footsteps behind me.

"Let's make fongoo."

"Fongoo" was a loose derivative of fondue, and it was our word for melting candy bars on the stove and then dipping cookies, marshmallows, or whatever else we had handy into the melted goo.

I said yes for several reasons: One, I love fongoo. Two, I'm not his mother—it is not my job to worry about his teeth or his lack of sleep. Three, my life is hurtling toward a point where I'm not going to know myself anymore, and while I do know myself, I sure as hell want to be making fongoo with my nephew.

We'd finished the fongoo and were playing Xbox when we smelled the burning. Ethan and I locked eyes.

"Shi—oot!" I said. "The fongoo."

I bolted for the kitchen, cursing. Burning the house down would do nothing to assure Jack I was a competent adult. I threw the door open, ready to reach for the fire extinguisher, but instead of finding it, I found the bathroom. I turned, opened another door. A cupboard filled with towels. I spun again. Where, in God's name, was the kitchen?

It wasn't the first time this had happened. I knew all I had to do was stay calm and wait for a few moments, and everything would come back to me. But the burning smell was getting stronger, and I couldn't see Ethan anywhere. And I couldn't even find my way out of the fucking *bathroom*!

That was when I heard Ethan scream.

According to Jack, after I ran in the opposite direction, Ethan tore into the kitchen and tried to take the saucepan off the stove. The handle was red-hot. He'd whipped his hand off so fast, he toppled the saucepan, splattering the burning chocolate onto his cheek. The worst part, except for hurting Ethan, was that it confirmed they were right about me. I can't be trusted with my nephew. I can't be left alone, even for a second.

"Knock knock."

I roll my head toward the door, which is eternally open, thanks to the skinny helper lady, who has an unnatural obsession with fresh air. Every time I try to close it, she appears like a magical air fairy—*fresh air, fresh air, FRESH AIR!* But this time when I look, Eric is there with a huge lion of a dog by his side. I feel my insides pull together to form an internal shield.

"Hey," he says. "How are you doing?"

"Fine." I address the dog since I can't seem to look anywhere else.

"Everyone being nice to you?"

"Yep."

It's a German Shepherd. Its teeth are yellow and shiny with saliva; its mouth is curved into that smile-snarl that dogs always wear to keep you on guard. *Am I happy? Am I angry? Come a little closer and find out.*

"Oh," Eric says. "Are you afraid of dogs?"

I try to put on a brave face, but I obviously fail, because Eric sends the dog out. On his way into my room he pauses at a watercolor of a leaf that Jack must have hung on my wall. It belonged to my mother.

"This is lovely," he says.

"Keep it," I say.

He frowns at me. "You know you don't have to just sit in your room all day. There's a bus that goes into town twice a day. Some folks like to go to a shopping center or to a movie."

I sit up. "I'm allowed to do that?"

"Sure. Trish, one of our staff, is escorting the bus group today."

I sink back into my bed.

"Or there are board games in the parlor," he says. "We try and encourage residents to congregate in there when they're home. We find that people feel isolated when they spend all their time cooped up in their rooms."

"I'm okay with being isolated."

Eric perches on the edge of my bed, a frown bobbing on his forehead. My heart sinks. It must be time for the pep talk. I actually feel bad for Eric. He doesn't want to give it any more than I want to hear it. Deep down he probably knows that if he were a resident here, he'd stay in his room, too. But that's not the dish they're feeding us.

"Fine," I say, cutting him off before he can start. (Mostly because I want him to get off my bed.) "The parlor? That's the place to be? I'll go there today. Promise."

Eric sighs. "You don't have to go to the parlor. That wasn't my point. My point is that I want you to be happy here."

"I know." Everyone wants me to be happy here. If I'm happy, they don't have to feel guilty.

Eric rests his hand dangerously close to my thigh. "Give us a chance, Anna. I won't pretend to know what it's like for you. But I do know that your brother didn't put you in here to wither away and die in your room. There's still a lot of life to be lived, but you need to stay in the game." He winks. "Jack told me you were an adrenaline junkie. I have to admit, I was pretty excited when I heard that. The most adrenaline we get around here is on bingo night."

He grins and I think I might actually vomit. "You're right," I say. "You have no idea what it's like to be me."

They say when you lose some of your senses, others get heightened. I think it's true. There was a time when I had a razor tongue. If there was a joke at the offering, I was the first to snap it up (and then deliver it with more pizazz than anyone else). Now I'm not as quick as I used to be, but I'm more observant, especially when it comes to people's state of mind. So when a young woman with spiky blond hair bursts through my door, I know at a glance that she's not only lost, but that there's something on her mind.

"Oh, um," she says. "Which way is the visitors' bathroom?"

Obviously, I have no idea. When I was diagnosed, my neuropsychologist (Dr. Brain, I called him) explained that memories tended to evaporate in reverse order. This meant my oldest memories would be the ones to hang around the longest, and new information, visitor's bathrooms included, were quick to disappear into the black hole of no return in my brain.

"I'm sorry, I don't know," I tell the woman. Her face, I notice, is crumpled and red. Wet. "Are you okay?"

She sighs, and I half expect her to turn and leave—continue on her search for the visitors' bathroom. But she stays.

"Yeah." She sniffs. "I mean no. It's my grandpa. He's . . . impossible."

"Who's your grandpa?"

"Bert. Bert Dickens."

"Oh," I say, though I have no recollection of meeting Bert. "Is he . . . okay?"

"He's fine, physically. Mentally, not so much. Sorry, I shouldn't have just barged in like this. Are you—?"

"I'm not busy." It's the understatement of the century. "What's going on with Bert?"

"Are you sure you want to hear this?"

"Sure I'm sure."

"Okay." She comes farther into the room. "The thing is—" She extends a hand and wiggles her fingers. "—I'm getting married."

I eyeball the diamond and smile like I'm supposed to, even though I've never seen what all the fuss was about when it came to those sparkly rocks. "Congratulations."

"Thanks."

I glance at own my ring finger, naked for almost a year. The knuckle seems to protrude higher now, without its anchor weighing it down. "Does Bert not like the guy?"

"No. I mean, yes. He likes him. But he doesn't want us to get married."

"Why not?"

"He thinks our family is cursed. Yeah, and he's not senile either. He's always thought that. His wife, my grandma, died when my mom was a baby. And Mom died when I was four. He thinks if I get married, then the curse will continue."

"I'm sorry about your mom."

"Thanks."

"Why does he think it's marriage causing the curse? Why not the baby?"

She gives me a strange look. This, I realize, is probably not helpful.

"Hey, I'm just pointing out that his theory isn't watertight. Maybe you could convince him the baby part causes the curse?"

"But what happens when I have a baby?"

"You want a baby, too?"

She nods. Somewhere deep in my soul, I think she's being a little greedy.

"Well, do you believe the curse?" I ask.

"No. I mean, my family has had bad luck, but . . . No. I don't believe it. But I want Grandpa to come to the wedding, and he says he won't. He says he can't bear to watch me seal my fate."

"Tell him if you don't get married, your fate will be worse than death."

She watches me through narrowed eyes.

"Tell him if you go to your grave with him as your husband, you'll go a happy woman. Tell him that even if he's right, you'd rather have a year of true happiness than die without knowing what happiness is." I think for a moment. "If he says you're wrong, ask him if he wishes he'd never married his wife."

"Wow," she says. "You're good."

There's an expression that says this exactly, and I try to conjure it up. Slowly, it starts to come. "A life lived in . . ." I try to continue, but the rest slips away. *Poof.* Gone.

"A life lived in fear is a life half-lived?"

"Right. Exactly."

"You're right. He adored Myrna. There's no way he wishes he hadn't married her. Besides, if I listen to his silly superstitions, I'm reinforcing the idea that this curse could actually be true." She sighs. "Thanks for being the voice of reason. I'd better get back." She cocks her head toward the closed bathroom door. "Do you think she's okay in there?"

"Who?"

"Your . . . grandmother?" She squints at the silver name-thingy on the wall. "Anna, is it?"

I often have trouble understanding things, so I don't worry too much that this goes over my head. I'm about to nod as if I understand completely—when suddenly, it dawns. She thinks I'm visiting an old person named Anna.

"Oh . . . yes. She's fine." I smile at the girl whose name I didn't catch, if she told me at all. "She'll be out of here really, really soon."